D0505818

The Food Detective

The Food Detective

JUDITH CUTLER

This edition first published in Great Britian in 2006 by
Allison & Busby Limited
13 Charlotte Mews
London W1T 4EJ
http://www.allisonandbusby.com

Copyright © 2005 by Judith Cutler

The moral right of the author has been asserted.

A catalogue record for this book is available from
the British Library.

10 9 8 7 6 5 4 3 2 1

ISBN 0 7490 8258 5

Printed and bound in Great Britain by
Bookmarque Ltd, Croydon, Surrey

Also by Judith Cutler

Published by Allison and Busby
Scar Tissue
Drawing the Line

Sophie Rivers series
Dying Fall
Dying to Write
Dying on Principle
Dying for Millions
Dying for Power
Dying to Score
Dying by Degrees
Dying by the Book
Dying in Discord
Dying to Deceive

Kate Power series
Power on her Own
Staying Power
Power Games
Will Power
Hidden Power
Power Shift

Romances
Coming Alive
Head over Heels

For Gill and Keith Bassett

– dear friends and mines of information

Thanks to Sue Manning for help with all sorts of veterinary facts you'd rather not know.

'He says he only wants a sandwich, Mrs Welford, and can he have just tap water with it,' Lindi reported, eyes wide. 'Weird, or what?' Pity she spoiled the effect by looking over my shoulder at her reflection in the mirror and fiddling with a strand of hair.

I put down my pencil. 'A night like this and a man doesn't want a decent drink! What's wrong with him?' I wasn't just humouring her: if I'd ventured from hearth and home through this sort of rain, I'd have wanted at least a twenty-year-old malt. In fact, I might just have one now, just as soon as Lindi had dealt with her latest crisis. She liked a bit of drama, did Lindi – in the absence of the real thing, she invented one every night. Though this seemed a mite more genuine than most, on a Lindi scale, at least.

She wound a tendril of hair round her finger. 'He might have a stomach ache.' No, not quick on jokes, either. I didn't know why I kept her on, flashing her boobs in her skimpy tank tops. It wasn't to please the customers. Kings Duncombe was hardly alive with testosterone-fuelled males ready to bed her in the hay. It was an ugly hamlet in the back of beyond, and until I'd started to make changes, the White Hart would continue to be the exclusive preserve of old men with weak bladders and foul teeth.

'Tell him there's no one in the kitchen tonight.'

'I did. But he says all he wants is a sandwich. And a glass of tap water.'

'Just the regulars in the bar?'

'Well, there's Mr Tregothnan, and Lucy Gay's dad, and –'

'The usual suspects. How many?'

'Seven. Maybe eight if you count this man.' She dropped her voice to a confidential whisper, thick with local burr, though we were the only people in the room, my sitting room, well away from the public rooms. 'Maybe he is bad, Mrs Welford. He do look ever so pale.'

'Better get him a bite before he fades away. Make sure everyone's got a refill before you leave the bar, though.' I wouldn't put it past them to help themselves otherwise. If they were as generous with their measures as they were with their puddles on the gents' floor, I'd be bankrupt within a month.

Back to my calculator, then. The White Hart wasn't going to be a failing country boozer much longer: not if I had a say in it. Alehouse and restaurant was how I'd remodel it. The present snug would become the restaurant, and the filthy storeroom in which rumour insisted the last landlord had kept his prize shagging-sheep would do nicely for a replacement snug. Some would say the regulars wouldn't notice if I left it as it was. But I'd do the decent thing, make it warm and cosy and the sort of place you wouldn't mind joining the locals in if you were waiting for your table. It wasn't as if the present snug owed anyone anything. There wasn't a comfortable chair in the place. The settles were old, which equalled murder for any modern spine, and the plastic patio chairs were almost as horrible as the green aluminium patio tables they were arranged round. Poor sandwich man would no doubt be stuck at one of them – the yokels would be huddled round the fire, their backs firmly to him. Oh, he'd practically feel the draught from their ears as they listened in to any conversation he might be having, but that was all he'd feel. Nothing of the fire, what was left of it after Lindi had almost let it go out – she was always surprised when she was left with nothing but ashes – and after they'd coughed and hawked and spat.

She was pithering with her damned hair again. I'd have sacked her weeks ago, except the only other girl in the village interested in working for me was Lucy Gay, and since she was only sixteen I couldn't let her do more than serve meals and wash up. Oh, yes – the Law and I were Best Friends these days. It had been hard enough work to get my licence – can I help it, I said, an innocent woman, if my husband gets sent down for a few years on some trumped up charge?

'Lindi! We have a customer, you said!'

She sauntered off.

I was just about to treat myself to that whisky when she came back upstairs again. Anyone else with an expression on her face like hers would have managed a canter, if not a gallop.

'You should see his hands! All bloody!'

'Bloody as if he's killed someone?'

'Bloody like someone's had a go at him, more like. And not just any old how – as if, as if they've tried to – you know, do what they did to Jesus!'

I awarded marks for imagination. 'People don't get crucified in the autumn, Lindi. They do that at Easter. Come on, he hasn't got bleeding great holes in his hands, has he?'

'Not as such. But you can see the blood through his plasters. Here!' She pointed to her outstretched hand. 'Right in the middle, here!' Hand still splayed, she touched the other palm. 'And,' she dropped her voice again, 'he's got deep scratches round his forehead. At least they're not bleeding now. But they have been. Like he'd been wearing a crown of thorns.'

I ought to ignore her, but what else was there to intrigue me on a wet Sunday in the foothills of Exmoor? 'Has he got sandals, long brown hair and a Che Guevara beard?'

Frowning a little, she said, 'His hair's like my dad's.'

Short back and sides with little pretension to fashion, then. Dead boring too, if he was anything like Lindi's dad.

'Palestinian or Israeli accent?' I pressed. Maybe I shouldn't have that single malt. They always said landlords drank their profits if they weren't careful. In any case, that glass of Rioja I'd had with my supper seemed to have gone to my head. I mimed a Shylock shrug: 'Oy vey?'

She chewed the strand she'd played with before, as if I'd set a desperately hard GSCE question. 'More like yours.'

Someone from Birmingham! I wasn't sure I liked the sound of that. You come down somewhere as remote as this to leave your past behind you, don't you? Not that I had a past, of course. Tony did, of course, God rest his soul. The sort of past that might encourage some of his old contacts to look me up, more's the pity. It's one thing having your old man being on the wrong side of the law; it's another finding you're supposed to be jolly chums with a whole lot of other ex-cons. And their wives, girlfriends and general hangers-on. No, anyone coming to look me up would get the shortest of shrifts. Whatever a shrift is. I'd have to look it up. A very cold shoulder, anyway.

'He's not local, then?' I asked, wishing I hadn't got into this.

It might have been mildly entertaining, but the last thing I wanted was Lindi getting the idea there was something about me to gossip about.

'I'd have known him if he was, wouldn't I?'

I nodded. Round here local meant this village. 'Better go and keep an eye on things. And if Mr Tregothnan gets too frisky, get rid of him.'

'Oh, I don't like to. It's only a bit of fun. He don't mean nothing by it, does he?'

So fondling the kid's breasts was only a bit of fun, was it? 'Don't they teach you anything about sexual harassment at that school of yours? Arm's length, Lindi – that's the best way. Off you go now.'

She set off, but hesitated by the door. No. Not to say anything. To give that hair of hers one last fiddle.

'Go on! Shoo!'

People didn't normally spend long in the gents. In, quick slash, out. That's the usual. And who could blame them? Stinking black hole. It makes me retch just to sluice it with a hose every day. But this guy did. Mr Sandwich and Water. Then he shot out, wiping his mouth and shuddering. That was normal, at least. As was his haircut: the boring sort I'd imagined. And then I twigged: it wasn't just normal. It was familiar. I nearly retched myself. The bastard. When I paid him a visit the next day it wouldn't be to ask after his health.

'It's harassment: that's what it is, Inspector Thomas!' I stood on the step of his mobile home – one of the fixed ones in the Happy Valley site – and confronted him.

He put his hands up as if to fend off my words. No, let them ricochet round him.

'Sending the filth down here to check up on me.' I stepped inside uninvited, just as he must have done countless times when he was a cop.

'Josie Welford,' his mouth announced as he backed away. He looked as surprised as I felt. Maybe I was wrong: maybe he hadn't come down here to spy on me. In which case, I gave him

Brownie points for recognising me. I'd lost the best part of four stone, changed my hair from the big brassy with black roots that Tony liked to a gentle bob, silvery gold, the best colour the priciest salon in Exeter could manage. Before I'd mostly sported dramatic flowing Kaftans, which never did disguise all my flesh; now I was country practical in a hooded waxed jacket and wellies. Most of all I was minus those grotesque fancy specs, more appropriate to a stage transvestite. Not only could I see better with my contacts, you could see that I had serious cheekbones.

But I still didn't buy the coincidence. 'Harassment!' I repeated, as if I'd just paused for breath. 'Typical of the filth, to have the brass neck to send you chasing round after me. You! The one who had Tony sent down. The one who ruined the best years of my life.' I'd always been known for my swearing, so I slung a few profanities at him, just like the old days but with less venom. Actually, maybe with more style.

He stared, his face working. Any other man, any other time, he could have laughed and got away with it. It was hard to take myself seriously, when each swear word was accompanied by a drip from a Barbour. But to laugh at the old me was to invite a kick in the balls and a crack on the skull as you went down. Unless I laughed at myself first.

'Twenty years. It must be all of twenty years,' he said. 'Birmingham Crown Court.'

I almost pitied him. Those days I was a big-haired, big-mouthed virago, calling down all the curses of heaven on him for what he'd done to my man. 'Fifteen years!' I'd screeched. 'Fifteen bloody years! For a man Tony's age. A decent man! Now he'll never go to his son's wedding, never see his grandchildren.' Blame the Gippo blood a couple of generations back for the bad language. Tony had hated it and made me clean up my act, except, he said, when circumstances merited it.

It had been teamwork, of course: I knew it even as I cursed him. The Drugs Squad; a bright young forensic scientist; a good prosecution lawyer; a jury brave enough to withstand the threats exuded by Tony's henchmen surveying the court (they'd made even me feel sick, and I was on their side); a judge handing down the long sentence. But it was easier to pick on one man as the villain. So I'd followed him all the way down Corporation Street hollering and shouting. I'd thrown more than words: I'd pulled off my stiletto shoes (quite a relief – the damned things always did cripple me – and hurled them at his head). I must have run fifty yards on the wet pavement before I'd realised I was barefoot.

On bad days, the really bad ones, maybe he'd remembered those curses. In detail.

He probably remembered how I'd had to stop and peel my laddered stockings – no, not tights, which Tony loathed – and rip them off and sling them too. He'd insisted on returning the shoes. Quite a nice grin and a courtly bow. He'd had a little bit of style in those days. These days? Something seemed to have taken the heart out of him. It was as if someone had rubbed him out and forgotten to colour him in again. Apart from the deep scratches on his forehead, that is.

And all that must have been – what? eighteen? twenty? – years ago. Tony Welford, love of my life for all he'd been old enough to have been my father, grandfather even, had been gone eight years now. And not a day when I didn't miss him, even if it was only to thumb my nose at his memory when I did things he'd have hated. Like losing my blubber.

'What about a bucket?' I waved my golfing umbrella at him. Not that I played, you understand. But the weather they got round here you needed all the protection you could get. If I didn't need the brolly, I carried a useful walking stick, to fend off overenthusiastic dogs and brambles.

'Bathroom,' he said, taking it and disappearing.

Protection like wellies, for instance. Tony would never have had a woman of his seen in wellies. Maybe he'd have thought the Barbour was a way of getting in with the local hunting and shooting toffs. More like he'd have thought it showed solidarity with his beloved monarch. Yes, he kept a photo of Her Maj on the wall of his Long Lartin cell. He'd been known to land men in hospital for expressing republican views.

When Nick got back I was still in his living room, half-sitting on the arm of the settee, trying to push one boot off with the other foot. I'd slung the Barbour across a standard household remover's cardboard box. I had my choice of a dozen or more, some already opened, the rest still taped closed. Where on earth could he possibly hope to stow so much in a place as small as this?

He'd always been the man to offer civilised gestures. Today he didn't look as if he could remember any.

'You're the first visitor in my new abode,' he managed. Suddenly he bowed deeply, sweeping his arm in an ironic invitation to admire it. At least I hoped it was ironic. The place was a tip. Well. It would be. He'd only moved in over the weekend, according to Molly at the shop.

For answer I stuck out my left wellington boot – he could pull it off. And the other one. Even when I'd been big, I'd had nice feet. I was still proud of them. Size four and nice high arches. 'How about offering a lady a coffee? Though if it's instant muck I'll have tea.'

'Only powdered milk anyway,' he said.

'You're joking! In the heart of some of the best dairy land in the country and you haven't got any bleeding milk! What the hell are you doing, man?'

'Settling in. Only arrived yesterday. Too late to get proper supplies. I just brought the bare necessities.'

'Including no doubt your booze and a pack of cards. Oh, everyone knew,' I said, standing up to peer into another box. 'Though all that came much later, didn't it?'

'No booze; no cards,' he said.

'Proper little plaster saint you've turned into, I must say. What about that tea, then? So long as you make it weak, I'll manage without milk.' I patted my hips. Only another stone to shed, but they said that was the hardest.

He opened his mouth, but thought better of it.

I nodded as if he'd spoken. 'WeightWatchers. Tony liked a bit of flesh on a woman. Now he's gone before, God bless him, I can lose a bit. Try, anyway. They say it's harder after fifty and they're bloody right. Don't you need to switch the kettle on? Or does your water boil itself?'

'Sorry.' He swilled mugs, shaking them dry. 'You said weak?'

'Like a nice healthy pee specimen,' I agreed. 'And no sugar, either.'

'I ought to offer you lemon.' He was making so much effort you could see it.

I looked slowly round the kitchenette. 'Oh, yes? Well, mind you get one in for next time I come.'

He stared: was I pulling his leg?

'Hey, get the teabag out! It'll be stewed.'

'Sorry. Here – is this OK?'

I peered at the tea. 'It'll do. Thanks. So what are you doing down here, if you're not harassing me?'

'A new job. Starting in about an hour's time.'

'Job? My God, the lord high Inspector Thomas must have retired! Why did you never get further than inspector? You'd got enough between your ears. Yes, you were a bright lad. We all thought you'd go a long way.'

He shrugged.

'After all, your face always used to fit.'

'I'm not so sure about that.' He swallowed. 'I've done my stint and taken the retirement cheque. But what with one thing and another, I – well, I needed another job.'

I dug in one of the boxes – he'd already started to empty this one, and came up with a photo of girl celebrating something with a glass of bubbly.

'Elly,' he said. 'When she got her A level results.'

'Pretty kid. Not much like you. I suppose you had the usual police marriage. The wife comes third after the job and the boozer. And then she ups and offs. Good for her. So you've got to work because you're still paying maintenance and there's the kids to put through college. It'll do you good to do a decent nine till five job for a change.' So what was it? I wouldn't give him the satisfaction of having me ask.

'Tea all right?'

I mimed a spit. 'Typhoo!'

'I always thought it was a perfectly good tea.' He put on a

poncy expression: 'What would Madam prefer to go with her lemon? Assam? Earl Grey?'

'Cheeky sod. No breakfast things?'

He flushed like a guilty schoolboy. 'I was just shaving when –' He stopped, grabbing his stomach as if he'd been stabbed.

All that stuff about food last night, and then looking as if he'd thrown up in the gents – did he have an ulcer? 'Tablets?'

'In one of these boxes.' He looked helplessly around.

'You'd better eat something. Dry toast.' I dug out a toaster and plugged it in. 'Where's your bread?'

He passed a Sainsbury's carrier.

'You'll have a round with me?'

Thick white sliced? I didn't think so. 'I've already eaten, thanks. You'd better take yourself off to Dr Cole.' I pointed at his midriff. 'He's twenty years behind the times, but at least that means he doesn't feel bound to experiment on you.' I perched on one leg, put my boots back on, first the left, then the right, then reached for the Barbour.

'How did you get the idea the police were after you?' he asked, twenty minutes after I'd expected him to.

'Obvious. A stranger in the village. Short hair. Keeps himself to himself in the bar. It doesn't take much to put that lot together.'

'*Keeps himself to himself!* They bloody froze me out. You should have seen them!' What a surprise. 'And what would they be looking for, the police?'

Tony's fortune, of course. 'If you can't work that out you're a bigger fool than I took you for. But they'd have it all wrong. I earn my own living now.'

He managed a thin smile. 'Josie, anything in your bank account, even in an old sock under your bed, is none of my business. Now. I'm not DI Thomas, West Midlands Police. I'm plain Nick Thomas.'

'So why are you here?' I paused, the Barbour zip halfway up.

'I told you. New job.'

'Which is?'

'The Food Standards Agency. Investigating officer.'

'Jesus Christ! You are going to be little Mr Popular round here, aren't you! You'd be better off letting the police rumour grow.'

He bridled. 'I don't see why. If people have nothing to hide.'

'Nothing to hide? People here make their living out of agriculture and don't need some government spy living slap in the middle of them.'

'If I spy it's to protect the public: I mean, farmers round here need protection from –'

'Spies like you!'

'Come on: how did BSE get into the food chain? Because feed manufacturers wanted quick profits and thought it would be nice to feed total herbivores recycled meat products. Those farmers didn't know what was in the feed. So it's my job to make sure manufacturers are putting into feed what will be good for animals. And for us. If you've ever seen a case of new variant CJD –'

'Oh, it's all stuff got up by the media. Old folk die every day of Alzheimer's.'

'And kids of sixteen? Eighteen? Who ate beef burgers made from nice fresh beef thinking they were safe?'

A man with a stomach like that shouldn't get so aerated. I changed gear a bit. 'Do you remember that politician – the Minister of Agriculture or whatever – trying to force his kid to eat a burger. And the kid had more sense than he did and shoved it away? Oh, Nick, they're such fools, aren't they! Thinking we'll buy that crap.'

'But people do. More to the point, people sell it to them,' he added. 'People sell over-age cattle, complete with spinal cord material —'

'That's coming in from Europe —'

'And some farmers are doing it here. Why not? They get good prices for beef that's less than thirty months old —'

'Pitiful prices, more like!'

'But virtually nothing for stock that's over that magic thirty months,' he overrode me. 'Wouldn't you be tempted? To take it along to a mate's place, way out the back of beyond, and set up a little abattoir? If I were a farmer down on my uppers, I'd be tempted.'

'But I don't suppose you'd succumb.' I stared at him. 'You reckon this meat – this thirty-month-old meat – wouldn't be kosher?'

'Neither kosher nor halal!'

'Eh? Oh, I get you.'

'Not the sort of thing I'd want to eat,' he added, 'with or without my ulcer.'

I found myself grinning. 'I don't half miss the food, Nick. A good curry. Down Ladypool Road. All that halal meat being made into wonderful curries and baltis. Tell you what, I've found a good place in Exeter: you can stand me a meal one night. When your stomach's better.'

I flapped a hand and picked my way through all his boxes to the door. He flapped one back. Lindi had been right about the plasters on his hands, too.

'You want to look after yourself, you know. Especially with this job of yours. Tell you what, you just tell folk you're a civil servant. Altogether safer, if you ask me.'

Chapter Two

The one person I didn't want to meet on my way back to the village was Sue Clayton, our curate. She always insisted on giving you a lift, even if you'd rather be on your own thinking, or, in my case, exercising off another calorie. She looked so hurt, almost resentful, if you tried to refuse that I'd given up trying, accepting each time as graciously as I could.

'I thought I was an early bird,' I said, cramming myself into the passenger seat of her Fiesta, 'but you've obviously been working already.'

'Yes,' she said, ignoring the implied question and grinding a gear.

How anyone could do that to a modern synchromesh gearbox always defeated me, as did the idea that anyone could see through her windscreen. She'd never mastered the controls that directed hot air on to it, and dealt with condensation by polishing with the palm of her hand. So she had not just a runny screen, but also a greasy one.

'I hear our newcomer has stigmata,' I said.

'Not really.'

So she'd met him already.

'But I've seen them – with my own eyes.'

'Scratches,' she said.

'Where did he get them from, I wonder?'

She shrank further from me, but then had to crane forward to see through a clearish patch the size of a postcard.

'Someone put plasters on his hands at least,' I prompted.

'Yes. I hate this corner.'

So did everyone with any sense. I always slowed to walking pace so I could get into first. Sue tried it in third. To be fair, she tried most things in third. The poor little car would probably die never having got into fifth. I glanced at Sue. She probably wouldn't either. The dream of my life was to get her to go on the town with me. You know the sort of thing: shop for England, nice lunch, another shop. Maybe a hairdo and a facial. She certainly needed the hairdo. Ponytails are fine and dandy when you're young with thick, shiny hair; when you're in your forties and your hair's not just fine but thinning and very dull, it's a pretty unforgiving style. Especially if you use rubber bands to confine it. If only she'd have it all lopped off and a spot of colour. Was it her dog-collar that stopped her, making her eschew the pleasures of the flesh, as it were, or lack of cash?

'What did you make of him?' I asked, when we were safely on the straight again.

Yes, straight but still narrow. And deep – we were probably eight feet below the level of the fields. No room for mistakes.

'Boorish.'

Sometimes her choice of word surprised me. 'Boorish?'

'I was driving back from Evensong at Abbots Duncombe last night in the pouring rain and found him in the hedge. So I offered him a lift.'

My face pulled itself. 'Sue! A complete stranger! Was that wise? OK, OK! I've read my Bible too, but – anyway, what was he doing in the hedge, for goodness' sake?'

'He said something about an unlit lorry. He'd jumped into the hedge to avoid it. And he'd got scratched to bits. And all he'd talk about was car maintenance and driving techniques. Mine. Boorish.'

Biting the hand that drove you. I couldn't fault his intentions, just his tact. 'He fetched up in the bar last night. Gave Lindi quite a turn, I can tell you.'

'I don't know why. He was quite presentable by the time I'd finished.'

'You'd done a good job with the first aid, but he still didn't look very well.'

She stared at me, not reducing her speed. The car slewed towards the hedge. 'Is that why you went to see him?'

'I didn't go to see him,' I lied flatly. Close as the grave Sue Clayton might be, but my past was mine and mine alone, and Nick might feel the same. 'I met him on my morning walk, that's all. He seemed better. I gave him the name of a doctor, just in case.'

'It must be strange, living in a mobile home. Especially at this time of the year, when all the other caravans on the site are locked up for the winter.'

This was the closest you got to girlie talk with Sue. All my life I'd had at least one decent woman friend, often two or three, the sort you can share that day I described or just ring up when you want to let your hair down. I'd never have got through all Tony's years of bird without Claire and Nesta, and then his McMillan Nurse Nell had become a mate – we still emailed each other at least once a week for a good natter. Sue didn't seem to have a natter-mode.

'Strange – and very lonely.' I thought about my early days in the village. 'Why don't you rope him in as a bell ringer?'

'What if he isn't a churchgoer?'

'Ringing bells would certainly make him one. Go on – it's hard to make friends in a community like this if you're not a playgroup parent or doing our sort of job.' I could feel her eyebrows shoot up. I didn't pursue images of the confessional and counselling, tasks shared by priests and publicans alike. 'You know: working with people.'

'What about his new colleagues?'

Talk about stony ground.

'He can't be at work all day every day. Any idea what he does, by the way?'

She shrugged. 'He didn't say.'

How could anyone be so incurious? Someone in her line of work, too. Tired of pushing on closed doors, I sat back and watched the countryside go past, the little I could see, that is, through the foul windscreen. So Nick had told her off for bad driving, had he? Ten out of ten for good intentions, zero for tact. He used to have something very like charm. What had changed him? I couldn't see him surviving very long in a job like this new one unless he mended his ways.

Sue dropped me not at the pub but at the vicarage, because I'd insisted I wanted to go to the village shop and an extra quarter of a mile would be good for me. I was glad, all the same, when she pulled off the main street into the road leading to her house. She mistimed the turn: if she often cut it as fine as that, in her place

I'd have moved the terracotta pots a bit. In any case, they weren't bringing much beauty to the garden – whatever the plants still growing in them had been, now they looked totally woebegone.

She didn't invite me in. Well, that suited me. I had a day's work ahead of me.

My electric kettle had other ideas. Just as I fancied a decent cup of tea, it gave up the ghost. I suppose the logical thing would have been to use the pub kitchen's kettle, but I didn't fancy having to trot upstairs every time I wanted a cuppa. A trip to the outskirts of Taunton, then, to Comet or wherever. That was the trouble with the rural life, as Nick Thomas would soon discover: there was no popping down to a convenient shopping mall. Though out of town shopping might have ruined many a town centre, at least it meant I didn't have to tangle with Taunton's traffic. And it was easy to park, especially on a wet Monday morning.

I'd chosen my kettle and was just sauntering round checking out anything else that might take my fancy when I noticed Nick Thomas. He too was clutching an electric kettle, and like me seemed to be browsing. He'd just fetched up by the TVs. All I meant to do was wave. Then I saw his face.

God, not an other terrorist attack. I too stared at the banks of screens. But all I found was some daytime TV pap.

And he wasn't moving. Not even blinking. His face was ashen, pouring with sweat. What the hell? He wasn't having a heart attack, was he?

I moved closer – you can't do straight lines in enticing consumer mazes. He looked like Tony's kid brother Sam, who scared us all witless with his sleepwalking. But you don't fall asleep in the middle of a superstore. Before I could get to him, or even call, he seemed to shake himself and toddled off to the checkout.

He'd be embarrassed if he thought I was spying, so I thought about a new hairdryer and pondered an electric carving knife.

'That man you just served,' I said at last, plumping the kettle on the desk. 'Was he all right?'

The young man rocked his head. 'Looked as if he'd seen a ghost, didn't he? But his money was good, so who was I to argue?'

Who indeed?

There was no sign of him when I came out.

Although there wasn't much call for suppers, which is why I could take the odd evening off, lunchtimes often attracted a little knot of villagers and a few serious walkers. You'd have thought weather like today's – it was sluicing down now – would have put off all but the most hardened drinkers, but several of the big-boot brigade were huddled at one of the patio tables, casting envious glances at the locals monopolising what I'd made sure was a pretty good fire.

'Tell you what,' Reg Bulcombe said, leaning on the bar as if hoping I'd be as generous in my display of flesh as Lindi, 'I wouldn't mind one of your steak baguettes. Well cooked, mind. Nice lot of onion.' Since he said exactly the same every lunchtime he graced us with his presence, which was three or four days a week, I didn't need to write it down. But I did, jabbing the slip of paper on the bills spike just to tell him he wouldn't get away without paying, as he'd tried, a couple of times when I'd broken routine.

While his drinking partner, Ted Gay, Lucy's dad, stared at the menu as if he could afford anything on it, I said, 'All this beef, Reg – are you on this Atkins Diet or something?' Maybe I was trying to drop a hint: he was carrying four stone more than he should – yes, I know, there's no one like a convert for being sanctimonious, his face that bluish red I associated with high blood-pressure and heart disease.

'Bit of good meat never hurt anyone, did it, Ted?'

Ted mumbled something into the pint he couldn't afford. Six children at school, the oldest Lucy, and his wife, virtually the breadwinner with all the cleaning jobs she'd gathered, died of cancer. Lucy did her best, bless her, making sure the others got their free school meals and had the best food she could manage at home. But Ted had never been much of a one for a hard day's work, and with so much booze inside him – no, not from the White Hart but from supermarket cans – only the kindest of his old employers now employed him for old times' sake. They were braver than me: I quailed at the thought of an alcoholic on the business end of a chainsaw or machete.

Reg leaned even more confidentially towards me. His breath mixed beer, fags and halitosis in equal proportions. 'Your freezer must be pretty empty by now. You want me to fix you up with another delivery?'

I dropped my voice to match. 'You're sure this isn't off the back of some lorry?'

He flinched as if I'd struck him.

'Come on, Reg: only joking. But it's such a good deal you're getting me.'

'All local grown. No middleman, see. No need for this talk of lorries.' He sounded genuinely offended.

I hesitated. 'Thing is, I need the invoices and receipts you promised for the taxman. And it's coming up to the time when I need to get every last shred of paperwork to my accountant. You promised them last week.' And every week since I'd taken delivery.

'I did say it was cash only, Mrs Welford.'

'And I paid cash, didn't I? But I need the paperwork, Reg. Can you fix it?'

'You can rely on me. And in the meantime, another load for that freezer of yours? Come on, the amount I eat it must be empty by now.'

'So must you be. Come on, Reg – one thing at a time. I've got to go and work my magic in the kitchen. Hi, Lindi! It was cold first thing.'

'I didn't think it was so bad. Wet, of course,' she conceded.

'What I'm trying to say, very kindly,' I hissed, as she shook her coat and hung it up, 'is that you're twenty minutes late. Again. Come on, Lindi – I can't serve here and cook lunches, can I? Wash your hands, and then see if those hikers want to order. Go on. Shoo!'

The meat looked good; it smelt good; it certainly tasted good. Damn Nick Thomas for making me wonder whether it *was* good.

And damn him for making me spend an afternoon in front of the computer. I'm old enough to prefer books, but I couldn't see me flagging down the mobile library and asking for all they'd got on

BSE and CJD. Not someone who ran a pub, for goodness' sake. It'd be all over two counties before you could say mad cow. In any case, when I'd been a mature student I'd learned at college how to surf, so I might as well polish my skills.

First I got through all the official stuff – including that put out by Nick Thomas's very own Food Standards Agency. Then I started following trails. And wished I hadn't. It was one thing dying a paralysed gibbering shadow when you were ninety, quite another to go like that at nineteen. I looked at photographs of kids who'd thought all they were eating was a harmless burger – just like that one Nick and I had talked of this morning. God, I'd have liked to force feed the wretched politician, cram him like a Strasbourg goose. Was he terrified every day his daughter had a headache or forgot something? Did he quake every time she stumbled in the street? I hoped so.

My feet took me inexorably downstairs. To the freezer. I hated throwing out good meat. But if it wasn't good meat, what else could I do with it?

Chapter Three

I distributed plates of lunchtime ploughman's to Tuesday's walkers – who well might have been yesterday's recycled – and sauntered over to collect a few glasses from the regulars. Yes, of course Lindi should have been doing it. But if there was any gossip going, I wanted to hear it.

For some reason the group round Reg fell silent as I approached, so I started a conversational hare myself.

'What's this new bloke doing out at your campsite then, Reg? Not the weather for the open air life, I'd have thought.' Though the pub walls were nearly two feet thick, and the windows in deep recesses, you could still hear the rain sluicing down, as if someone had forgotten to turn off a celestial tap. It was a good job I'd already started my improvements: I'd just had the gutters cleared and the drains rodded.

'Oh, ah. He's a funny one all right,' Reg guffawed, slapping his leg. 'You know what I found him doing this morning? Trying to bury a cat, for God's sake.'

'A cat? Did he bring it down with him?'

There was a tiny shuffle from the others, which took me straight back to my long-forgotten schooldays when someone was trying not to snitch.

'Found it, he says. Dead. I told him to shove it in that there council paper bin, but seems that was too easy. He wouldn't even put his cardboard boxes in there. Said it'd mess up the recycling or summat. "Come on, man," I says, "who's going to tell? Not me, that's for sure." But no, he squashes everything into the back of that car of his and off he goes. Said something about the recycling centre.'

'He took a dead cat to the recycling centre!'

'Well, no. Reckon he must have left that back at his caravan. Said he'd dispose of it tonight. With a bit of luck, I says, it'll wash away and spare you the trouble.'

'Dispose of it? How can he dispose of it? I mean, it isn't likely he'd have brought a spade down here with him, is it? No garden,' I explained, as Reg and his mates looked as if they couldn't conceive of a life that didn't involve a spade.

'Ah. Suppose not. Anyway, he said he'd put the poor bugger under his caravan and deal with it this evening. If it isn't washed away by then.' Reg repeated. He hawked and spat. 'We might be needing Noah's Ark, but there's only room for live moggies, that's what I told him.'

I joined in the general mild laughter before disappearing back to the bar. Lindi finally registered there were glasses to be washed, and I withdrew to the kitchen to await developments – like Reg huffing and puffing round to find out why there was no meat on the menu and why I hadn't pressed a repeat order into his hand as soon as he'd appeared.

By now the whole village must have heard I'd tipped all that meat into the big kitchen waste bin, which had been emptied this morning. With luck, there must have been as many theories as villagers. I wasn't sure what to tell him. There was no point in falsely accusing people of selling unlicensed meat. Not until I knew. After all, it had seemed to be good quality. But the receipt business bothered me. Any legitimate supplier would surely provide the paperwork another business needed. Meanwhile, I had to source some more meat, and if my prices went up to match, tough. When the restaurant was open serving high quality food, customers would expect to pay accordingly. What if I went one step further and made it a completely organic restaurant? Would that be possible? Not just Reg but all the locals would huff and puff, but their days in the snug were limited anyway.

Upstairs in my quarters the phone rang. I decided to take the call. It wouldn't do Reg any harm at all to wait. And I'd always wanted to try my hand at vegetarian cooking.

'Beans on toast? I'd rather been hoping for one of your steaks,' Nick said that evening as I poured him an extra-long G and T.

'Do steaks and gastric ulcers mix?'

'I saw the Boots pharmacist. She's given me some wonder drug, the best you can get without prescription. I thought I'd test it out.'

'Unless you want to risk the pickled onions in a ploughman's, it's beans on toast or a salad,' I said. 'Problems with my freezer,'

I added innocently.

He held my gaze. I looked over his shoulder. If I started talking food supplies it might blow his cover. I assumed he'd had the sense he'd been born with and was taking my advice.

'So how was work? Tough being a new boy, I should think.'

He nodded. 'Not just the new boy. Pretty well the only boy. There are only five of us in the whole country.'

'So you're the cat that walks –'

'Cat?'

Ah.

'You know, that cat that walks by itself. Or were you thinking of another cat?'

He nodded. Fred Tregothnan erupted into the snug with a great swagger.

'Tell you what, Nick,' I muttered, real side of the mouth stuff, 'come up to my flat and have a coffee before you go. Now, Fred, what can I get you on this foul evening?'

'You know what I want,' he said, loud enough to draw everyone's attention to his pelvic thrusting movements. 'What I always want, of course.'

'Didn't your mother teach you anything?' I asked tartly. '*I want doesn't get*, remember.' But I had to sound as if I were joking: landladies aren't supposed to tell their customers to go and take a running jump. I waited till Nick was preoccupied counting out change, and dropped my voice. 'Mind you don't try anything on with Lindi or young Lucy, Fred.'

'Oh, they don't worry about that!'

'But I do. In Lucy's case I'm *in loco parentis* and I owe them both an employer's duty of care. A joke's a joke, but you touch up either of them and you'll answer to me. Your usual?' I added, back at normal volume. 'Now, I don't think you've met our newcomer, Mr Thomas. He's down here working in Taunton as a civil servant – but you mustn't hold that against him!'

There: cue for a lot of jokes about things in triplicate and the rest of the rubbish. And a chance for me to back out gracefully. 'Beans, was it, Mr Thomas, or that salad?'

'So Reg Bulcombe didn't offer you a lift back, then?'

Nick looked round my living room as if he'd arrived in heaven, as well he might, after that tip of a mobile home. I followed his eyes. The genuine beams, the colour-washed walls hung with small but good paintings, the oak furniture polished to a glow with elbow-grease and wax. The floorboards were wide, with cracks between them that would swallow pound coins without noticing, and mostly covered with the best rugs I could afford. Yes, it looked good. What was the point of having money if you didn't use it? Only I knew how much money was left – but I had a lot of receipts, all giving proper provenance. If the receipts showed a good deal less than I'd actually paid, that suited me and the dealers, who'd never objected yet to a little cash in hand.

'No.' He looked at me seriously. 'Did you expect him to?'

'Don't see why not. You could take it turn and turn about, drinking and driving.'

'Makes sense. But I didn't come from the campsite. ' He was about to add something but seemed to think better of it. After a false start, he continued, 'They're not exactly night howlers, are they? Pooping their party at nine-thirty!'

'Their cows prefer to be milked at five-thirty,' I said.

'Of course. Not a lot of working farmers in Brum. You've got this looking lovely. Will you be doing the same with the down-stairs?'

'If I have my way I will. And I've got planning permission.'

'From the authorities, but not the locals.' He wasn't going to hand out advice to me the way he had to Sue Clayton, was he?

'I didn't ask the locals. The amount they bring in wouldn't keep a mouse in cheese for a week. They'll be all right anyway. Provided a bit of fresh paint doesn't kill them. You've not been out back yet?'

He snorted. 'I'd rather —'

'— piss in a hedge than use the privy. I don't blame you. I hose it and I bleach it and I hose it some more, but it still stinks. Ordure of ages. So it's coming down. The temporary replacement's out there. See.' I pulled back the curtain and pointed at a couple of Portaloos. 'My bathroom's across the corridor if you want it. I'll make the coffee.'

'Would you mind,' he said awkward as a kid, 'if I passed on the coffee. Water. I'd love a glass of water.'

'Whisky in it?'

'When the tablets have worked properly. But if you –'

'I'll stick to coffee, thanks.' But on reflection I joined him in water. Ty Nant. I'd bought it for its sexy bottles. The glasses were elegant, too – I was buying different styles here and there to consider for the restaurant.

Goodness knows why I was going to so much trouble for the man who'd sent down my Tony. To prove I could, I suppose. No, it wasn't a matter of gracious forgiveness. It was to prove I wasn't just the widow of an ex-con who preferred to live on the cheap on a council estate in Brum's Bartley Green. We could have afforded somewhere nice – we had a lovely apartment in Spain – but Tony was obsessive about what he called his roots. Though why he could have for one moment thought his roots were in Bartley Green when in real life his folk came from Milan to run a chippie, no one, not even himself, could have said. It was a mistake, of course. If we'd bought the sort of house I'd wanted, just down the road in an altogether nicer suburb called Harborne, the way property values had risen I could have been a millionaire by now.

'Sit yourself down, copper, and tell me about this cat,' I said, curling up in my favourite chair.

'Cat?'

'The one you wouldn't let Reg Bulcombe pop in a bin.'

'It was a paper bin! A clinical waste bin, I'd have shoved it in there without blinking. But I don't know that I'd want bits of dead moggie in my morning paper. Seriously, it could have contaminated a whole batch.'

'So what did you do with it? I take it all your garden tools are in store somewhere. Unless you planned to go prospecting in them thar hills.'

He got up and pulled the curtain again. It had stopped raining. The village doesn't run to streetlights, so even though just a few stars shone between the hurtling clouds, you could see the loom of Exmoor in the middle distance.

'Another reason for going home early,' I said. 'You're only a couple of miles out of the village. Some of these men have front drives that long. And a five mile drive to get to them. They've got their own private worlds. Some of them are literally monarchs of all they can survey from their front step. Tough lives they lead, some of them. Most of them. And they can't afford more than the pint they nurse all night.'

'But you're not prepared to subsidise them.' Question or accusation?

'Hang on. They'll get a better snug than the one they've got now. You're not telling me there's any comfort in those settles or in those awful patio chairs! And just before you say anything about it, I've made sure they'll have another authentic snug. I've bought the contents of another pub further up the valley. Bought up as a grockle's holiday home, if you're interested. Chic restaurant I may be opening, but I'll make damned sure the locals have somewhere to swill.'

'All right, all right. Sorry. I was out of order there. Right out of order.'

'Yes. You were trying not to talk about the dead cat.'

He stared at his glass and took a swig. His face convulsed. And he started to hiccup. I'd have laughed, but they were great, racking hiccups, and the way he grabbed his stomach suggested he was in a great deal of pain.

'Stand up. Stand up and walk around!'

Gradually the hiccups subsided.

I whisked away the Ty Nant. 'You'd do better with still than sparkling, maybe. I bet champagne's a killer, too.'

He nodded. 'Thanks.'

'And the dead cat?'

'Oh, for fuck's sake –'

'No swearing in my pub, Mr Thomas, thank you,' I said, prim as I could. But meaning it, too. And determined to get to the bottom of his story. 'You might as well tell me your version: there'll be at least eight swirling round the village tomorrow.'

He'd have won an Oscar for his sigh. 'I found a dead cat by my caravan. I had to dispose of it.'

'You didn't feel like shoving it under a hedge and letting Mother Nature dispose of it.'

He pulled a face, almost as if he was ashamed of his sensitivity. 'Someone's pet. The least I could do.'

'Might equally have been feral.'

'That's what Sue Clayton said.'

'Sue? How did she get involved?'

'She happened to drive past as I was dealing with it.'

Happened, eh? Like hell she *happened*. The waste bins were near the road, sure, but you had to pull on to the camp reception car park to see them.

'She had a spade and we buried it. End of story.'

Except it wasn't. I could see he was holding something back. 'I'm surprised it didn't get dragged away by foxes during the day. They wouldn't know you were planning a full-scale funeral for it.'

'I think they might, you know. After all, second time round, someone had chained it to my front step.'

I made it my business to be at the village shop immediately after nine, the time I knew Sue Clayton would be there to buy her paper. In my mature student days, I'd taken up some offer that meant that if I bought a regular *Guardian* I got it at discount and I'd stuck with it ever since. It was one of two put aside for regular customers; the other was for Sue. So we had something in common, including, this morning, a shared interest in dead cats. But I wouldn't point that out straight away.

Nick had bowed himself out almost immediately last night, furiously refusing to discuss the matter of his chained corpse, though I thought his anger was directed at himself for having mentioned it, not at me. I hadn't argued, partly because he really didn't look at all well and mostly because I really couldn't understand why I'd invited him up in the first place. He certainly wasn't the sort of man I'd have checked out from a personal ad. Mind you, he was better than some I'd actually agreed to meet. A couple you'd have expected to see beaming out at you from the Sex Offenders' Register. Others were still labouring under the illusion that a gay man needed a woman to be respectable, and I wasn't going to be any man's 'beard'. Or the other woman, of course. For all an erring man claimed his wife didn't understand him, I always had a strong suspicion she understood him only too well. No, my Holy Grail was a nicely set-up man who could offer all that Tony had offered. Actually, rather more. Being married to someone doing a great long stretch forty miles from home isn't my ideal of conjugal satisfaction. While he was banged up, I'd had plenty of offers, don't doubt it, but I'd never fancied anyone enough to want to divorce Tony – always assuming his family and friends would have let me. Oh, they didn't seem to mind the odd fling, so long as I was totally discreet, and word never seemed to get back to Tony. Except once, when – more in sorrow than in anger, he assured me – he told me he'd have my lover's balls cut off and shoved down his throat if I didn't give him up.

Sue was fingering a couple of overripe bananas in the special offer basket Jem and Molly Hawk used to dispose of outdated fruit and vegetables. They might have made a good banana cake, but otherwise they'd have been inedible even disguised in a dish of muesli. Still, there was no accounting for taste, especially if you're on the lowest of incomes. I wouldn't have touched the young onions she bought, either. Young? Suffering from senile dementia, more like.

I waited till we were both outside the shop, busy with brollies and hoods, to say, 'I heard that you'd seen Mrs Greville and refused to attend the next meet to bless the hounds. I tell you, Sue, that was downright brave of you.'

She snapped her fingers. 'I don't give that much for the Grevilles of this world. It isn't as if they've ever worked for all those acres of hers. And I'll bet all their titled ancestors were descended from some yob who picked up his estates as blood money when he'd slaughtered a few innocent Anglo-Saxons to please William the Bastard.' All good *Guardian*-reading stuff. From Sue, however, it sounded more personal than theoretical. I opened my mouth to ask why.

But Sue was tracing a line in the mud, just like a naughty toddler. 'On the other hand, it won't have done me a lot of good with the Powers That Be. Especially my hunting and shooting bishop.'

'Moral stands are exactly what a curate should be making,' I beamed. 'And the Powers That Be should be pleased with you. Especially at the Highest Level. Bother bishops,' I added more loudly, as the rain bombarded our brollies. 'They're no more than middle management!'

'It's those in middle management that hand out jobs,' she reminded me.

'Heavens, Sue, you've been vicar here in all but name ever since Mr Ellis had his stroke. Surely they won't deny you the promotion.'

'It's wheels within wheels,' she said, as gloomy as the weather.

'I thought they were supposed to grind very small.'

'That's the *mills* of God. At least, thanks to you I have another bell ringer. Mr Thomas. It'd have been better if you'd come along too.'

So the ground had been more fertile than I'd realised. I awarded myself a Brownie point – and, had she not suddenly carped, one to Sue. But I hated being put on the defensive. 'I couldn't leave Lindi on her own. And I'm more use behind the bar than Lucy Gay, who's not allowed to sell booze for another eighteen months yet. In any case, she's one of your stalwarts, isn't she?'

'Apparently. I'm always over in Duncombe Parva the night they practise. I suppose it does mean she comes to church.'

Why did she sound so grudging? I said as quietly as I could against the gusting wind, which made the umbrellas more of a liability than an asset, 'It's amazing she finds time. But bell ringing's the one night in the week she regards as her own. She runs that home, you know. Well, her father's about as much use as a chocolate lavatory. Five of those children to feed and clean and wash for. Five lots of homework to check plus her own to do. A couple of evenings working for me. And she still seems to be doing well at school.'

Sue's lips tightened. 'But she doesn't bring the others to Sunday school. And she refuses to be confirmed.'

'In her situation I'd have my doubts about a benevolent divinity.' I'd rather put my trust in a benevolent if bullying employer. Yes, the one who let her study in the kitchen if it was a quiet night and made sure she always had plenty of odds and ends to eke out her food budget. But I'd sworn her to secrecy about that – threatened to cut off supplies if so much as a whisper got out.

'All the same.'

I'm afraid I have a very short fuse. Even that silly bit of intransigence lit it. And as usual, my mouth got into gear before my brain did. 'I hear you've added undertaking to your other clerical duties.'

She flushed, and – to her credit – tried to laugh. Mistake. It meant I knew she had something to hide.

'Though I don't suppose cats qualify for consecrated ground. Clever of you to carry a spade in the car just in case.'

But this time I'd gone too far, and she greeted with apparent delight and no doubt real relief the church organist, the only man

I know who can make 'Away in a Manger' sound like a military march. I left them to it.

So she must have taken Nick back to the parsonage to bury the cat. Weirder and weirder. But I'd never asked about her antipathy to the Grevilles. My job for another day.

Whatever the weather, I went for an afternoon walk. Bother the idea that every pub in the land should be open all day and half the night too. The White Hart was firmly shut between two-thirty and seven, and, unless there was a party, seemed to close down naturally between ten and ten-thirty. It'd be different when the restaurant opened. Even then, I'd always gone on the principle that if people found it hard to get into a restaurant, the more cachet it got. I was even toying with the idea of set sittings, but given you virtually need an Ordnance Survey map to find the place, I supposed a bit of flexibility was more sensible.

Today I struck out up the footpath alongside the stream that in summer makes the village so attractive to tourists. Shoals of them, dropping bits of ice cream cone as they looked for trout, would hang over the deep V-shaped recesses presumably built in the parapet to allow yokels to cower out of the way when the lord of the manor and his cronies came whizzing along in their curricles and chaises. Or, if you want to be less controversial, when the haywain trundled past. Actually I suspect it was something to do with controlling water flow, something about which I knew zilch.

There had been talk of pulling down the old bridge and replacing it with one wide enough for Euro-monster lorries, but in a rare burst of energy, Sue Clayton's vicar, Rupert Ellis, had managed to get it listed as a grade two historical building, with a star banged on it for good measure. And somehow the idea for an extra bridge had quietly died.

The footpath was steep, strewn with large stones. When it was dry, it was like climbing a flight of overlarge steps. In this weather, there seemed to be almost as much water coursing down it as in the stream-bed itself. Even with gaitered boots and water-proof trousers, I didn't feel very dry. Poor Tony: what would he have thought to see his relict – I got that word from some of the memorial tablets in the village church – dressed up like an apology for a deep-sea fisherman? He wouldn't have been able to conceive of the pleasure I got from my walks. Nor of the reason I started in the first place. I'd read somewhere that simply walking half an hour every day reduced your weight by half a stone a year, even if you didn't do anything else. Walking half an hour seemed a mammoth task when I started – and I'm not referring to my weight, though I shudder to think that once I filled the clothes I'd kept as a dire reminder. Oh, I got rid of most of them – you could probably have housed a couple of asylum seeker families in one of my tops. Except you mustn't joke about such things down here. They assured me solemnly when they saw my choice of reading that everything, from BSE to the Iraq War, was the fault of 'they danged bogus asylum seekers'. Since I'd never seen a non-white face down here, I wondered whence they'd drawn their conclusions. Anyway, all but a couple of my circus tent dresses had gone, and I only kept those because I liked the material and planned to turn them into proper garments when I'd finished losing weight.

Meanwhile, I actually liked walking, now it didn't chafe my thighs and now my lungs had got used to the idea of expanding. So I was furious to find a coil of barbed wire across a public right of way. OK, since no one else ever seemed to use it, my private right of way. Nice, new, shiny barbed wire. Why the hell had anyone done that? It was against every right to roam law in the country.

Meanwhile, should I take the path to the left, which meant crossing a bridge I wouldn't have fancied even when the water was low, or to the right, which would take me towards the campsite of which Nick was the solitary inhabitant? Consulting my map – oh, yes, I did the thing properly, a large scale OS map folded into a protective cover, even a pair of field glasses to help me spot birds or landmarks – I grasped my walking stick firmly and set off towards the camp. And then I turned back. I was waterproof, pretty well thornproof. No one was going to stop me going down that path.

But it wasn't just barbed wire. I realised as soon as I tried disentangling it that there was razor wire in there too. My gloves weren't up to tackling that. But if I could lay my hands on some leather gauntlets and some wire cutters, I'd be back.

The snug filled up slowly with the regulars, but there were a couple of gaps where two of the bell ringers usually sat. There was no doubt they'd started their practice, nor much as to where the expression 'dropping a clanger' came from. Nick, no doubt.

'Well, we all have to start sometime,' I told Lindi, covering her ears ostentatiously. 'Remember those early pints you pulled? Now, make sure you're ready for the rush after practice.'

'I wouldn't have thought three was a rush. After all, Lucy can't drink.'

However did people cope with teenage daughters? 'I believe they've got a new person on the team. And Mr Tregothnan always comes in just as they do. Now, I'm telling you, Lindi – you keep him at arm's length. Flirting's one thing, touching up's quite another. And if he thinks he can get away with it with you, what about poor Lucy?' Wrong. There was no love lost between them, as Lindi's exaggerated shrug and pout reminded me. Damnation. And she'd have picked up my description of Nick Thomas as 'a new person on the team'. Why hadn't I simply named him? Nothing like a bit of reticence to stir up gossip, was there?

First in was Ron Snow, rubbing his hands with what looked like a mixture of cold and glee. 'Be able to do Bob Minimus soon,' he crowed, before he even savoured his pint of cider. 'That new lad don't look much, but he'll manage, you mark my words,' he added, looking round as if someone was prepared to challenge him. He got in half of bitter for his crony, Wally Hall.

Aidan Carr, managing to look dapper despite his layers of thick sweater, sashayed in for his G and T. He always camped it up in public, knowing, I suspect, how many fingernails he got under by doing so. He lived with his long-term partner Carl, a younger man who insisted on stripping to the waist to chop wood. Women who hadn't twigged the nature of their relationship lusted after him; those who had complained such a hunk was wasted.

'Such a vile drink,' he murmured as I poured for him. 'I'd adore a decent pint, Josie darling, but think of my image. Now, when are you going to grace our humble board with your fair presence?'

I bobbed a curtsey. 'Whenever you ask me, Sir, she said.' An evening *à trois* with them was an invitation to be cherished. While – with a huge flourish designed to set every old codger's teeth on edge – he unzipped his handbag, I glanced round. No sign of Nick, or of young Lucy.

No. Surely not. I'd got him down as a decent man, for all he was an ex-cop. If he started messing round with the young, Tony's threats to my young lover would pale into insignificance beside my actions.

'Sue said she'd got an extra recruit for you – Mr Thomas, who's staying on Bulcombe's campsite. Didn't he turn up?'

'Indeed he did. And provided a moment of drama.' Aidan leaned forward confidentially.

'He never broke a bell!'

He shook his head, his face serious. 'I was afraid he was having some sort of attack. One minute he was chatting away, if not easily then with due social enthusiasm, the next he was ashen white and literally speechless. I was quite concerned. And what poor Lucy must have thought, goodness knows.'

'Lucy?' I asked sharply.

Aidan raised an eyebrow. 'That poor child has borne more than her share of burdens, Josie, but having a strange man look at you as if he'd seen a ghost can't have been pleasant. However, he pulled himself together and joined in –'

'We heard!'

'– and has promised to come next week, work permitting. Have you any idea what his line of business might be?'

'Some sort of civil servant, he said.'

'Totally respectable, then. Which is fortunate, since he insisted on walking Lucy home. He said he wouldn't let his own daughter walk around after dark on her own.'

'You think that was a good idea?'

'Lucy seemed to think so. She was asking for some information for one of her school projects. But you can ask him yourself

– here he is!'

Ron Snow was on his feet faster than I'd ever seen him move. 'Well, young Nick, it's time for your scrumpy. Tradition, isn't it, missus, that we wet a new ringer's head. Come on, pull him a pint. And then it's down in one, isn't it, boys?'

I did as I was told. After all, it was his fuss to make, not mine. Then I had an idea. 'We've got this all wrong. It should be a yard of ale.'

He might get drunk, but at least ale might be kinder to that ulcer of his. Imagine, tipping a pint of pure acid on to an open sore. His throat worked as he swallowed saliva. Or it might have been one of those clever tablets of his. With a wonderful impression of nonchalance, he reached for the vile liquid and downed it in one.

He acknowledged the cheers and stamps of the little group of regulars, and looked as if to join them. But they returned to their allotted chairs, any gap seamlessly closed. Was it their rudeness or his ulcer that turned him ashen white? He waved a perfunctory hand in farewell, and, whatever his hopes or intentions might have been, turned and left the bar.

Chapter Five

They'd gone! My brand new Portaloos had gone! When the hell had that happened? And why? I was on the phone before you could say urinal, before I was even dressed, staring down at the spot where they'd been while I was still mother naked.

'Collected! Why should they have been collected?'

'You phoned yesterday morning, or your barman did.'

It was hard to stay furious when the old guy had such a gentle Mummerset burr. But I did my best. 'I shall have to speak to my barman,' I lied tartly. 'In the meantime, I want them replaced, and – are you listening? – I want you to write in big letters on my file that they will not be removed again except on my personal request. In writing. With my signature, which you will check against the signature on my contract. Yes, of course service them regularly. But don't take them away. Or I'll ram you head first down one before it's emptied. Understand?'

He understood.

I was due for a talk with Dominic Webster, my architect, so I had to forego my early walk. Calories apart, it wasn't much loss. The hills and the sky were both the same leaden grey, and the roads awash. Definitely a day for headlights. I picked my way slowly into Taunton, slashing through puddles halfway across the road. At last I parked on the far side of the cricket ground, which was convenient for the architect's office if not for shopping.

Only to have Dominic's receptionist telling me, in that singsong delivery so beloved of estate agents and flight attendants, that his car *had* broken *down*, but that she was sure that Dom *would* be with me *as* soon as *possible*.

'How soon is soon?'

We established that his diary was clear for the rest of the morning, flooded foundations preventing him from making the scheduled site visit to somewhere near Exeter that had necessitated my early appointment. So I might slip to the shops for an hour. Actually I wanted to go to the library and have a root round. After all, if Mrs Greville owned the area, that barbed wire would be on her land, and it would no doubt give Sue enormous satisfaction if I could make the old bat remove it. OK, not with her own bare hands. But it would be a peace offering.

Head down, umbrella up, I ran slap into Nick Thomas, in a brand new Barbour. Was this the sincerest form of flattery? More likely the only practical choice. 'Not working, Copper?'

'I've run out of milk.'

'Don't you have a minion?'

'I work on my own. I told you.'

'I didn't realise it was as alone as that. Come on, I know a place where we can get a decent cup of coffee. I want to pick your brain. And you can get your milk on the way back. And some water biscuits – they're supposed to be good for bad stomachs.'

'So what did you want to know?' he asked warily, as we sat at right angles to each other in the bay window of a café that wanted to be chic but ended up chi-chi. Our waterproofs, dripping on to the floor beneath the curly hat stand, didn't help the ambience.

'Land law. Can a landlord just block a public right of way if he feels like it?'

'You know as well as I do that he can't.' Was I meant to take that as a compliment? 'But it's not land law. It's an offence under the Highways Act of 1980. Section 137 as I recall. The same legislation we used to make demonstrators move on, as it happens. You report the obstruction to the county council, who'll have some sort of team devoted to such offences. Their officers will serve notice requiring the obstruction's removal with a specified, suitable time. Failure to comply will result in prosecution at a magistrates' court, the maximum fine being £1000.'

I sat back, mouth agape. 'Well, I'm blessed. You know, you almost grew back your white shirt and epaulettes before my very eyes. Sir!' I gave a mock-salute. 'So all I've got to do is go to the council and they shift it. Pouff!'

'In time.' He returned to his washed out self. 'It rather depends on what else they've got on their plate. And in this weather they may have other fish to fry. Or other obstructions in the form of fallen trees to worry about. Do you know who owns the land? Sometimes a simple face to face request is sufficient.'

'I'm averse to curtseying. And grovelling in general. And that's what Mrs Greville would want before she even consented to see me. Aristo of the old school, according to Sue Clayton. The sort whose *noblesse* obliges others to do things. She owns your campsite, by the way. Bulcombe's just the manager.'

'I'll practise my underwater bowing, then. Wasn't there a Greville in some sort of political scandal?' Ah, would that explain Sue's ire? 'Luke Greville? Must be twenty years ago. Would they be related?'

'I've no idea. What sort of scandal?' And why didn't I remember anything about it? What was I doing twenty years ago that would blot out something like that? Ah. Dealing with Tony's threats to have Mike's wedding tackle removed and used as stuffing.

'I can't remember. I had other things...' He shook his head, like a dog disliking water. He managed a grin. 'Oh, some sort of grubby little hands in till scandal, I dare say.'

'Not sex? No bondage and S and M with half the Cabinet? How disappointing.'

'Not that particular scandal, not as far as I remember. In any case, if they were Maggie's favourites they seemed to be able to get away with a few sexual peccadilloes. Money would be my bet. Anyway, he got deselected, and then they found him a safe Euro-constituency, and he's off there now, legislating from Brussels.'

'Perhaps they went on the same principle as Claudius's for shipping the mad Hamlet off to England – one other bit of corruption wouldn't be noticed in the shambles of European administration.'

His eyebrows shot up. He needed to trim them – four or five hairs, already old men's tufts, were growing wild and unruly. 'Since when did you read Shakespeare?'

'Since I did my Open University course. You never asked how I qualified to run a pub, Copper. I'll tell you. The hard way. When I'd done my first course with the OU, I thought it'd be more fun to study full-time, so I became a mature student. So if there's a catering qualification going, I've got it. I practically took root at the College of Food. Waitressed, maitre d'h'd, administrated – oh, and cooked. There.'

'Well, good for you. I have to hand it to you, Josie – you're a woman of parts, aren't you?'

'Most of them much smaller than they were. Come on, Copper, just because I'm not going to eat one of those gorgeous cakes doesn't mean you can't. Good for the stomach, I'd say.'

He hesitated.

'You took a risk, sinking that muck last night.'

'Had to, didn't I?' He took a chocolate shortbread.

'You men and your face-saving.'

'Fortunately the stench in that open sewer of yours was enough to bring it all back without it hanging around. Hell, Josie, I've smelt some vile things in my time, but nothing like that.'

'That's why I had those Portaloos installed.'

'Had.'

'Hmm. They seem to have disappeared, don't they?'

'Dead cats; disappearing loos. Are the villagers usually like this?'

'I wouldn't know. It's the first time I've crossed one of them.'

And so to the library. It was such fun to be rooting around again. One of the best bits of all those years of study was going through the archives of a Midlands stately home and finding Elizabethan recipes and cross-referencing them with herbals to find the appropriate ingredients. I wouldn't end up with highly-spiced mince pies (made with minced meat, not mincemeat); I might end with a spicy bit of gossip about Mrs Greville's son. And I might find out why Nick stumbled when he referred to the scandal. Something that had affected him. Something that had given him his ulcer, stopped in its tracks the career of a highly talented police officer (yes, as Tony always used to say, praise where praise is due, and you don't get to be a DI before you're thirty, not without something between the ears) and now occasionally paralysed him. Like in front of all those TVs. And, from what Aidan said, in the middle of bell ringing practice.

Who's Who didn't go into Luke Greville's deselection, of course. It did confirm that he'd been born Lucas Cornelius Hetherington Greville in 1958 in Somerset, and had been educated at Eton. He hadn't gone on to Oxford or Cambridge, however, or any other British university, but to a place in Germany I'd never heard of. His hobbies were cricket, polo and philately. He'd been an MP in a safe as houses Tory constituency from 1988 to 1993. In 1996 he'd become a Euro MP. Three years for the scandal to die down. It must have been a big one – had he stolen a Penny Black?

Or the cricket or polo equivalent?

OK. Microfiche time.

My decision about which story to pursue first, Greville's or Nick's, was made for me. The library had only national newspapers on microfiche, and in particular the *Times*. If Nick's case hadn't been prominent enough to reach that, I'd have to get one of my Birmingham cronies to do digging for me. Almost rubbing my hands with glee, I started on Greville. Only to find my mobile chirping illicitly away. Dominic had arrived at the office.

'Go to a library!' Nesta screeched loud enough for Dominic's receptionist to raise an eyebrow. I held the mobile away from my ear for safety's sake.

'Not just any library, Nesta. The Central Reference Library. Failing that, the *Evening Mail* offices. And ask to see copies for 1984 to 1988. You're looking for the biggest police stories – front page news.'

'Anything in particular?'

'Good girl – you always did give in gracefully. No. I've got one or two ideas but I want you to come up with the biggest. And report back to me. Friday?'

'Make that a week on Friday. I've got a new fella and –'

'New fella! Tell! Hell, Dominic's ready for me. Talk to you soon!'

I spent the afternoon talking to my new meat suppliers, Dan Troman and Family. At least, they'd be my suppliers if the test run proved satisfactory. The prices were very much higher than those I'd been used to, a fact I floated across our negotiating table, which was, incidentally, a refectory table dating from the year dot in the middle of a huge kitchen in the family farmhouse. If I'd been them I'd have used a photograph of it in my publicity material; I might well in my own, provided all went well.

'How much did you say?' Dan's eyebrows headed for what had once been his hairline. He might have been a caricature of a farmer, big and broad with hams for hands and a ruddy outdoors complexion emphasising the blue of his eyes.

I repeated the figures.

He shook his head. 'Even with conventional farming I couldn't do it for that. Here, Abigail!' He summoned his wife, a rangy woman who looked as if she'd be more at home in a classy solicitor's office than in a farmyard. 'No wonder we only cater for niche markets.'

She looked long and hard at me. For a moment I was reminded of Nick in his keen young days, sniffing out a lie. 'Is this some loss leader? Does his poultry cost twice as much as usual?'

'I've never used him for chickens.' They came free-range from a neighbour, who also supplied me with eggs.

'Pork?'

I might have been on a witness stand. 'I've not used it enough to have a regular supplier.'

'Has he ever offered it to you?'

'Look, I'm only asking you to price up a regular delivery of beef. If you can offer pork and bacon – yes, I'd kill for good old-fashioned bacon, the sort that doesn't leave white goo in your pan – then let's talk about that too. Meanwhile, let's stick to this particular issue, shall we?'

Over a cup of Earl Grey, served by Abigail in a china cup after we'd come to an agreement, I asked, 'Why were you so concerned about my original supplier's price?' But I knew the answer already.

'If it's not off the back of some lorry,' she said, despite Dan's warning cough, 'I'd say it was old stock illegally slaughtered and put into the food chain.'

'There's no call to make accusations,' Dan protested.

'Oh, there is,' I said. 'The thought had crossed my mind, too – why do you think I've come to you? Yes, just to celebrate, just this once, I will have one of those scones, please.' It came with clotted cream, and jam. In my mind's eye I could see the judder of the scales. But it was worth it. Every last gram.

Chapter Six

Friday morning was Josie-time, my own private quality time. Each week I left the village at eight thirty-five prompt. If I passed anyone – and today it was Fred Tregothnan apparently arguing the toss with Nick Thomas as they stood outside the village shop – I waved, but no one in the village knew where I went. Maybe they thought I had an assignation with a secret lover – and I was happy to keep it that way. Actually, they'd have been half right. Piers, the instructor, and I did have the odd highly pleasurable shag, and it was always nice to know I could pull a bloke half my age, but the main business of the morning was a flying lesson. I'd gone on the principle that if Sarah Ferguson could fly a helicopter, so could I. I'd no ambition, as she did, to write children's books about choppers. Certainly not *children's* books about *choppers*! I just did it for the pleasure. It invigorated me for the whole of the next week. Well, the flying or the recreational sex.

I always got back in time to open up the bar, remind Lindi exactly what she was supposed to be doing and get into the kitchen. There was more passing trade on Fridays, people nipping off to their holiday homes or heading back to the city a day early to beat the weekend M5 jams. Today I was gratified to have quite a run on the organic steak I'd brought back with me, and plenty of favourable comment. I'd made sure I marked it up as a Special, lest people compare the price with the one in the menu. When I had a new menu printed, the prices would be even higher, so I could sell it at a profit, not just little more than cost.

As soon as Reg Bulcombe registered the offer on the blackboard, he strode over to me, jabbing at my chest. I stared down at his parsnip of a finger.

'Yes, Reg. What can I get you?' I asked before he could speak. 'Your usual?'

'I can't have my usual, can I? 'Cos you've slapped a fancy great price on its head. Going organic, are we? We'll see about that. You mark my words we'll see.'

'If you mean to get rid of the Portaloos again, you'll find I've trumped you. Now, do I draw you a nice cool pint or are you going to throw your toys out of the pram and stump off with your thirst still raging?'

There was a murmur from his cronies. His round, was it? I filled half a dozen glasses, some scrumpy, some bitter, passing them over in pairs.

As he took the last, he hissed, 'You turn your nose up at good meat at my prices – you're off your head, woman.'

'I told you, Reg – I need paperwork for my accountant. You come up with the documentation: I might do business with you again. We'll have to see, won't we? After all, like it says on the board, this is an unrepeatable offer. Or did you leave your reading specs at home?'

'Your fancy writing, that's the problem. That and the fancy prices.'

'He's right,' Fred Tregothnan, who'd just appeared, butted in. 'You need to keep your prices down, if a man's going to eat and pay his vet's bills before Christmas! You'll just have to get in the queue, Josie.' His tone was jocular enough, but I fancied the message wasn't. Reg's farm never had paid well, according to the village, which is why he'd turned the flattest of his fields – coincidentally the one most prone to flooding - into the mobile home site. I didn't know how campers rated such facilities, but I couldn't imagine Reg earning the equivalent of a Michelin star. His preferring the foetid old privy to the Portaloos didn't augur well, did it?

Fred had his usual brandy and soda. It was unlike him to drop in in the middle of the day, still less like him to order food and sit on his own to eat it. He had the last of the organic steaks.

'So is there any real difference,' I asked as I took it to his table, one of the patio ones, 'between organic meat and your bog standard commercial stuff?'

He shook his head. 'Some folk even think ordinary husbandry's better for the animals, because they get more preventive medicine –'

'As in antibiotics,' I put in.

' – and I'd be hard put to tell the difference between the two. But I can tell the difference between any meat and that from beasts given Angel Dust –'

'Angel Dust?'

'It's highly illegal, so you won't be asking me to prove it with a blind tasting.'

'Where did you have it?'

'Over in the States. It's a hormone-based growth accelerant, banned throughout Europe. They even have the sense to ban the US meat produced with it. It makes the animal grow very quickly, and to my mind gives nasty, spongy meat. Pap.'

'But you won't be top of the queue if I go completely organic.'

'There are good organic farmers and bad organic farmers. A lot depends on the butcher, too – how long he hangs his meat, and in what temperature. Beef, now, it needs to go really dark, not this bright red stuff people like from their supermarkets.'

I didn't point out I'd spent more years at college than I liked to recall learning about the colour of meat. Customers liked to think they know best. 'These new suppliers said they knew every animal by name – oh, I know they were playing the sentimentality card – and had them slaughtered locally. At least they died happy.'

'That's a factor. The enormously long journeys the poor beasts make to slaughterhouses – they're unforgivable. But that's the government's fault, all this bloody red tape they tie us around with.'

I nodded. I'd come across Compassion in World Farming during my travels on the Net.

By now he was well into his stride. 'No wonder more and more vets are turning away from large animal practices and sticking to tabby cats and terriers. Which reminds me,' he said, smiling ironically, 'will you be serving the stirrup cup to the hunt this year?'

But at that point one of the walkers asked for his bill, and I didn't quite hear Fred's question. Accidentally on purpose. I still hadn't made up my mind. But if Sue could refuse to bless them, I was that much closer to refusing to serve them. Why didn't they do what other hunts did, gather at some big house? I could have volunteered Mrs Greville as hostess there and then.

Now, why hadn't Fred joined his mates? For all he was a professional man, educated and not short of a pound or two, he usually mixed with the settle crowd. It was their highest praise, that he didn't have a bob on himself. Maybe that quip about money had offended them. Maybe it wasn't a quip at all. Both Reg and Ted Gay had got up to lean over his table, talking earnestly. Or was it meanly? Gay was jabbing the air, his dirty finger an inch from Fred's nose. How on earth had dear little Lucy managed to spring from loins like those?

Fred managed to ignore any threat, smiling and leaning back in his chair as the others slouched off.

Lindi began to saunter round collecting glasses, and, even as I watched, what did the bloody man do but put his hand up her skirt and goose her?

I was at his table before he could remove it. 'Mr Tregothnan, if you can't treat my employees with more respect I shall have to ask you not to patronise this pub. Lindi, there are people waiting to be served.'

'But it was only a bit of fun, Mrs Welford,' she bleated.

'It may be, until you decide to sue me for not protecting you from sexual harassment. Off you go. And you, Mr Tregothnan, have to choose whether to keep your hands to yourself or drink elsewhere.'

I wasn't surprised when there was a thundering on the kitchen door five minutes later. I hadn't seen him off the premises, nothing confrontational like that, so I should imagine this was his way of proving he wasn't going quietly. I stepped out, closing the door behind me. No rows in my food preparation area. Not with all those knives ready to hand.

'How dare you, you cow?' he began.

I summarise: every word was accompanied by a profanity. Not that I could complain. I was about to use quite a few myself.

'I'll tell you how I dare,' I said. Years before I'd heaped curses on Nick Thomas's head. I repeated them now with interest. My voice never got above a quiet monotone. I might have discussed the weather with more animation. But he got my drift: you didn't mess with Josie Welford. 'So now you know,' I finished.

'You're welcome here any time, any day. But you do not lay a hand on my girls. Ever again. Now, go and castrate a cat and chew on my words.'

I turned on my heel and returned to the kitchen.

A few minutes later Lindi appeared, lower lip trembling. 'All those things you said, Mrs Welford – did you mean them?'

'Of course not. But he needed scaring. Men have to learn that "no" means "no", Lindi, and we're the only ones to teach them as far as I can see. And that means some of us have to learn to say it. Go on: have a try. Go on. You don't have to be rude. But you mustn't giggle and wiggle your bum while you're saying it. "Stop that, please. I don't like it." Go on. I mean it, Lindi.'

I was out and about early on Saturday too, equipped with seca-teurs and leather gloves. Sue had persuaded me against my better judgement that I had flower-arranging skills that could be used by the women decorating the church. Women? Silly me. Ladies, of course.

In the summer most of the flowers came from local gardens. At this time of year they came from a flower wholesalers in Exeter, Sue setting out well before six every Saturday morning to collect them. We tended to work in threes, the rota apparently having been worked out at random. But Jem and his wife had decided to sneak a rare weekend away from the shop so I'd been pulled in as substitute for Molly.

Sue had put the flowers – gladioli, asters, dahlias and chrysanths – in a couple of deep black plastic buckets that could, with the addition of a wodge of Oasis, double as vases. More than half, a vivid mix of colours with Michaelmas daisies and some of those imported daisies, turquoise and orange and bright blue, which always reminded me of a child's scribble, had already been removed and lay on a groundsheet. You'd need sunglasses to work with them.

We had three or four displays on ordinary Sundays, and they'd usually last, with a bit of judicious dead-heading, for a couple of weeks, and maybe, in chilly weather, even longer. Our church didn't, after all, run to much in the way of heating.

I checked the vase on the altar – no, nothing could be retrieved from that. And the water was so rank it turned my stomach. Out to the compost heap, then. I propped the empty vase under the stand-pipe we use, hoping the force of the water would wash away some of the green sludge, and wandered off to look at the graves, pulling weeds here and there as I went. My route took me down towards the stream I'd walked beside earlier in the week. How many folk had died in times past because they drew their water from a stream polluted by the graveyard, innocent, clear water, but far from pure? I leaned on the wall and peered.

Pink water? Not pink as in strawberry ice cream, but pink as in the water left when I soaked Tony's handkerchiefs he really should have thrown away after one of his nosebleeds. Why should the stream be any sort of pink? It wasn't as if we'd got any industry to turn it that colour. I'd once been to some ancient abbey up in Yorkshire only to get hay fever from the river – it ran past a shampoo factory, and frothed myriad bubbles, giving off the richest of pongs. Unforgivable, of course, but in those inno-cent days before tight environmental controls it was almost funny. Our stream didn't smell, though.

The altar vase still did, but not so much. I gave it another swirl, resolving to bring rubber gloves and a scourer next time.

By now the other lady was back from wherever she'd gone. No explanations for arriving, sorting flowers and then popping out again.

'Those are my flowers,' she greeted me, flexing her secateurs.

I didn't need to ask which. 'Very well. And where are they to go?' Though I could have put money on the answer.

'On the altar, of course. Where is the altar vase?'

I passed it to her; it was still dripping, of course. How she'd deal with the wet bottom and the altar's pristine white linen cloth, I had no idea.

'I don't know you, do I?'

How could some only five foot two look down her nose at me? 'Josie Welford.' I put out a friendly hand, ready to shake hers. She neither shook it nor responded with her name. 'And you're…?' I prompted.

'Mrs Coyne. You're from?'

From? Ah, which house! Brean Park or Teign Court, that sort of from. 'The White Hart.'

'The publican! What on earth are you doing here?'

'Arranging the flowers beside the lectern.' I suited the deed to the word.

'A publican. Arranging flowers.'

The conversation didn't develop much. I didn't know my Bible well enough to tell her exactly what dealings Christ had had with innkeepers, but I did want to mouth words like 'pharisee' and 'whited sepulchre' under my breath. Anyone else I might have made a quip about water and wine and the pink stream, but any more snubs and I might forget Whose house I was supposed to be decorating.

Mrs Greville's, I suppose, to judge by the memorials and brasses. Well, Mrs Greville's husband's ancestors, at least. It wasn't a terribly distinguished church, every period having had a little go at it, the Victorian Grevilles most of all, with a floor tiled in glossy blood and custard. But I enjoyed decorating it, all the same, tucking vases into niches that might once have held statues, before Cromwell or someone knocked them off their perches. I was happy to let Mrs More Money than Taste go wild with her colours. My restricted palette did very well as far as I was concerned – whites and yellows, yellows and oranges, oranges with russets. Halfway through, I produced the flask of coffee I always shared with my usual partners, Jem's mother Rose and an aunt of Lucy's. I unscrewed a cup – would she like to join me? She shook her head abruptly: she was busy on far more important things, the gesture said. She was, too. Her masterpiece was no more than halfway complete.

The church door opened gently to admit a lady in her sixties, terribly thin with the consequence that she looked amazing in her jeans and jerkin. Sue's *bête noir*, Mrs Greville. She smiled vaguely at us both. 'Barbara. Mrs Welford. I'm sorry I'm so late. One of the dogs… I waited ages for Mr Tregothnan but there was no sign of him at his surgery this morning. I suppose he must have had an emergency somewhere.' She looked around the church, spreading her hands as if genuinely embarrassed. 'There doesn't seem much for me to do.'

'Is the dog very ill?' I asked. 'I'm Josie, by the way.'

'Caro. I take it you and Barbara have already introduced yourselves.' She put out her hand for me to shake. She could have
done with a good manicure. 'Spud? He's just off his food. So
unlike him, though. Now, why don't I make amends by sweeping
up? That's coming along beautifully, Barbara – such verve. And
Josie – now, there's only one thing wrong there, my dear – no
one'll see it, tucked away down there. Let's pop it onto a kneeler,
shall we? Did I ever tell you about my favourite kneeler? It's in
Hereford Cathedral. The SAS one. Such a hoot. You can just
imagine them all blacked up for some terrible mission and one of
them saying, "Hang on, Sarge, just got to finish this corner."'

Our laughter rang round the church. Why on earth had Sue so
taken against her?

We lifted the vase as she directed and stood back to survey it.
Yes, I felt quite proud.

She applied herself to the broom, me busy with the dustpan
and brush. While we waited for Barbara to stick in the last few
dahlias, I asked, 'Have you noticed the stream recently? It's gone
a funny colour.'

'The rain, of course,' Barbara cut in.

Why didn't she ask what was funny about it? 'I'm sorry?'

'All that rain – it's bound to discolour the water.'

'But to turn it pink?'

'Pink?' Caro repeated, the same disbelief in her voice as in my
head.

'Have you never noticed how red the soil is in parts of Devon?'
Barbara snipped an end, letting it fall on to the floor. Caro bent,
rather stiffly, to pick it up. Yes: her knuckles were slightly swollen
– maybe her knees or hips were already arthritic.

Actually, I had. I'd been to a sleepy little village with some
bloke I'd met on the Internet. Dawlish. And the stream there was
a deep terracotta colour after a thunderstorm. Not pink, though.
And come to think of it, we weren't in Devon, but in Somerset.
Just.

One part of her perfect triangle stood up too high, mocking

the rest. It would have been the work of seconds for me to nip it out, but I refrained. Caro, winking with the eye Barbara couldn't see, gave it a deft shove.

'Ladies, I'm sorry to be such a bore, but I must have another go at seeing the vet. Can I offer you a lift, Josie?'

She was the sort of woman to whom I could pat my buttocks and say, 'I need the walk, thanks. I hope your poor Spud improves.' Then I had a spurt of courage. If Sue could do it, so could I. 'Actually, there's something I need to ask. I'll walk with you to your car, shall I?'

She raised a well-plucked eyebrow, but held open the door with a friendly smile.

'I was wondering if you'd mind the hunt meeting at the Court,' I began. 'I hate to break a village tradition but –'

'You're anti-blood sports too.'

''Fraid so –'

She gave a snort of laughter. 'My dear, I loathe them too! Why do you think it stopped gathering at the Court and moved to the White Hart? Tell you what,' she added, dropping her voice to a stage whisper, 'Ask Barbara Coyne. She'd love to think she's one up on me!' With a wink, she let herself into her car, not the huge four-wheel drive I'd have expected but a fairly elderly Volvo Estate. Spud lay in the back looking, even to a non-doggy person like me, pretty miserable.

I got back to find some of Barbara's flowers in my arrangements – my lovely golds dotted with turquoise, that sort of thing. 'I found I had some to spare,' she smiled graciously.

'But there are a couple of gaps in your own,' I said, pointing them out and returning my lectern arrangement to the original. 'There.'

By the time she'd rearranged them to her satisfaction I'd retrieved some bright pink carnations from my bronze chrysanthemums – not my favourite flower, I have to admit, but it would have been churlish to spurn Sue's choice.

'They stick out a bit,' I said, aiming for apologetic.

She pulled her half-moon specs a little lower down her nose, and looked slowly from me to the flowers and back again. She didn't need to say it: the interlopers were a metaphor for new-comers to the village. I was a shocking pink carnation amid the mature, sensible natives. I could have pursued the theme: we were more fragrant, easier to arrange and a good deal less unyielding. As it was, I simply held her gaze longer than she thought comfortable.

To do her justice, she fished the carnations out and shoved them into her medley. If I'd been more charitable, I'd have said it was a wonderful floral image of a multicultural city like dear old Brum. As it was, it simply added to the mess.

She might see my suggestion about the hunt as a peace-offering, or even as a desire to appease. Hell. In any case, was it my place to ask her? That had never stopped me yet. I plunged in.

For all I might have been suggesting she host a drug-taking convention, she was tempted. I could see that. She agreed, with a show of reluctance, to discuss it with the Master. We bade each other extremely courteous farewells and I left.

The feel of the secateurs in my hand reminded me of another job involving cutting. The obstruction on the footpath. When I took my walk that afternoon I went armed. First of all I photographed the tangle of barbed and razor wire. Then, with my pliers, I attacked it, piece by vicious piece. It wasn't as easy by any means as I'd expected, and I was glad of my old outsize gardening jacket over my Barbour, not to mention two pairs of leather gloves. With my walking stick, I shoved the stuff into the brambles beside the path. I didn't want to be accused of theft, did I?

Rain came squalling down. I ignored it for a couple of hundred yards, but it was really so unpleasant I gave up with ill grace and headed back to the sanctuary of my living room.

There was an excellent turn out for Sunday lunch, the organic rib of beef earning a lot of plaudits, which I was happy to pass on to my Sunday chef, a bone thin lad called Tom Dearborn, who looked as if he couldn't tell the time of day, but had the nose and palate of an angel. He responded with a close inspection of his clogs.

'Thing is, Mrs Welford, I don't think as how I can work here any more.'

'Tom! But you know I was hoping to take you on full-time as soon as the restaurant was up and running. You're more than good enough.' He was: he was wasted on simple Sunday roasts.

A further inspection of the clogs.

'Have you had a better offer? I'll match it if I can.'

''Tisn't that, Mrs Welford.'

'And you'll be working in a brand new kitchen, with all that state of the art equipment.'

'I know. It's just that …'

I closed the kitchen door so we wouldn't be overheard. 'Just what?' As he hesitated, I asked, 'Has someone suggested it would be better if you didn't work for me? Just because I'm a grockle? Hell, Tom, there aren't many employers round here who aren't grockles! There aren't many employers round here full stop.'

'I know. And you're a very good one, don't get me wrong. And I told him –' He wrung his hands miserably, the big knuckles crunching.

'Told who, Tom?'

If there'd been a crack between the floorboards, he'd have tried to disappear down it. 'This bloke. You don't know him.'

'Did he want you to work for him or just to stop working for me?' I didn't need to wait for an answer. 'Did he threaten you? What'll he do to you if you don't do as he says?'

'He says he'll stop me seeing my Sharon.'

'Come on, he can't play Montagues and Capulets in the twenty-first century! And you're a bit old for Romeo and Juliet,' I added, in case he hadn't followed me. He still didn't, of course.

'Thing is, she still lives at home. And – I'm going to be a father, Josie.'

I hugged him. 'That's wonderful!' If bringing a child into the world without a roof of your own was wonderful. 'When?'

'In February. Thing is, he knocks her about when he's had a few – I –'

'Then the first thing to do is get her out of there. Now. Today.'

Even as his eyes lit up, reality hit him. I fancied it had hit him quite a lot in his short lifetime. 'But where –?'

'Here, of course. You'll have to rough it in the B and B rooms for a bit. But I always did plan to turn the old stable block into accommodation for the chef – we discussed the plans, remember.'

There was a bit in Shakespeare, *Hamlet*, as I recall, about one auspicious and one dropping eye. That was Tom to a T.

'Go and talk it over with her. It's not the Ritz, and everything's pretty tatty. But it's better than being beaten up and putting a baby's life at risk.' Even as I said it, I wondered how much more they might be at risk if they accepted my offer. If a violent father didn't want his daughter's young man even working for me, how much more of a provocation would it be if his daughter sought refuge under my roof?

Chapter Seven

My Monday morning walk established that Nick Thomas had either left for work extremely early or that he'd spent at least the night, and possibly the whole weekend, elsewhere. An old flame? He hadn't looked like a man with a current flame: anyone with less ardour it would be hard to imagine. Even his hair and skin resembled long-cooled ashes.

The ground near his mobile home was wet enough to suck off my wellingtons, which I'd bought in Wellington, the nearby market town, in an emporium called – wait for it – the Wellington Boot Shop. The deep footprints I left – I could have done without the strains of 'Good King Wenceslas' running not quite inexplicably through my head – simply filled with water. In fact, it was so hard to walk through what was now a quagmire that I cut across to the lane, preferring to take my chance with any traffic to the ignominious loss of a boot - especially as there'd be no one to rescue it for me but myself. As I passed the paper skip in which Reg had wanted Nick to bury the cat, Reg himself emerged from his bungalow, which, like the rest of the administration buildings, was on a rise. I suspected he wanted to meet me as little as I him. As he shoved a spade and waders in the back of his utility truck, he glowered at me, logging my visit; any protests I made that I was just having a walk and certainly not visiting Nick would only make matters worse.

So I took the fire to his line. 'Any chance of a lift, Reg? It's no fun, swimming in wellies.'

'Not going your way, am I?' He wasn't as good as the game as I was. 'Got to look at that stream. Making sure it flows OK.'

Was he, now? And what colour would it flow when he'd seen to it? I'd make a point of checking later.

It was hardly flowing at all. My afternoon walk would have to be a bit longer, wouldn't it, to find out exactly what Bulcombe had been up to. No good, if I knew him. The shortest way was along the footpath I'd cleared the previous day. It'd be good to check if my activities had been noted. It was going to be slippery enough under foot for me to take my stick, certainly, but I didn't lug the other gear around – if the razor wire was back, I'd go and yell at the council in person.

No – I wouldn't have to! I'd triumphed over it. It was still where I'd left it. Brilliant. Like a conqueror, I set out on my victory march. Nearly. If I hadn't gone flying I would. I never thought I'd be grateful for a bank of brambles and nettles, but I was this time, once I'd gathered myself up and sorted myself out. So why had I fallen? A quick swish with my stick told me. Someone had stretched at shin height a piece of green wire, the slightly roughened sort I use to train my clematis up, between a couple of clumps of gorse. It actually cut a little notch in the walking stick. And then I went flying again. Yes. Another trip-wire, a couple of feet from the first. Had they been there all the time, just as back up? Or had someone found the mess and set them up in revenge? Maybe they hadn't bargained on the bramble cushion. Maybe they'd hoped for a broken ankle to keep the trespasser out in the cold and wet till they were found. No. For 'they' read 'she'. Or 'I'.

This was beginning to feel personal.

'Hello, stranger,' I greeted Nick Thomas that evening. He looked pale and drawn, but managed a smile of sorts. The sort he'd probably once used as he sat down to interview suspects. So where had he spent his weekend? 'You should have been in yesterday – lovely roasts for lunch, there were.'

'I supposed there wouldn't be a slice or two left to make a sandwich?' He looked like a Bisto kid sniffing in vain.

'I wouldn't be surprised.' If I had to sacrifice that nice slice of roast turkey breast I'd been keeping for my supper, I might as well ask outright. 'Where have you been all weekend?'

'I had a case in Hampshire –'

'Hampshire?'

'Yes.'

'So you work weekends?' When he didn't respond, I said, 'I suppose you're used to working weird hours –' I bit off what I'd been going to say. It was I who'd started this idea that he was a civil servant – no need to blow his cover.

He nodded absently.

'I'll get that sandwich, then.'

He was still nursing his drink, the backs of the other boozers firmly against him, when I carried it through to him. Not a bad sandwich, either. Occasionally I went really wild and baked my own bread, freezing batches of loaves or rolls. Sometimes, at three in the morning, when I really did panic over the future of this place, I'd sneak down and fish out a roll, microwave it and smother it in butter fresh from the Taunton farmers' market. Bliss. Even if I could almost see calories massing. I hadn't given Nick one of these special small rolls. But he had a couple of chunky slices of organic loaf, thickly carved turkey with home-made mayonnaise and a neat little side salad in case he was the sort of man who usually ignored the five portions of vegetables rule.

'If you work in Hampshire, why did you come to live here?' I asked, setting it in front of him. He could hitch himself up on a bar stool or take it to a patio table.

'It seemed a good idea at the time.'

'But you'd do better somewhere nearer Exeter and the M5.'

'It's not so very far from the M5 here, is it?'

I wasn't going to spend the whole evening discussing road communication, so I smiled and turned my attention to bar stock. He withdrew to a table.

When he'd finished, I drifted over to collect the plate. 'Tell me, why should rain make a stream turn pink?'

He shrugged.

'The sort of pink Sue's water must have been when she bathed your scratches.'

He flushed deeply. 'She was kind. A good sort. I suppose I should have gone to church yesterday.'

'It never hurts to swell the numbers,' I agreed.

'I wouldn't have put you down as a devout Christian.'

'My beliefs are my own affair. But if you don't support the ancient institutions that keep the village together how will they survive? And they'll be missed when they've gone. Like this pub and the village shop.' Maybe it was time to hop off my hobby-horse. I grinned. 'And you could have seen the stream for yourself. I called the water company but they couldn't have been less interested.'

'That's officialdom for you. Good sandwich,' he said, heaving himself to his feet. 'I'd best be off – I ought to unpack a few more boxes.'

'You could check the stream, too – it rises on Bulcombe's land. At least, it's not really his, of course, any more than the campsite is – he rents it from the Greville estate. And this morning he was off in his waders with a spade.'

'Problem?'

'Only that the consequence is that the stream is hardly flowing at all now.'

'So where has all the water gone?'

'You tell me, Copper. You tell me.'

Telling Sue Clayton about our joint triumph over the hunt was the least I could do. In private, not with a couple of dozen parishioners milling round shaking hands and smiling after morning service. Should I beard her in her den, possibly catching her unawares, or do the decent thing and ask her back to my place when I accidentally met her as we were buying our *Guardians*?

Any plans had to go by the board, however, when I arrived to find the shop seething with gossip. It seemed that Fred Tregothnan had disappeared. I didn't think he'd been so upset by our tiff that he'd have flitted. But one or two people looked surreptitiously in my direction, and one or two quite pointedly, so I took care not to mention it. In any case, I pointed out when it was clear I had to shove my oar in, he was a grown man and, like the rest of us, was allowed to take a break when he needed it.

Barbara Coyne was standing by the counter, hand held out for her regular papers – the *Mail* and the *Telegraph*. 'Totally irresponsible,' she declared. I wasn't sure whether she meant Fred or me. 'You've obviously no idea how much a rural community depends on its vet. Just skipping off without a locum. Poor Caroline Greville had to take her dog all the way to Taunton.'

Mention a dog in the village, and of course everyone goes doolally. The topic of Tregothnan was swamped in enquiries about the animal's health and anecdotes about dogs – and vets –

the speakers had known. I didn't want to draw attention to myself by offering my real opinions of what Tony used to call mobile poo factories, so I simply took my paper from Claire, Lindi's older and more responsible sister, and slipped out. Sue was just parking – or rather, abandoning her poor vehicle with its front wheels jammed into the kerb. The rear ones were still calling for help from the middle of the road. It would have made an interesting project for Nick to teach her a few police driving skills. Even cleaning the headlights – necessary on a day as dark as this – might have made a difference.

She got out slowly, hunching her shoulders and turning up her raincoat collar. The wind lashed her hair across her face: she had to pick strands from her mouth between sentences, which meant her coat flew open. Why didn't she simply button it and have done? But that was Sue for you.

'What's this about you and the hunt, Josie?'

'You've heard already?'

'From about ten different people.'

'Pleased or otherwise?'

'Mrs Coyne was chuffed. But too disgusted with you to admit it. I suppose the rest were divided fifty-fifty. I'm surprised no one buttonholed you after morning service yesterday.'

I wasn't. I'd long since perfected the art of catching only the eyes I wanted to catch.

'Sunday lunch to supervise,' I said tersely. 'Anyway, there's more news to put mine in the shade. Fred Tregothnan's done a flit.'

If only there'd been enough light to read her face. Or less wind, so I could have worked out whether she really was swaying on her feet. 'Why?' she asked after a perceptible delay. Though it might have been caused by that flying hair.

I shrugged hugely. 'Maybe because I told him off. Maybe because he's got a new girlfriend in Plymouth. Who knows?'

'But – missing? Really a missing person?'

'That's what rumour says. Hey, let's go round to his house and have a look. Come on, Sue, it's your morning off. Come and do something schoolgirlish and then I'll brew you your best cup of coffee this week.'

In the half-light, which was obviously all we were going to get this morning, Tregothnan's house looked unexpectedly forlorn. He'd never maintained it to the picture postcard standards of most of the village. Judging by the slippery moss beside the front door, one of his gutters had been blocked for some time. The paint was peeling, too, and what we could see of his curtains suggested they hadn't seen a cleaner's since they'd been hung. The side entrance, to his surgery, was better maintained, and his brass plate was like a beacon.

Sue set off round the back like a greyhound

'Hey, where are you going?'

'To look for the key, of course,' she said, over her shoulder. 'His mother always used to keep it under a flowerpot. I'll bet he does too.'

He did. We stood and stared, Sue at the key, me at Sue. 'You really can't use it, you know,' I said. 'Go on, cover it up again.'

'But if –?' She was wild-eyed, pointing at the house.

I patted her arm – time to bring her back to reality. 'If he's officially a missing person, the police will have checked he's not lying ill inside,' I said, quite gently.

'But if they haven't –'

'And if they found us in there we'd have a lot of explaining to do. I'm sorry, Sue, it was a stupid idea. Really stupid. Let's go and have that coffee.'

Her lower lip trembled into a stubborn line. 'As the village pastor –'

Trying to sound grudgingly reluctant, I said, 'OK. I'll come with you.' The key almost leapt into my hand.

Leaving our muddy shoes on the mat, we stepped from a tiny scullery, still with a crock sink and a utility electric cooker, into the kitchen. Apparently he'd shared the house with his mother, inheriting it when she died in her late eighties. He must have been a child of her middle age. It looked as if she'd stopped decorating the moment he was born, and he'd made no changes since her death. It smelt of damp and toast and bacon. The kitchen led into a short passage to the front door. To the right was a door that must lead to the surgery – I wasn't interested in that. The bedrooms and living room were more my line. Especially the latter – though just for the record I went upstairs first, to make sure we weren't sharing the place with a corpse. No, the bathroom, cheerless as you'd imagine a monk's, and both bedrooms, were unoccupied. There was a frowsty male smell, bedclothes including an old-fashioned quilt tumbling onto the unvacced floor as if he'd just got out of bed. The back bedroom, once his mother's to judge from the floral wallpaper and framed prints, was just a junk room.

Downstairs, then.

To my amazement Sue was ferreting through his bureau. 'Address book. Bank details. The police'll need them.'

And would have been happy to find them themselves, no doubt. However, her good-heartedness gave me the chance to look at his books – he had a row of what looked like first editions of scientific books, with a scattering of philosophy – not at all what I'd have expected. If ever a man was a porn man, it was Fred. I'd bet a week's takings there'd be some highly dubious stuff on the hard disk of the state of the art computer sitting uneasily on a fifties table next to a well-worn armchair. I could almost see him sitting there perving away. What I couldn't work out was why a professional man with a decent small animal practice, not to mention his farm work, should live in such a museum piece. What did he spend his money on? Not clothes, not car, certainly not home.

'Have you found anything?'

Sue shook her head. 'I wonder where else I should look.' She peered round the room.

'His dispensary? I mean, he'd have to keep all his practice records somewhere – perhaps he lumped everything together.' I went through into the hall and stared at the door. It had a couple of serious locks – all the drugs he needed to keep, I suppose. I put my nose to one of the keyholes and sniffed. No, nothing but the smell of doggy wee that veterinary disinfectant never quite eradicates. Not a body, I'd stake my life on it.

There was a loud rattle at the front door. Sue and I grabbed each other. I twigged first. 'Post, I suppose.' I toddled off to have a look. Yes, a heap of what looked like circulars, nothing personal. I leafed through it twice, just to make sure.

Shrugging, I called, 'Time we left the experts have a go, Sue.'

She followed me reluctantly, hugging her coat round her and slipping her shoes on as slowly as a bullied kid on the way to school. She was clearly in two minds over the key. With an ambiguous glance at me, she replaced it under the pot.

'You said you'd told him off,' she said, turning back slowly to the street.

'I found him with his hand in Lindi's knickers. Literally. Broad daylight. Stupid girl stood there giggling. God knows why she didn't tip his drink over his head. I would have.'

She laughed, the sound brushed away by the wind. 'I'll bet you would.'

Tuesday night was WeightWatchers night in Taunton, and it would take more than a drop of rain to put me off. Actually, it was rather more than a drop. It hadn't stopped all day. Much to my disappointment at lunchtime the snug had been almost empty – I'd have loved a good turnout of settle men, all seething with speculation about Fred and eyeing me meaningfully. I doubted if there'd be many more that evening. All the regulars knew there wasn't much in the way of food on Tuesdays, and there'd be no passing trade, not if people had any sense. So I took myself into Taunton early, scuttling to the library so I could carry on checking Luke Greville. Actually, now I'd met his mother, I didn't want him to be an out and out villain. Perhaps if he'd just committed a sexual peccadillo with a consenting adult I wouldn't have objected. Especially one with a happy ending. But it was frustrating, all the same, to find that although the Fraud Squad had reportedly investigated his affairs, no charges were ever pressed. The papers were very cagey about making direct allegations – hadn't they ever heard of *Publish and be damned*? There was nothing obvious about Nick Thomas, either, though I noted a number of crimes in Brum that had been dramatic enough to creep into the *Times*. I'd get Nesta on to all of them.

* * *

After a cup of tea – yes, literally that, no milk, no sugar and certainly no sticky bun – I dropped into the WeightWatchers session and had the satisfaction of having lost another two pounds and a bit of an ounce. I stopped long enough for a natter with a couple of women I know by sight, before paddling back to the car.

Despite my elation, I wondered if I'd been foolish to come out. No. I didn't wonder. I knew. The A road was awash, and we got diverted well before Kings Duncombe. It was hard to tell road from puddle, and at times I was scared by the feeling that the car was being sucked away even as I drove. On one corner the flashing lights of a fire engine illuminated the ghostly figures of householders trying to rescue their furniture as their house was pumped out. Poor sods. Thank God the White Hart stood at the higher end of the village. I wouldn't give much for the shop's chances if the stream overflowed its banks.

Someone from the council, swifter to respond to an excess of water than the water company had been to an excess of colour in water, had already dropped off ROAD CLOSED signs. I got diverted several more times, before I saw the lights of the village ahead. Even as I pulled into the pond that was my car park, they started to gutter. Candles? Yes, I had plenty of those. Open fires. Food. Drink. No problem. I could hole up here as long as it took, and make the White Hart the centre of the community it was supposed to be. My predecessor had boasted that he'd never closed even when the village was cut off for eight days by six feet of snow. If he could do it, I could do it. Even if the water lapped and swirled round my feet as I stepped from the car, it was well clear of the four steep steps to the back door.

I stepped into total darkness and a girl's scream.

'Lucy? Is that you?'

'Mrs Welford?' A hand gripped my arm. 'It's only you!'

'Who were you expecting it to be?'

'I dunno. But –'

'Just pass me the torch from the hall table. Where it always is. Thanks. There, that's better. Hang on, what the hell's that lot?' I pointed the torch at a heap of white at her feet.

'Sheets, Mrs Welford. And blankets, like. I've been airing

them.'

'Airing them? Why? And why you? Where's Lindi? Oh, light some candles, girl, and then you can tell me exactly what's been going on.'

Chapter Eight

'It's not Lucy's fault,' a gruff voice from the darkness said.

I swung the torch. 'Nick Thomas!' The beam must have hurt his eyes. After a moment I shifted it. 'What are you doing here?' If I'd expected anyone to be needing a bed it might have been Tom Dearborn's girl, Sharon. So why hadn't she come? I must phone Tom. 'The candles are under the bar, this end, Lucy. And matches.' I pointed with the torch.

'Orphan of the storm,' he said, his clothes dripping on to the flagstones. Had he been swimming? He couldn't have been wetter. 'And Lucy said she was sure since you did B and B, you'd put me up for the night.'

Lucy returned, looking like Lorna Doone in the glow of a pair of candles she'd had the sense to put in pint glasses. As if in role, she almost curtseyed. 'I was just making up one of the en suite rooms.'

'Good girl.' I smiled, but seethed. It wasn't me but my predecessor but one who'd put up the B and B sign. I didn't know how he'd dared. I'd hung up a 'No vacancies' notice, but someone had absconded with it and I hadn't got round to replacing it.

The rooms were in a very poor state, and I didn't like to charge for them. I had nowhere to offer a guest breakfast – you could cut up the stale air in the bar and carry it out in chunks. This might pass as rustic atmosphere if you were downing a lunchtime drink but wouldn't go with cereal and skimmed milk. On the other hand, if I offered Nick free accommodation, it might put us both in an awkward situation.

'Leave one of those candles down here,' I said, passing her the bundle of bedclothes. 'Good girl. Careful how you go.' She was half way up the stairs when I realised something was wrong. 'Where's Lindi?'

The poor kid said awkwardly, 'She phoned to say… she couldn't come tonight.'

Did she indeed? 'Well, it was considerate of her to warn me. And to have the gumption to phone you. Off you go.'

Nick didn't watch her up the stairs. Brownie points for that, at least – unless he was afraid I'd throw him out if he did. 'The campsite's flooded. I waded over to get out as much as I could, but then the caravan just floated away, boxes and all.' He was taking great pains not to let his voice break.

All those little things he couldn't bear to leave in store. If I was kind, he might weep. I was brisk. 'Clothes?'

You could see the deep breath, the brace of the shoulders. 'Got a rucksack full. And some photos and things. But most of it's gone.' He swallowed hard.

I couldn't help myself. 'You poor bugger. Go on, upstairs with you. Lucy'll run you a hot bath and then I'll rustle up some food for you. No, leave all those wet things down here – I'll stow them in the boiler room. Oh, for God's sake, man – don't you think I've seen a man in the dark in his knickers before?'

At which point the lights came back on.

The really wet stuff still dripping in the boiler room, and his shoes stuffed with yesterday's *Guardian*, I'd ended up putting all the stuff in his rucksack through the tumble dryer. Though I drew the line at ironing it myself, I was happy to provide him with the wherewithal. I set up the board at one end of my own kitchen, and busied myself starting the living room fire – not so much to keep us warm as insurance against another power cut – and then preparing vegetables. He'd have to eat what I was going to eat, which was not necessarily stuff I served in the bar. Not that there were any clients tonight. If any was fool enough at this stage to venture out for a drink, Lucy could call me. Otherwise she could sit in front of the fire and do her homework uninterrupted, which may have been the reason she volunteered to take Lindi's shift. As for getting her home, I supposed I'd better chauffeur her. Usually she was happy to walk, on the understanding that her dad would meet her halfway, but I didn't see him leaving his fireside just for my peace of mind. His line was that Lucy was used to being on her own. He regarded as downright eccentric my city take on girls wandering solo down lonely lanes.

'The funny thing,' Nick said, resplendent in my black silk kimono, 'is that the far end of the village – you know, the shop end – is dry.'

'Torrential rain apart.'

'OK, not actually flooded. The stream's fuller than you said it was earlier, but certainly not to overflowing. Whereas this end, where you'd have expected it to be flood-free, the lanes are like sluices.'

'Not funny at all if someone rearranges the watercourse,' I said. 'Which is what I bet your nice Mr Bulcombe was doing when I saw him.'

'Why should he want to do that?' A rare smile told me I was interesting him.

'Come on, you're the copper – work it out. Either he doesn't want other people to know that the stream's running pink, so he sends the water another way. Or he's found out what you really do – and not, before you ask, from me – and he wants you out of here.'

'You sound like a cop yourself,' he said, taking the hanger I passed him.

'You spend as long as I did with a man the wrong side of the Law, you learn to think like a cop. Studying the opposition's tactics, you might say.'

'Sounds reasonable.'

'So who knows you're with the Food Standards Agency? No, don't tell me – Fred Tregothnan. Well, you were a fool to tell him.'

'I didn't tell him. One area of our work is meat hygiene. He's the vet responsible for checking a food packing company's premises near Barnstable.'

'Which you had to check out?'

'In a friendly sort of way, I told him I'd be paying a visit in the next few months.'

'If that was the conversation I saw you having last Friday morning it didn't look very friendly. Watch your iron, Copper! That's a decent shirt.' So he was rattled, was he? Any moment now I'd find myself offering. 'Was he upset enough to do a bunk?'

'What the hell do you mean?'

I passed him another hanger. 'Only that Fred's gone walkabout

– and the police have logged him as a Missing Person.'

His reaction was much the same as mine had been. 'Misper? But he's a grown man – they don't usually start worrying this early.'

'Perhaps they know things about him we don't. Or I don't?'

He concentrated on the next shirt, taking great pains with the right sleeve.

'Come on, Copper, any moment now your little pals'll come knocking on the door asking what you were arguing about –'

'Why? Who've you told?'

'All those years married to Tony, and I tell anyone anything I don't have to? But it stands to reason, doesn't it – if I saw you, half the village will already have blabbed. They're probably after me, too, because Fred and I had a pretty audible row about five hours after yours. He was groping young Lindi.'

'Which might explain why she didn't turn up tonight and Lucy filled in?'

'If she'd been upset. She seemed more anxious about my yelling at him than about having his fingers up her bum. Tried to say it was only a bit of fun,' I added in a Lindi-bleat.

'Did she mean it or was she afraid of offending Tregothnan?'

'She made me sound like a spoilsport,' I admitted. 'How much more ironing have you got to do? When the end's in sight, I can start on the supper. While it cooks, I'll run Lucy home – I'll put you in charge of the bar while I'm off.'

'Honoured, I'm sure. Wouldn't it make more sense,' he said, putting the iron on its heel and switching off, 'if I took her? Hell, Josie, don't look at me as if I'm some bloody paedophile. She's younger than my own daughter.'

'I'm sure that's what they all say.' I reached for my keys.

'I was hoping,' he said, suddenly as bright-eyed as the kid policeman I'd once thrown my stilettos at, 'to try out my new toy. You probably didn't see it. It's parked at the front, because I wasn't sure how big your yard is. Or how big the toy is.'

'Not another one with a bloody gas-guzzler! Jesus, you people! Have you no idea how much pollution they push out?' Not nearly as much as my chopper rides, truth to tell, but no one knew about those.

His face fell.

I might have gratuitously smashed a kid's train set. 'But at least you have the excuse that you need it for your job,' I conceded without waiting for him to plead, 'not just for the school run. And presumably you know how to drive the thing – unlike all the mothers round here who think they're giant dodgems.'

His smile was bleak. What nerve had I touched this time? 'It's the greenest I could find,' he mumbled.

'Well, why not give it a spin?' I checked my watch. 'There won't be any customers now. If there are, tough. I'll just give Lucy a shout.'

'Will you be doing the cooking for this restaurant of yours your-self?' asked Nick, now fully dressed again in garments so drab I almost wanted to tell him to slip the kimono on again. He broke a five minutes' silence. He leaned back from the table, dabbing his lips with the linen table napkin, smug as a paterfamilias at his board.

Double-damask linen tablecloth. Silver cutlery. Bone china. Well, the food deserved it. As for the decorative candles in silver candlesticks, they weren't meant to be romantic – they were there in case of another power failure.

'Some of the time,' I agreed. 'After all, I do pretty well every-thing now.'

'I should think you're guaranteed a regular clientèle, then.' He managed a smile.

'Local fresh vegetables, local free range chicken cooked in good quality wine –'

'Local?' He must be feeling better to try teasing me.

'My preference is New Zealand. It'd be hard not to make a meal taste good,' I said, clearing the dishes on to a tray – I'd never been good at clever waiting with plates stacked along my arm, especially with my own china.

When I returned from the kitchen, he asked, 'So you'll be going for a niche market?'

'For the restaurant. And as good as I dare for bar meals. You've barely touched that wine.'

'Best on a full stomach,' he said, drinking quite deeply. 'You neither, actually.'

'Best for a flat stomach. But I wouldn't object to another glass. There are times I'd love to go on a bender and eat and drink a whole week's worth of points in one sitting.'

'Why don't you?' He was topping up my glass, but paused to look at me.

'Because you don't lose as much as I've lost without a good deal of will power. And there's another stone to go. And it'll take even more will power not to pile it all on again. I've seen it dozens of times. The scales. The panic. The diet. And then you get bored or upset or plain greedy and on it all goes again. And then it's the scales, the panic and the whole lot all over again. Which is why I don't just diet, I exercise. Which is why I saw the pink water and the barbed wire on the footpath and Bulcombe armed with a spade. You're in a better position than I am to find how all these are connected. But I'll start you off. Your first weekend here, you found yourself flattened into the hedge. By a large, unlit lorry, Sue said. Which road, Copper?'

'The obvious one. The one leading directly from here to the campsite.'

I stood up to reach out my large-scale ordnance survey map, spreading it on the table in front of him. 'I can't see anything on here to attract large unlit lorries. Can you?'

He looked furtive, then embarrassed. 'Not without my reading glasses, I can't.'

'Go and get them then. That's how you're singing for your supper tonight – by helping me work this out.'

I'd loaded the dishwasher by the time he returned, clutching a swish-looking laptop, plus his reading glasses. He installed himself at the dining table again, checking for a place mat to go under it before I could even yell.

'I use this for the job,' he said. 'It's not got just large-scale maps, you can enlarge whole sections. And there's another programme that gives you aerial views of everything. Want to see?' He vacated his chair so I could look at the screen – I've never worked out why you can only see from one angle. Something to do with the plasma, I suppose.

'So you need aerial views for your work?'

'Hardly. But I do need the maps. And a handy in-car guide to where I am and how to dodge traffic jams. A manor this big, I can justify a few bells and whistles.' He paused. Was he waiting for me to apologise? He ought to have known by know that Josie Welford didn't do apologies.

'"People muthst be amuthsed",' I muttered.

He looked at me sharply. 'Orwell?'

'Dickens. So this is the White Hart, God's eye view?'

'Right. And here it is' – he leant across me – 'on the OS map. And this is how you enlarge it. See?'

'Clever,' I conceded. 'Tell me, does that chariot of yours have one of those on-board computers to say if you're parking safely?'

'Yep. And it changes out of four-wheel drive when I don't need it.'

'So it's got more whistles and bells than the Last Night of the Proms,' I said, amused and almost approving. 'And your campsite is here? And the road runs here. So what we need to look for is where your road intersects with my path. Right?'

'Right. Which would be –' he put a hand on the back of my chair and peered – 'there.'

'But there's nothing there.'

'Officially. So let's change programmes and look from the air. Do you know about grid references? Because that's what you need to type in.'

His turn for the chair.

'Explain as you go: I'd rather learn to fish than be given one.'

'If you can read a map you're halfway there,' he said. 'This is how it works…'

Apt pupil I may have been, but I soon reached out the Laphroaig and a couple of crystal glasses. 'So we're no nearer knowing what's there.'

'Only because these aerial photos may have been taken before the whatever it is was built.'

'I thought you said it was constantly updated by satellite or something.'

'Or because your path leads to another path that intersects with the road. No whisky, thanks.'

'Water? Plenty of that, after all.'

'Not even that, thanks.' He oozed embarrassment. 'Do you want to do another scan?'

'Not tonight, thanks. I need my beauty sleep. I don't yet run to a residents' lounge, but you're welcome to sit in the bar as long as you want. Or here, of course,' I added, not wishing to sound too offensive.

'All that swimming's left me weary, thanks very much.'

The lights flickered and died.

I lit two of the dining table candles from the dying fire, giving him one and keeping the other for myself. 'Did Lucy leave you plenty of blankets? What kind of landlady am I? I should have checked!'

'She left enough for an army. I suspect the towels she found were yours, by the way – they rather stood out against the utility tiling. And she'd found a kettle and tea bags from somewhere, even some little pots of milk.'

'She's got her head screwed on, that kid. Right: do you want a morning call or was your alarm clock amongst the things you rescued?'

I didn't exactly spring out of bed – my joints didn't go in for springing these days – but I got up more quickly than usual to check the power, which was mercifully back on, and the weather. It was no longer raining, even if it looked as if it might start again any moment. Though there were plenty of huge puddles, the roads no longer ran with floodwater. Good. It wouldn't suit me to be marooned. I was showered and dressed and just thinking about breakfast when Nick tapped on my door, shaved and wearing what I took to be his work clothes. He looked more on the point of leaving than demanding a full English.

'I was just wondering about the things in your boiler room,' he said.

'I doubt if they'll be dry enough to wear yet. In any case, you're surely not going into the office – you'll be needing to make insurance claims and generally sorting out your life.'

'Where better than the office? And I can buy some new clothes in Taunton.'

'Where you can also get some breakfast, no doubt. Don't be a fool, Nick – with a stomach like yours, you ought to eat before you do anything. I'm not much of a breakfast woman myself, but there's what the supermarket insists is freshly-squeezed orange juice, fresh fruit and organic bread with that marg that's supposed to reduce your cholesterol. Tea or coffee? Oh, and I eat in the kitchen, if that's all right by you.'

He nodded, looking more daunted than grateful, and followed me, sitting down like an obedient child.

'What you also ought to be doing,' I said, slicing bread and slotting it into the toaster, 'is finding out whether Bulcombe really did alter the course of the stream – it might be an insurance scam, and I'd hate to see him getting away with it.'

'You mean I might not be the target?' He sounded doubtful.

I turned sharply. 'What other threats did you have apart from the dead cats? Come on, Nick: what are you hiding?'

'A couple of headless rats. And I'm not sure the damage to the caravan was accidental.' He mumbled as if was all his fault.

'Damage? You didn't say anything about damage.' I plonked the toast rack on the table as if checkmating him.

'It could always have been a log, I suppose – there was a lot of debris floating around. The current was pretty strong.'

I reached across to tap his skull. 'Hello? It there anyone at home in there? Something stove in your caravan and you think it's an accident? On top of all those other things? For God's sake, Nick you used to be a cop. For how many years? Thirty? When we crossed swords, you were a bright young man, destined to go far. You wouldn't make it to parking warden on today's showing!'

He disappeared, like that cat in *Alice*. Not physically, of course. Just like he had in the superstore. Something switched off inside. I stared, almost as freaked out as he obviously was. I knew you shouldn't wake sleepwalkers, should stop people in epileptic fits swallowing their tongues. But what about men holding a piece of toast in one hand, a cup in the other, staring at something horrible I couldn't see?

At last he put down the cup, and swallowed. 'I suppose you're right.'

Though I couldn't see what bit of my diatribe he was agreeing with, I nodded. 'So are you going to get in touch with the village bobby, or am I?'

He blinked. 'Village bobby? Is there one?'

'Of course not. Not in these days of improved service to the community. But there's a decent sized cop shop in Taunton. There'd be someone there you could talk to, surely to goodness.'

'Not the most popular people, retired officers trying to tell those still serving what to do,' he mused, sinking into officialese as if it were a pair of comfy slippers.

'Not even when you come with evidence?'

'I have no evidence. Not unless you want me to exhume a dead cat from Sue Clayton's back garden.' He changed direction with an almost audible crunching of gears worthy of Sue herself. 'Isn't there someone from the church who could help her with that? Dig it over, plant a few low-maintenance shrubs? It's clear she can't manage it on her own.'

'Maybe you should lead the way by offering her driving lessons,' I said, hoping he'd spot the glint in my eye.

'I'll dare if you dare offer to put her car through a carwash first,' he responded, colour returning to his face. 'Thanks for the breakfast. Look, Josie, it's clear you're not geared up for paying guests at the moment. But if you're right, and there is something going on round here, it'd make some sort of sense for me to stay where I am. Would it be inconvenient? It's not as if I want five star service, bed linen and towels changed every ten minutes. And I could eat in the bar. And I'd pay in advance, if you want.'

'I don't see why not,' I said. 'Until you find your feet, at least.' Goodness knew what the village would say, the two of us holed up together. Half of me wanted to wave a couple of fingers in the air and tell them to count them. The other half wondered if a bit of chaperonage in the form of Tom's pregnant Sharon might not be a good idea. I'd phone Tom when he'd had time to wake up – apart from his Sundays with me, Tom worked one of the late night shifts at an M5 service station, a job he was hopelessly overqualified for. 'And there's no need to pay in advance. That room of yours is so... Seventies? Sixties, even?... I don't like charging for it.'

'You might as well – I shall be chalking it up for my insurance claim,' he said, getting to his feet. 'And meals, too.'

'You shall have a bill, then – all properly receipted. That's why I stopped buying my meat from Reg Bulcombe's crony,' I added. 'No paperwork. All cash in hand.'

He laughed. 'So you did take some notice of what I was saying about BSE, then!'

'I had a good surf round the Internet. I came to the conclusion you had to treat this thirty month regulation with respect. And if you don't know your steak's birthday, you can't send it a card, can you?'

'It's actually quite bad news for organic farmers,' he mused. 'Naturally reared cattle take longer to mature than your average commercial beast. So they're not past their prime at thirty months – they're well short of it, in terms of meat per carcass.'

'The stuff I'm going in for makes up in flavour what it lacks in growth. But I couldn't get Fred Tregothnan to give an opinion one way or another on organic food. Not in front of Reg Bulcombe, anyway.' I paused. Had there been real needle over the vet's bills? Enough for Fred to sit apart from his cronies?

Nick sat down again. 'Why should you mention Tregothnan in conjunction with Bulcombe?'

'Well, you saw them – their backs at least – round the fire.'

'Didn't you think it odd, a professional man hobnobbing with all those yokels?'

'*You can tell a man who boozes, By the company he chooses*,' I quoted.

'So who *got up and slowly walked away*?'

'The last meal he had here, he ate on his own. He had this little spat with Reg – something about not spending in the bar money he owed in vet's bills.'

'In public? Not very tactful.'

'Not a man for tact, Fred Tregothnan. When I banned him, he gave as good as he got, believe me.'

'No,' he said flatly. 'I don't.'

'Ah, you've been on the receiving end of my tongue when I was roused, haven't you. Sorry, Copper, if you took any of it seriously. No hard feelings, I hope,' I added lightly.

He didn't reply. My God, he had taken my foul words to heart, hadn't he? If not in the cold light of day, at least at three in the morning when you can only think of bad things.

I sat down again. 'What happened to you that made you think I'd really cursed you?'

'You see a lot of things as a police officer,' he said in a remote voice, and left the room.

It would have been better if he'd raised his voice or slammed the door.

Fred Tregothnan wasn't your sensitive type, not like Nick. He wouldn't have turned a hair. Surely he wouldn't. We'd talked once or twice about my distant ancestors after I'd told him off for calling someone a bastard gyppo. I'd told him I was entitled to have a foul mouth when roused – it was my only Romany legacy. But he had to watch what he called people, I said. He'd stayed away from the bar a couple of days on those occasions too.

But he hadn't left the villagers in the lurch.

Maybe I ought to take a trip into Taunton Police Station myself – get my word in first.

It was a good job Nick wasn't there to see me. I was playing 'confession is good for the soul' with all I could give it, complete with tears and some sodden paper hankies.

'I was very angry, Sergeant,' I told the bored young woman who'd been landed with listening to the rants of this hysterical old woman. The fact that she was a good five foot six and no more than a size eight, if that, didn't make her any more likeable. Even her hair was genuinely blonde. I pleaded, 'I had to make him realise that what he was doing was completely out of order.' God, I hated that phrase. What did it mean, for goodness' sake? But everyone on *The Bill* seemed to say it, so perhaps I should try it on her.

She nodded, absently, from the way she kept fingering it apparently more interested in a stray spot on her otherwise immaculate chin than in me. 'Are you saying a grown man would be so upset by a few hard words that he left the village and hasn't been seen since?'

I managed a rueful smile. 'Put like that it doesn't make much sense, does it? I'm sorry, I've obviously wasted your time.'

But she wasn't as bored or as stupid as I'd thought her. 'On the contrary. You've been very helpful. Tell me more about the incident that made you so angry. It wasn't you he was assaulting, is that right? But one of your staff. Would she have –'

'Lindi was inclined to think the whole thing was a joke, a bit of silliness. She didn't want me to say anything.'

'Have you discussed it with her?'

'Only in a motherly way. I made her practise saying "No" out loud. A bit of assertiveness training,' I grinned. There was no answering smile.

'It's a close knit community,' she began.

My ears pricked. So they hadn't dismissed the disappearance out of hand.

'Would anyone else have been offended on her account? A father? A brother? A boyfriend?'

'You'd have to ask them,' I said as blandly as I could.

'We will, Mrs Welford,' she smiled ominously, 'we will.'

OK, the interview wasn't going quite the way I'd intended – that was an exit line if ever I'd heard one – but maybe I could capitalise on my mistake. 'People are saying the police are taking this case unusually seriously.'

'I hope we take all our cases seriously, Mrs Welford.' She was shuffling some papers and any moment would close the folder and pick it up to show the interview was over. She did better. She got up, just managing not to yawn.

This was the moment to tell her about the bloodstained stream and the blocked path. That would bring her up short. But a series of intelligent observations wouldn't accord with my earlier ditzy persona, would it? Maybe I'd keep them to myself for a while longer. Until my photographs had been developed at least. First stop Boots, then, and their one-hour developing service.

I was just going back to collect my photos, having spent a miserable hour dodging low pointing brollies and those huge pushchairs with plastic covers looking like mobile intensive care units, when my phone rang.

'Nick?'

'I know it's an awful cheek, Josie, and I wouldn't ask if you weren't a wet weather walker, but would you mind showing me exactly where the path was blocked?'

'Not at all. Provided you've got the right walking gear, that is. Have you?'

'Er …'

'I'm in Taunton myself as a matter of fact. I'll meet you at your office and then we can sally forth together to get you everything you need. How do I get there? I'm just outside Brazz.'

'I could meet you there – '

'And expose me to all those tempting calories? Not bloody likely. OK, fire away –'

Nick's office was as soulless a place as it had ever been my misfortune to see. I stared at the blank walls and minimal furniture.

'I'd offer you a chair, but I think the Defra folk down the corridor may have borrowed it.'

They seemed to have borrowed his kettle, too – the one I'd seen him buy the other day, when he went into one of his brown studies. Should I remark on it or keep mum? 'I thought they were supposed to be improving farming and the environment, not nicking furniture. Shouldn't they get their own? Or are they too busy having *rural affairs*?'

To my amazement, the feeble joke made him put back his head and laugh, the sound echoing round the office as if it hadn't heard such irreverence before. 'Not with me, I'm afraid. Yes, it's a hole, isn't it? It's only when you look at it through someone else's eyes you see how bleak it is. Never mind, I'm sure I shall find a few posters about Colorado Beetle to brighten up the place,' he added, with an encouragingly sardonic grin. Perhaps there was still some life in him.

'A few pot plants, some nice bright mugs – you'll soon make it home. Not that you're here much, are you? On the road most of the time?'

'Apparently work comes in waves. The farm near Southampton I should have gone to today's been cut off by floods. My predecessor was a good boy and finished all his paperwork before he left, so I'm at a loose end.'

'You've spoken to your insurance company?'

'As soon as I arrived. They'd love to send an assessor but don't know when it'll be: I'm not the only one to have suffered.'

'I bet they'd love a few photos of the site.'

'My camera was one of the things washed away.'

'Mine wasn't. I've just bought a new film. Come on – what are you waiting for?'

The razor and barbed wire tangle was just where I'd left it, but no new tripwires had been set up. None that I could see, anyway. I photographed everything again, from a different angle, and then led the way up the path that would eventually take us to Nick's campsite. We didn't talk much. For all he must have been five, maybe seven, years younger than me, he was distinctly out of condition, puffing and blowing and ready to stop at every convenient vantage point.

'What happens if we go up there?' With his walking stick – yes, I'd insisted he bought one of those, to go with his new weather-proof gear – he pointed to his left.

'We get lost. Funny, I'd never even realised there was a stream there. I thought it was just a sheep track that was always a bit wet.'

'It's a bit more than a bit wet now.'

It was a full-blown torrent. How come I'd never registered it? I double-checked with the map: no, nothing. Weird.

Nick peered over my shoulder, tracing its probable route with his finger. 'What's that mean?'

'Some sort of building. Look, there's a track leading to it. From your lane.' I turned. 'Do you suppose the track's wide enough for one of your unlit lorries?'

'I'll bet it is. But I'd rather check it by car than on foot.'

'Yep. The scenic route would be nice on a fine day. OK. Right here, then.'

I snapped away at the campsite, no longer flooded but clearly awash, from a variety of angles. Then we dropped down to the level of the reception area. I was relieved to see that there was no sign of Reg Bulcombe. Nick's staying at the White Hart was one thing; his walking out in the rain with his landlady was another.

Nick quite understood. While I hung back, he peered ostenta-tiously. 'Maybe he's busy contacting the owners of the late, lamented country retreats.'

'"Retreats"? More like last stands!'

'There'll be some corner of an English field that is forever matchwood!' he offered.

Cackling with silly laughter, we headed through the oozing field. I took some record shots, including some of a suspicious gash in the front of Nick's desirable residence, stacked up out of reach on top of other victims, so we couldn't rescue anything more. Then I took some weird ones too. Not quite Man Ray, but pleasingly abstract.

At last, the rain, no more than occasional if vicious spots while we were walking, returned in good earnest. I stowed the camera under my waterproof, patting the pregnant looking bulge.

As we trudged back, Reg's car pulled up.

'Leave him to me,' I muttered, wondering, all the same, what I could say. 'Just smile like a daft grockle.'

But no subterfuge was needed. Head down, Reg kicked the cab door shut and strode head down into his house. If he saw us through gaps in the greying net curtains, he gave no sign.

Chapter Ten

Since there were a couple of the regulars in the snug, Nick had his lunch in there, his face deep in my *Guardian*, though their backs presented such an impregnable barrier that they probably didn't even register his presence. I gambled on their not noticing that his sandwich wasn't exactly standard, and that he drank mineral water from an elegant blue bottle unavailable at the bar.

As soon as the last one had grunted his farewells, Nick retired to his room. What he was planning there I don't know: all he was doing when I tapped on his door and went in was sitting on the bed, hands clasped between his spread knees, apparently deep in the study of the carpet.

Hands on hips, I surveyed the place. 'I ought to be paying you to stay here, not the other way round. I reckon that's a post-war utility mattress. And as for the wallpaper – you don't suffer from migraine, do you? Ugh.'

'It is a bit lively, isn't it? But I won't notice it for the next hour or so. I'm just off to check where the stream and the path meet.'

'On your own.'

He looked around. 'I don't see the Fifth Cavalry anywhere, do you?'

'No, Kimo Sabe. But I see your faithful Tonto. And I reckon that vehicle of yours might just class as Silver.' When he didn't reply, I said, 'Come on, Copper, you've seen enough of this area to know never to go anywhere on your own if you don't have to.'

'*You* do.'

'Oh, ah.' Those were a peculiarly Midlands couple of syllables. They could mean absolute agreement to complete cynicism, and pretty well everything in between. 'Sure I do,' I agreed. 'But only because in this weather I only ever walk routes I know every inch of from my summer walks. Even then I'd never set out in rain like this, not with the clouds likely to roll down the valley and blank out all your landmarks.'

'I'll be going by car.'

'And I suppose you'll have your mobile to hand to summon back up should you need it.'

He looked huffy. 'And is there a problem with that?'

I put my head back and roared with laughter. 'No, no problem at all. Not if you install a couple of radio masts as you go. Haven't you noticed, Copper, that this area's got as many mobile black spots as a Dalmatian?'

His grimace turned into a grudging smile. 'Don't you have a pub to run?'

I clapped my hand to my head. 'Hell, I've got a phone call to make! Just give me five minutes and then you can whisk me away in your shiny new transport of delight.'

'Tom's left! What do you mean, left?' My screech down the phone must have been painful.

Tom's landlady meant exactly what left usually meant. Gone. Vamoosed. Quitted. And no, Tom hadn't left a forwarding address. He'd paid up in full and disappeared.

The work number he'd given me – for use in only the most extreme of emergencies, he'd always stressed – was answered by a ratty Welshman who told me that personal calls were forbidden. I assumed my sweetest phone persona, telling him I was chasing a reference and that I wasn't paid enough for him to be so unpleasant to me.

'In that case you can tell your boss that Dearborn cooks like an angel and left here giving ten minutes' notice so you can imagine whether I can recommend him or not.'

If I'd been my own PA I couldn't have thanked him any more politely. But my scalp was creeping. Why had Tom done a runner? Was it simply because of Sharon's brutal father? If so, why hadn't he come to me?

'You know what these kids are,' Nick said, as if such a platitude might reassure me.

'I know what Tom is – the most wonderful chef who was aiming to work for me full-time as soon as the renovations were finished. Staff accommodation for him and his girlfriend and baby, too.'

He raised a disbelieving eyebrow. 'That'd be in the pub itself?'

I cackled. 'A wailing brat on the premises? No, thank you! No, the old stables and garage are doomed. And very chic accommodation they'll make, too. The planners passed the alterations without a murmur. I even got a pat on the back for developing the local economy.'

'But Tom Dearborn no longer fancies living there.' He looked serious.

'He'd have started in one of the bedrooms like yours,' I admitted. 'But not even the thought of that should have made him bolt without telling me.'

'What about his mobile?'

'First thing I thought of. Zilch.'

'But he'll call back in response to your message.'

I looked him straight in the eye. 'I have a nasty feeling he won't.'

The track we'd decided to follow hadn't been asphalted, but thickly enough covered in hardcore to give a decent surface, at least to Nick's four by four. Some heavy vehicle with a wider wheelbase had dug ruts in it, and the branches of the hedges had been broken off as if a giant had tried out a new hedge cutter.

I pointed. 'Your unlit lorry?'

'Could be.' There was glimpse of a low roof a couple of hundred yards away. 'Our building, I presume.' He pulled the car as far into the hedge as he could without risking its shiny metallic paint and got out, shutting the door without a slam. I followed, by dint of hitching myself over the gear lever and handbrake and sliding across the driver's seat.

'It's a bit small – not even a barn,' I observed, dropping down beside him and closing the door equally quietly.

He sighed. 'I'd rather you'd stayed put.'

'I know. I never take hints, though.'

'I gathered.'

We retrieved our boots from the back, the carpet of which he'd protected with heavy-grade polythene sheeting. Boots, not wellies – we were obviously to be a pair of walkers out for a stroll in a temporary lull, just happening on the place. Walking sticks, map holder round my neck – we looked the part as we donned hats and pulled on gloves. My camera disappeared into the waterproof's front pouch.

A hundred and fifty yards we trudged in silence as some walkers do. Simultaneously we stopped. Nick snorted quietly. 'If the planning people object to your wire, they won't like that,' he said.

They wouldn't. Although the wire mesh fence he pointed at wasn't more than four foot high, it was topped with razor wire. It certainly prevented legitimate access to our right of way. The wind gusted our way a mixture of smells, none of them pleasant and some of them all too identifiable.

'Enough to make you turn vegetarian,' Nick muttered, shoving a mint into his mouth and offering me one.

Hang the calories: peppermint over cowpats and blood any day.

'It'd take a lot to make *me* turn vegetarian,' I muttered. 'Is this where they slaughter them or rend them?'

'Oh, there's a perfectly legitimate rending plant up the road,' Nick said blithely. 'Not a lot of people know about it, and I should imagine even fewer talk about it, but it's all above board.'

'What! So why are we farting about here?'

'Because it's not a problem. My predecessor checked it a couple of months before he left. It's not due for another inspection till next spring.'

'All the same!' I could have screamed. 'A rending plant – isn't that the likely source of my blood.'

He shook his head firmly. 'Not if it meets regulations.' He pointed at what lay behind the gates. 'That doesn't. The planning regulations first and foremost. And probably all the other food hygiene and veterinary and disposal of waste regulations too.'

'So what'll you do?'

'Nothing.'

'What?'

'It's a job for the local police. Not me.'

Arms akimbo, I turned to face him. 'Now you listen to me, Copper, and you listen good. If I can risk ruining my pub by cancelling my meat orders because they don't have paperwork, you can damned well get off your arse and do something to something to close an illegal abattoir. Whatever law you have to invoke.'

'Evidence, Josie. We'd need evidence. And the police are the ones to get that.'

'And what sort of priority do you think they'd give it?'

'Depends. They might even say it's not their job but Trading Standards'. Which it may be. The laws are very unclear – lots of loopholes.'

I stared him in the eye. 'OK, if you won't get evidence, I shall. Whatever it takes, however it takes – I shall close that place down.'

It would have made a great exit line. But here I was in the middle of nowhere dependent on this guy for a lift. A diversionary tactic was called for. Fishing the camera from my pouch, I strode up to the gates, snapping the huge padlock and chain, and then standing on tiptoe to take what was little more than a corrugated iron shed. My eye fell on something else first. Dog turds. So any nocturnal adventures on my part might be noisily revealed. Noisily and possibly viciously. I was too much a townee to love any dog simply because it had four legs and barked.

I inched my way round the perimeter fence, taking photos from every angle. There was no separate office block, just the shed, which would only have been able to deal with a couple of beasts at a time, surely. Even so, inside there must be stun guns, chains, lifting tackle. And no paperwork, of course. If ever a business looked as if it worked with cash, this was it.

At the furthest point from the gates there was a loose section of mesh. With a little effort even I could ease it away from the fence posts. But what was the point of gaining access if I was about to be torn limb from limb?

The light was fading fast, the clouds whipping like torn sheets across the sky – we were obviously in for more rain. So the second half of my circuit was a good deal speedier than the first. At least, it would have been, had I not found myself flat on my face in a knot of brambles. Somehow I'd managed to shove my hands forward, so they took the brunt. But there was nothing to lever myself up against except thorns. And I needed leverage. My left ankle wouldn't work.

It didn't hurt. Not yet. It was just anchored. Somehow I'd

have to roll to see what was going on. Rolling needed leverage too. As would trying to fish my mobile from my camera pouch. And it was a fair assumption that either Nick's would be switched off or we'd be in a damned black spot.

Would he come looking? He'd made no effort to catch up so far, and I must have covered some four hundred yards. Where the hell was he?

I opened my mouth to yell. And shut it again. What if he was no longer alone, but trying to explain himself to some driver with a lorry load of cattle to be slaughtered? Surely I'd have heard – the one thing you took for granted in the country was silence, so the rumble of a lorry over those stones would have been obvious, even accounting for the roar and wail of the wind, which might have been auditioning for the soundtrack of *Wuthering Heights*.

Damn it, I was hanged if I was going to lie here any longer. If I'd been walking on my own and had been upended like this, I couldn't have hung round waiting to be rescued. I'd have cursed and yelled, but at myself. Which is what I did now. It wasn't ever going to be pleasant, so I wasn't surprised by a bit of pain. But I was shocked by the sudden agony in my ankle. I did a sort of press up, easing back till I looked like a runner in the blocks. But I wasn't going to run anywhere, not with a gin trap for company.

It was driven very deeply into the ground considering it was only meant to catch a small animal. But a small animal, mad with fear, could be very strong, I told myself. In any case, if I sat down, I could ease the wire noose back into shape, and extricate my foot, albeit very gingerly. Once free, I managed to yank it out, and prepared to carry my trophy home. There was nothing badly wrong with the ankle, I decided – thanks to my boots. I hobbled a few more yard, scanning every blade of grass as I went.

Yes – another trap. This one wasn't anchored as well as the one that had noosed me, and responded quickly to a good yank, sending me reeling and staggering, landing this time on my bum. Still no bones broken. All the same, this time I was glad to use the wire fencing as a support. It wasn't much fun letting go of it to stumble back to where I hoped the four by four still waited.

It did, and Nick with it. I waved and called, but he didn't

respond. He was staring deep into something that wasn't any-where except in his head. This time I was too much in need of TLC myself to worry about wounding his psyche or whatever. I shook his arm roughly. 'What the hell's going on?' I demanded.

Chapter Eleven

I bundled him back inside the car, shoving him across into the passenger seat. 'Is it some sort of epilepsy attack or what?' I demanded.

'I don't know. No, I do know it's not epilepsy. I got it checked out – some Well Man clinic,' he gabbled, 'you know, where they check everything from cirrhosis to in-growing toenails.'

I was meant to get so absorbed by detail I lost sight of the problem. I didn't. 'So did you tell the clinic exactly what happens? For Christ's sake, man, you drive a lot of miles in a lethal machine – you can't just lose it like this when you're driving.'

'Funnily enough I don't.'

'D'you see me laughing? Just because it hasn't happened yet doesn't mean it won't ever. Why does it happen at all? Yes, I've seen you like this before – in Comet or wherever the other day, for a start. Is that why you left the police – ill health?'

He shook his head emphatically. 'I did my full thirty years. Nice plump pension and a new job I could do in my sleep. That was the idea.'

'So have these … blackouts… just started?'

The headshake was less emphatic. 'I've had them on and off for a while. They've got worse recently. Since I left work.'

'What's Dr Cole say?'

'I haven't had time to register, yet.'

I threw my hands in the air in exasperation.

'What have you done to your face?' he asked. 'And what's that you're holding?'

A peer in the mirror told me I looked like Dracula's mother, blood trickling from a lot of scratches I hoped were superficial. Now I was back in the warm they were starting to sting. I waved the gin traps. 'The latest variation on the trip wire that caught me the other day. Or illegal animal traps. How do you push this seat back? Ah.' I pulled my jeans up and my sock down. There was a thin red weal all round, but a fine black bruise already forming where I'd taken most of the force, where the shin just becomes the top of the ankle. 'The thing is, the harder you struggle the tighter this noose pulls,' I said, demonstrating in the gear lever. 'It's really designed to catch rabbits or foxes, whatever the landowner considers vermin.'

'In this case, you. You're lucky not to have broken your wrists when you fell, a wom –' He bit back what he was saying, blushing furiously.

'A woman my age, eh? These days women of my age know all about preventing osteoporosis, Copper, thank goodness. But you're right. And I'm lucky the thorns missed my eyes, too. I think these might be evidence, don't you?'

Suddenly he lunged for me, pulling some lever that tipped the seat right back, and swarming all over me like a demented lover.

'What the *hell*?' And then I heard the lorry, and returned his embrace with interest.

At last we straightened. 'I never knew undercover work could be so interesting,' he said, rather spoiling the effect with an embarrassed laugh.

'D'you think they clocked us?'

'What, with the windows all steamed up, as if we've been snogging for hours? Doubt it.'

'You're going to have to acquire a girlfriend, fast. The whole village knows you've got a new set of wheels. I don't want it to be known that it was me in here.'

'Hang on – if I'd have been going to snog *you* I'd have done it in the comfort of the White Hart. So I should think your reputation will remain lily white. Now what are you doing?'

'Going to take a few photographs, of course. A bit more of the big E. Evidence, Nick.' Despite my ankle, I was out of the car and running in that crouched way that film cowboys or soldiers use when they mean Business. What I'd thought was a lorry turned out to be no more than a horsebox towing a trailer. But horses didn't low.

I didn't risk getting close in, just in case they'd got any dogs with them, but hey, what's a telephoto lens for except to protect the snapper from being snapped? The lens gave exceptionally good definition – it damned well ought to have done for the price I paid for it – and I focused on the registration letters. Then I got a couple of the poor beasts in the trailer, and one of the driver, just as he was getting out of his cab. After that, discretion overcame valour, and I scuttled back to the car, apparently doing up my flies – anyone seeing me might have thought I'd been having a quick wee.

By now Nick had turned the car – no mean feat in such a narrow space. 'Where next?'

'Taunton. Boots. To pick up my original film and drop this one in.'

'Have you taken that many photos? A whole film? Already?'

Had he seen it, my look would have withered him. 'I'd rather not be caught with this on me. For Christ's sake, Copper, Tony was a criminal. Big time. He didn't get where he did by taking risks with evidence. Would these guys, if they so much as suspected we were interested?'

'Where he got was Long Lartin, for Christ's sake,' he snorted. 'A stretch in a maximum security jail's scarcely a pinnacle of achievement!'

'That's because he got careless and you people got canny. Won't this thing go any faster?'

He took the hint. I have to admit he drove very well in appalling conditions – wet roads, some running inches deep in water draining from the banks, mist rolling in and occasional bursts of driving rain.

'Anyone would think we were being followed,' I said as he did a particularly nifty piece of overtaking.

'Are you sure we're not? Look, Josie, in Taunton, I shall try to overtake a bus and drop you at the next stop. Catch it to Boots.'

Splitting up made sense. I nodded. 'And what about you?'

'I shall take this to a car wash and then back to the garage to get another.' His eyes, narrowed in concentration, relaxed into unexpected crows' feet of amusement as my jaw dropped. 'It's on appro, Josie – hell, you don't fork out the umpty-ump thousand pounds this sort of vehicle costs without trying it for size. I shall say I'm not sure and try another in the range – rather higher, so don't worry, they won't object. It's either that or false plates,' he added. 'Which would you advise?'

After Boots, which I reached too late for their same day-service, my next trip was to the post office: I wanted to send the negatives I already had to someone no one would think of, preferably someone I could get them back from without any problems if necessary. Piers, my flying instructor, would do. He was ex-RAF, and was still enough of an overgrown schoolboy to relish a bit of subterfuge. I photocopied the prints of the barbed wire and popped them in an envelope to Dom, my architect: he wasn't as silly as Piers, but was rather more accessible. And as a friend, rather than a lover, he might be even more reliable. And then I drifted in and out of the shops, buying early Christmas cards and decorations and wishing I had a few more people on my presents list. Being an only child and then childless myself limited the options, especially as I was no longer on speaking terms with most of Tony's lot, the epitome of awful in-laws.

By now my yanked leg was complaining, and my lower back having a really vicious moan: a quick call to my osteopath established that he could slot me in after his last patient. He added that we might even have a quiet drink together if I was up to it. By which, of course, he meant excellent sherry, a brilliant bonk (he'd studied anatomy, after all) and usually a particularly nice meal.

'Got a pub to run tonight, Morgan: we'll have to take a rain check on the drink. Plus I've had to fix a lift back,' I told him as I arrived. 'No, don't ask…'

In bed or out of it, Morgan did wonderful things with his hands, this time involving a ruler and my camera as he photographed my bruises and recorded them. 'It probably ought to be a GP doing this,' he said, 'but better me than no one. Now, that lower back looks a bit lopsided…'

I loved it when he talked technical.

'Clunk click on every trip,' I grinned at Nick, as he picked me up outside Morgan's door. 'I feel a hell of a lot better – I was really beginning to stiffen up.' As was Morgan, of course, but I didn't tell Nick that. 'The thing is, once you pass fifty the body doesn't bounce like it once did.'

'That's why rugby's a young man's game,' he said inconsequentially. 'Terrible thing, isn't it, growing old.'

'It sure as hell beats dying young,' I snapped.

Our progress in this even bigger gas-guzzler was distinctly more sedate than the journey into Taunton. Nick seemed to be disconcerted by the very size, and embarrassed (rightly, in my humble opinion) by the amount of space he took up in the heavy rush hour traffic. I felt like some very superior mortal, looking down into microcosm of lives you see in other people's cars. Perhaps therein lay the monsters' appeal – Peeping Tom-mobiles. I peered entranced at cars littered with fast food packaging, toys and a couple of really gross used condoms.

Apropos of nothing in particular, I said, 'Maybe it would be better if you dropped me just outside the village.'

'Hmm,' he agreed. 'It's not raining too hard. And the less we're seen together the better.'

'I hate to suggest it, but I think you ought to find somewhere else to eat –'

'Already thought of that. It's bell ringing tonight, so Sue offered me a snack at her place.'

So she'd changed her confirmation class for him, had she?

'Is that OK, ringing on a full stomach?'

'Actually, it'll be after the session – she's busy earlier, apparently.'

'In that case you should have a snack before you start,' I said maternally. Oh, no, not Nick and Sue Clayton – what a joyless coupling they'd have.

Where the hell was Lindi? As soon as I'd lit the fire and set up the first round on the house to apologise for keeping the fire-hoggers waiting, I checked both the pub phone and my own for messages. There were none. I phoned her home number: it rang on and on. She'd not even had the nous to organise the automatic message service. Her mobile was switched off. I left a message, hoping to sound more in sorrow than in anger.

What did she think she was playing at? Even as I cursed, a ghastly thought struck me – she hadn't actually gone off with Fred Tregothnan, had she? True she'd phoned Lucy yesterday evening, but she could have done that from anywhere. I'd have to ask Lucy if she knew any more as soon as I got the chance – which wouldn't be tonight because it was bell ringing, and she was their star.

Anyway, here I was, knackered after all my walking and stiff with a combination of my falls and Morgan's yanking me about, and I had to turn to and pull pints. And wait up for Nick, as though he was a kid out on an unsuitable date, because he'd forgotten to take his key, and there was no way in the present situation I was going to leave the place unlocked. What a good job I had plenty of accounts to check – my very favourite occupation. I don't think. I felt like Lucy doing her homework as I worked in front of the fire in the snug.

It was only eleven when Nick returned, using the pub entrance, looking distinctly self-conscious. Surely they hadn't been to bed on their first date, her being next thing to a vicar?

He gestured with his thumb. 'That thing's so bloody huge it almost dwarfs the pub. But I thought I ought to stow it round the back – it'll be less obtrusive there.'

'You reckon? Hey, you look as if you could do with a drink and I know I've earned one – bloody VAT.'

'That was one thing Tony never taught you, eh, Josie? He never paid a penny of tax all his life, did he?'

'If that's a roundabout way of asking what happened to all his worldly wealth –'

'Ill-gotten gains, more like!'

'Forget it. We seem to be rubbing along quite nicely, young Nick. But you'll find we won't any more if you persist in talking about Tony. Do I make myself clear?'

'Abundantly. I'm sorry. But you must expect an ex-cop to be intrigued – we never found a bean, you know.'

'Well, as you can see, I have to earn a living. So draw your own conclusions.' I led the way to my quarters. The fire was low, but I didn't intend to make this a long evening, so I slung on just a couple of logs. 'Red wine or white? And then you can tell me what information about Lindi you extracted from Lucy. I trust you did?'

'I tried,' he conceded, 'but Mrs Greville was all over her.'

From the kitchen I shouted, 'Mrs Greville?' Yes, an estate-bottled Pouilly Fume. I grabbed a pair of glasses and the opener and headed back.

'She's one of the team – on an irregular basis, apparently. Anyway, she might have stepped back a couple of centuries, all Lady of the Manor, charming the Lower Orders.'

'Really? She didn't seem to have any side when I spoke to her the other day – the church flowers,' I explained.

'Plenty of side tonight. Snubbed me to kingdom come, she did. Anyway, it seems she's got some sort of function coming up and she wants Lucy to do some waitressing.'

'So you didn't get a chance. Damn and blast.'

'No. But I did ask Ron Snow where Lindi was – you know, I made it sound like a laddish nudge nudge, wink wink.'

I didn't want a discussion of histrionics. 'And…?'

'And it seems she's around in the village – but for some reason she's not coming to work here any more.'

'Hell! Did you get any idea why not?'

'As soon as I started asking questions he clammed.'

'Guiltily?'

'Clammily.' He swirled the glass, sniffing appreciatively. 'This is very good.'

It was outstanding, wonderfully flinty but with plenty of other aromas and flavours. 'I only drink very good wine. I don't want to get hung over. Anything else to report? Come on, what did you pick up at the vicarage?'

He sat down carefully and took a couple of appreciative sips before looking up at me. 'I'm not your junior officer, Josie. I went to ring the bells because that's what I do; I had a bite with Sue because she's a decent woman and she asked me. I wasn't there to spy.'

It was too good a wine to throw over him. In any case, I wasn't one to give up at the first hitch. 'But…?' I prompted.

'But nothing.' He sipped again. 'I think Lindi may be going to work for Mrs Greville, too, though I'm not sure on what basis. You'll have to ask Lucy.'

'Assuming, of course, *she* reappears. Copper, why should two of my staff disappear without a word in the space of one week?'

He looked at me as if I were a recalcitrant sergeant. 'Are you a good employer?'

'I'm fair. I work them hard and expect the highest standards. But I also pay well over the odds. Very well over.'

'Rumour has it you bullied Lindi.'

'Me!' I didn't know which to disbelieve more, the accusation or the sudden flood of tears to my eyes. Me, tears?

'Over the Fred Tregothnan business.'

'I only tried to teach her how to tell a groper to push off – politely. Duty of care, Copper – I've got a duty of care to my employees!'

'You don't have to justify yourself to me. But if they think you bullied Lindi, how d'you think they feel about your treatment of Tregothnan?'

'Proud, I should hope – the women, at least.'

'Not all women like their assertive sisters.' He emptied his glass in one gulp – a sin with such a classy wine. Maybe it would irritate his ulcer as much as it irritated me. 'Anyway, tomorrow I really do have to spend a day at work, and I ought to be in early. So if you'll excuse me –'

I got to my feet. 'What time do you want breakfast?'

He was within an inch of saying he didn't have time to eat, or that he'd catch something on the way. But he quailed before my eye like a kid before its head teacher. 'Is seven-thirty too early?' he asked humbly.

Chapter Twelve

Friday started badly and got worse. First there was a phone call from Piers, saying he'd gone down with a throat infection, which had given him absolutely solid ears and that he'd have to cancel our lesson. He didn't even sound up to what we referred to as theory lessons, our nickname for our other activities, so I wished him well and resigned myself to a dreadfully mundane day, kicking pebbles as I headed for the shop and my paper like a sulky schoolgirl.

And at the shop I might well have been back at school. Oh, any of the schools I'd been inflicted on. Back then, as soon as the kids twigged I had Romany blood in me they'd start on me – hurling abuse (though not as much as I hurled back at them), jostling me, pulling my hair. Others, less brave, just gave me the silent treatment.

There was no hair-pulling at the shop. But plenty of silent treatment. Jem and Molly were nowhere to be seen, but that was nothing unusual – the hours they kept the shop open they couldn't be there all the time. They employed on the till a rota of school and college kids, a couple of hours here, three there, just scraping together the national minimum wage to pay them. Usually, if I didn't have to buy anything else, I'd just catch the kid's eye and they'd hand my *Guardian* over the heads of those with full baskets – they all knew I was on that prepayment scheme.

Today, all my efforts to catch young Al Tope's eye were in vain. So in vain I thought maybe someone waiting had complained about my queue jumping and would berate him, not me, if I did it again. I did the obvious thing: I picked up a basket and worked my way along the narrow aisles, coincidentally finding a couple of things I needed and remembering others. But as I reached for the Thai fish sauce, someone stepped in front of it. And stayed there, big impregnable back towards me, ignoring a firm but polite tap on the arm and a clear, 'Excuse me.' Bar applying a shoulder and heaving there was nothing I could do.

The same thing happened by the cheese and again by the vegetables. If the first man was a stranger, the other two weren't –

one was Reg Bulcombe's brother, the other an occasional crony of Wally Hall, the regular drinker. If I dodged sideways, so did they. Well, well, well. If they thought that was going to upset me – OK, they were right. But they'd never get a hint of it. The people who'd really suffer would be Jem and Molly, because I always made a point of buying as much as I could from them, no matter how much cheaper the supermarkets might be. Damn it, I had a contract with Molly's sister-in-law to supply daily fresh vegetables.

What if they extended the Coventry treatment to the bar itself? What if they boycotted it? Well, that'd be their loss, because there wasn't another boozer for six or seven miles; with the last bus running at six on the days, of course, that it deigned to run, they'd be on detox pretty fast, unless they could find someone to drive them. As for me, I'd lose a steady but not major source of income. Most of the profitable food trade was from passing motorists and walkers, apart from people who came every Sunday from miles around for the lunches Tom Dearborn and I cooked. Well, just me, now, by the look of it.

I joined the queue, not attempting to engage in conversation and risk a snub. When my turn came, I simply asked for the paper and reminded him it was pre-paid.

Al stretched a hand for it. Wally Hall's mate coughed loudly. 'Don't know anything about that,' Al said, flushing and addressing the till.

Et tu, Brute! "Course you do. Every Thursday for the last twelve weeks you've known about it. But if you want to make an issue, take this – and pop the change in the Air Ambulance tin.' I dropped a tenner on the counter.

Exit, pursued by barely concealed hostility.

The answerphone was flashing when I got in. It could bloody well wait until I'd had a good strong coffee – and not the beans I use in the bar, either. Some I had in mind to go with liqueurs when the restaurant was open. A real gourmet glug. And all that nice caffeine to brace my shoulders.

Which, irritatingly, needed a good brace. And even more after I took the call. Nick. It seems that the Food Standards bosses had heard he wasn't hard-pressed down here and wanted his assistance with a really nasty case in the South East. He might as well stay there until it was done, given the warmth of his welcome here, hadn't he? But he'd pay for the room, the same as if he were occupying it.

Would he indeed! Patronizing bastard. Thinking I needed his money to keep my head above water – though perhaps that wasn't the best of images, in all the circumstances. And, of course, it wouldn't be his money but the anonymous insurance company that paid – a nice victimless bit of fraud.

Possibly. But I wasn't worrying about insurance premiums right now.

Maybe he was just reserving it, so if a coachload of stranded tourists turned up, I wouldn't be able to oblige them. As if I could, with no cook and no bar staff.

So what about his company? Now the natives were restless, would I have preferred the presence of a man about the place? Or was it Nick they wanted to be rid of, not me at all? Was all that hostility meant to make me get rid of him? Did I put it around that he'd left or keep very mum indeed? Maybe a visit to Sue might be in order. If anyone had her finger on the pulse of village life, she did.

She was out. I left a message.

I shrugged. She probably regarded anything Nick said as in the Confessional anyway.

As for Nick, what on earth did I make of him? Talk about Jekyll and Hyde – not that I could ever remember which was which, and he certainly didn't sprout fangs and do dastardly deeds. Quite the reverse. In an off moment, he could make a mouse look manly. Other times he was passive aggressive. And sometimes he was a decent man I was sorry I'd ever cursed. Well, I could un-curse him. Maybe it'd be better in church.

Or maybe I was being fey, and it was nothing to do with me, but a result of something in his police days, something Nesta should have reported on by now. It must be a week since I'd asked her to check on Brum's headline news. It was all very well of her to say she'd got a new man and was too busy – you have to get out of bed now and then, even with the best bloke. I poked the numbers on the pad as if I were driving in nails.

Nesta – technophobe Nesta, who hadn't even been able to retrieve her messages till I'd shown her how – had only gone and recorded a new message for her answerphone. 'I'm sorry I can't be with you at the moment – I'm on holiday in Madeira with the sexiest guy in the world!'

Stupid cow, giving tempting information like that over the phone! I'd bloody well stood over her to make sure her original out-going message didn't say anything about being out – and now she was telling all and sundry her house was empty. What kept her ears apart? Certainly not brains.

Lunchtime was terrific. I could have done with two bar staff and a couple of helpers in the kitchen. The media were in town! Well, three of them. The reporter, whose face I knew, of course, Nicola Rodway, her soundman, Chaz, and Wills, her cameraman. They'd come from Exeter to film the floods, and now they needed liquid refreshment. And some decent food. So I had another newsworthy story for them – *floods prevent staff getting to work, but heroic landlady does all herself*! And so she did. Thank God for microwaves and extendable lunch hours. Raiding my own collection, not the official cellar, I produced loads of wine on the house to compensate for their having to wait a little: that might have helped. I abstained totally, not wanting to present a cheery Santa Claus face to the camera, and talked solemnly about the harm to the tourist industry, not to mention the poor farmers, at this very moment struggling heroically to rescue their livestock. And what about the poor folk who'd lost their mobile homes? Their treasured possessions? Their memories? Then we all drank some of my connoisseur coffee and had a liqueur or two and they stowed their gear and went off into what might have been a sunset had there been anything other in the sky than bulging, rain-filled cloud.

But it wasn't raining yet, and since when had I been a fair-weather walker? It wasn't as if calories took any notice of the weather. As I laced the boots, I'd no idea where I was heading. My feet took me back towards the village shop. Not into it, though. Not after this morning's treatment. In any case, there was something, now I came to think of it, that I wanted to check. I came to a halt on the bridge. There was plenty of water in the stream now. Enough to have brought out one or two sandbags by old doors well below modern street level. It was turbulent, swift-running water too, laden with detritus that snagged and tore at the banks, sometimes sticking, sometimes dislodging more. And it was muddy brown. No, not a sign of any pink. So what had happened to floods in the campsite? If my calculations were correct, the water should be going down nicely now. I'd love to check.

It was quite a step, however, and darkness was definitely falling – after all, I'd set out well over an hour past my usual time. For all I was used to moving briskly, today I felt vulnerable, and the car beckoned. Sure I'd eventually drunk a little with the media team, but not enough to turn a breathalyser the palest shade of green. And first, of course, find your breathalyser. If the rural police weren't up to tracking down Fred Tregothnan, I didn't expect them to be lurking in a lay by on the off chance of nailing me. Nor were they.

No, any lurking was the province of none other than Reg Bulcombe, whose lacy curtains twitched into action as soon as I parked. Ideally I'd have snook into the site unnoticed, but, caught in the act, I positively beamed at him, waving my fingers in an irritating little twiddle as I strolled up to his door.

I could hear his footsteps: I could almost hear his brains trying to work out what I was up to and debating if he cared enough to find out. Curiosity won in the end, and he poked his head round the door.

He could have warmed himself on my smile. "Afternoon, Reg. How are you? I was just passing and thought I'd collect any mail for Mr Thomas.'

'Ah. They said he'd shacked up with you.'

'That's what pubs are for, Reg – to accommodate people washed out of their homes when the floods come. Has the water started to drop yet?' Playing ditzy, I set off for the field, Bulcombe padding after me in grey tweed carpet slippers. 'Oh, it's not so bad now, is it?' I cooed. 'But you'll have such a lot to do salvaging all those caravans, you poor man. Such a shame. I hope you can make the insurance folk dance to your tune, because you'll be losing such a lot of money until people can come back. Oh, I'm so sorry.'

He shifted awkwardly, his slippers glooping in the mud. 'Well, I'll just have to pull my belt a notch tighter,' he muttered.

'What about other folk? Have they been as badly hit?'

'Reckon no one's escaped,' he said, doom-laden as if the plague had struck and Kings Duncombe were a latter-day Eyam. He sucked his teeth.

My headshake was a mirror image of his, my sigh gusty enough to shift a cloudbank. I hated myself for ingratiating myself with him, as I'd done countrywide with the TV performance, but I had to live. By which I don't mean make a living. Fred Tregothnan, a strapping man, had disappeared. I didn't want to join him wherever he'd gone.

At least I could excuse my involuntary shiver. 'This damp makes it feel so cold, doesn't it – and you'll catch you death if you're not careful in those slippers of yours.' I turned. Halfway back to the car, I asked casually, 'Did you say if there was any post for Mr Thomas?'

As if there wasn't enough wetness around, he spat, copiously. 'I suppose I'd better go and see.' He didn't invite me in, despite spiteful little slashes of rain.

I could hear him chuntering away to himself, no doubt trailing mud from his slippers wherever he went. Hell, the man would know if there was any post for his only winter tenant – it wasn't the sort of thing you'd forget, now, was it? He came back empty-handed, however. 'No. But I'll bear it in mind, Mrs Welford. If I get any, like. Be staying with you long, will he?'

'He'll be wanting his own place as soon as maybe, I'm sure,' I said. 'Maybe not even in the village.'

'You mean he's pulling out already?'

'He's said nothing to me either way,' I said. 'So long as he pays his bills, what is it to me? Mind you, they'll need another bell ringer if he does go. You ever thought of joining in, Reg? A big man like you would take to it like a duck to water.'

The washing up regarded me balefully the moment I ventured from my accommodation into the pub kitchen. Yes, all that and what I suspected might be something of an ordeal tonight – not that I'd let on by so much as a smudge of my mascara. Assuming anyone turned up to make it an ordeal, of course. Even as I donned rubbed gloves and apron I stripped them off again. I had a phone call to make. If anyone in the village were woman enough to brave public opinion, it was Lucy Gay.

As I dialled, there was a noise in the bar. I froze. What were they up to now? Grabbing a bottle as a weapon, I tiptoed through.

Lucy was placidly raking the ashes and adding wood to the fire.

It would have been easy to get very emotional. Instead, I tried to be breezy. 'You're nice and early!'

She shrugged. 'Don't know how you'll manage if I don't come,' she said matter-of-factly. 'And that's what I told my dad when he said I shouldn't. He knows about all what you send pretending it's left-overs, though his pride tells him to say nothing. Knows when he's on to a good thing, my dad. But truly, Mrs Welford, what I get here is the only decent food the kids get to eat. All this good fresh produce in the fields round here, and the school meals are just junk. I don't know what they think they're doing.'

I let her gabble on, pretending not to see how embarrassed she was. But sooner or later we both knew I'd put a simple question to her. It might as well be now.

'Why doesn't your dad want you to work here any more?'

She stood – God, I wish I were that lithe these days – wiping her hands on a tea towel she'd tucked into her waistband.

'Well? The whole village is sending me to Coventry – not speaking to me.' Funny she hadn't recognised the idiom. 'Any idea why I'm suddenly so unpopular?'

She shook her head. 'Not exactly. They know I like you so they don't spell it out, not when I'm around. But they say you're too nosy for your own good, sneaking round people's property even when it's raining.'

So it wasn't a particular problem about sneaking into

Tregothnan's house. 'I've always gone for walks on my own in the rain. They didn't mind before.'

'They've always minded. But then you brought your boyfriend down and he's a sly old bugger too. Never stops asking questions.'

'Boyfriend! I haven't got a boyfriend!' I was surprised my squeak didn't crack the glasses.

She looked reproachful. 'You have that, Mrs Welford. Mr Thomas. One look at him and you can see he's smelling of April and May. You can't look me in the eye and tell me he didn't come down here to be with you.'

'I can and I will! It's true I met him once before, but it was in most unfortunate circumstances and I certainly never wanted to see him ever again.'

'First night he's down here you're out there at that caravan of his.'

'Correction. First night he's down here I recognise him and the following morning I go out to his caravan to tell him to shove off.'

'So how come he's living with you now?'

Jesus, was it something in the water or was it all the inbreeding? 'Come off it, Lucy,' I said. 'You know as well as I do he was flooded out. Damn it all, it was you who gave him the room! I'd have left him to fight his way through to a motel in Taunton.'

She turned her eyes, huge in that underfed face of hers, full on me. 'But seems to me he's got his feet well and truly under your table. Doesn't eat down here like any other guest.'

For answer I took a deep, deep sniff. 'Tell me honestly, Lucy – would you ask anyone to eat a meal in here?'

'Well, it's all according, isn't it? Seems to me the food side of the business is really taking off.'

'It is indeed. Anyway, Mr Thomas isn't here any more. He's working in another part of the country. I've no idea when he'll be back. And as soon as he's got that caravan of his sorted out, he'll be out of here. Or go somewhere else if he can't fix it. Got that?'

Her nod was a bit on the perfunctory side, as if to please me rather than express conviction.

'And you'll tell the others.' Damn, that sounded like pleading.

'If I see them.'

How noncommittal can you get?

'Why's Lindi not coming any more? And before you say I should ask her direct, I can't get hold of her. And Tom, the chef, has done a bunk too. Next thing I know my builders'll decide they don't want the job.'

Head on one side, she considered. 'No. They're a Taunton firm. No one from round here. Of course, you really ought to have asked Mr Barnes – that's Mr Bulcombe's cousin, on his wife's side.'

'George Barnes? I did. He said it was too big a job. And his nephew. He said it wasn't big enough. But he quoted for it, just on the off-chance, and he was ten per cent higher than the firm that's doing it.'

'Ah. Deliberately pricing himself out of the market,' she agreed. 'Business Studies GCSE, Mrs Welford,' she added as my eyebrows went up. 'But I don't know why Tom Dearborn should do a flit. He was telling me how much he was looking forward to coming here full-time, ah, and that soft-headed girlfriend of his too. Getting herself in the family way at her age.'

Marvelling how she could veer from a child to a middle-aged matron in the course of a paragraph, I patted her on the shoulder. 'If you see young Tom, just talk to him, will you? Make him see a bit of sense?'

'If I see him. Now, was there anything special you needed doing, like, or shall I just see to the kitchen – saw you on TV, I did,' she added over her shoulder. 'Reckon you could have done yourself a bit of good there.'

I followed her, wincing at that damned washing up. 'D'you reckon the other villagers will approve? I said nice things about them, after all.'

Rolling her sleeves, she shook her head. 'They all watch the other side, don't they?'

I was showing her how I cook one of my chicken and vegetable pies – and pointing out how many vegetables you could disguise so her family would eat it without whinging – when the door to the snug clicked open. So surprised I nearly dropped the pie funnel, a traditional blackbird that always made her smile, I wiped my hands, and smoothed my apron, for all the world like one of Lucy's kitchen maid ancestors. Then I remembered it didn't do to look too eager – too desperate, even – I strolled to greet my only customer so far.

'Sue! What can I do for you on a night like this?'

She shrugged expressively, looking round the empty room. 'More like what I can do for you, I'd have thought. Provide you with a customer.'

'Bless you. But it's warmer in the kitchen – Lucy and I are working in there.'

Lucy, a smudge of flour on her nose and the deepest triumph in her eyes, was surveying the pie she'd handsomely decorated with leaves cut from spare pastry as she prepared to pop it into the oven. She nodded shyly at Sue, who had the sense to talk bell ringing for a couple of moments.

'You go and keep an eye on the bar, there's a good girl. I'll call you when this is ready,' I said. 'If you don't mind roughing it in here, Sue?' I added.

'Roughing it? It's beautifully warm!'

Yes, her vicarage kitchen was the coldest hole I'd ever been in. 'What will you drink? There's a lovely drop of Australian Grenache left over from this lunchtime.' I showed her the bottle, and reached for a couple of glasses.

As she took the first sip, however, her mouth prissied up. 'Lucy – are you sure it's all right for her to work in the bar? At her age?'

I jerked my head towards the door.

Sue accepted the tacit invitation and peeped. 'But she's sitting by the fire reading!' she squeaked, having the sense, at least, to close the door first.

'Doing her homework, more like.'

'You pay her to sit her and do her homework!'

'I pay her to sit there and keep an eye on things. To react in an emergency – take the other night, when Nick Thomas turned up while I was out and she insisted on making him up a bed. She

found the bed linen and towels and did all that was proper.'
Which neatly introduced the topic of Nick, of course. And made
Sue blush.

I was too busy stacking newly washed china to notice officially,
of course. A tea towel might not be as good as the confession
box, but it gave people the idea of anonymity.

'The police came to see me,' she said at last.

'About Fred Tregothnan?'

'About our going round his house. Someone in the village ...'

'Snitched. Just like them to finger outsiders, and say nothing
of their own misdemeanours.'

'Motes and beams,' she mused.

'So what did you say?'

'That we'd been concerned he might be ill inside and had let
ourselves in – and out – without finding him. Or anything else,'
she added with venom. 'They practically accused me of armed
robbery!'

'Even the police should be able to tell you're as honest as the
day.' What they'd make of me was another matter altogether, of
course. 'Don't worry. Here, there's another bottle of the
Grenache upstairs. Or would you prefer white? There's some
cracking Chilean stuff here – also courtesy of the meedya boys
and girls.'

'It was a good interview. Pity no one in the village'll have seen
it. No one would have guessed they were trying to drum you out
of town.'

'*Drum me* – it's come to that, has it? Whatever did I do to
them that they should want to get rid of me?'

There was a long silence. 'I think it's got to do with Nick
Thomas,' she said, with something sounding suspiciously like a
sob.

Chapter Thirteen

In the end Sue revealed very little more than Lucy had already told me. And it seemed to me that she had introduced Nick's name into the conversation simply for the pleasure of hearing it. So I was glad I'd made it plain that he'd been staying at Lucy's suggestion, not mine. 'You know he's moved out for a while?'

She winced as if I'd slapped her face. 'No?'

'Oh, he's kept his room on,' I said as prosaically as I could. 'But he's got an urgent job in the South East and says he may just as well stay there until he's finished. He didn't actually say it aloud, but he implied that this place was hardly the Ritz and that he might as well have a bit of comfort while he could get it.' I laughed; she didn't. 'Goodness knows why he ever moved down to a place like this in the back of beyond.'

'His daughter,' she said. 'Apparently she always wanted to live in a cottage with roses round the door.'

Ah. The girl in the photographs I'd seen on his very first Monday morning.

'Was she planning to move down here with him? Not a lot on offer for a young woman her age, is there?'

'He just hoped she'd come and visit him. She lives with his wife. Ex-wife. They've got a son he never sees either. Phiz – some such name. And she's Elly. The daughter. No idea of the wife's name, have you?'

Most of this was news to me, of course, but I simply shook my head vaguely as if he'd confided in me all but that. Now, had he discussed those blackouts with Sue? I got on to safer ground. 'But that doesn't explain this as his choice of base. I told him to his face he was nuts to come so far off the beaten track.'

She looked wistful. 'I think he wanted to become part of a community.'

'He didn't choose a very welcoming one, then, did he?' Him and me both. 'I suppose you had to go where you were sent.'

'Where they thought I was needed.' There was a hint of huff.

'And where they could screw the most work out of you for the least pay.' I pulled myself to my feet. Wonderful smells were coming from the oven, and I didn't want the pie to burn. Gingerly I peered. No. Another five minutes was all it would need, however. 'Any comeback about blessing the hunt? You know something,' I added, 'I'm beginning to understand why I'm off hunting. I'm beginning to empathise with the fox. Being drummed out of the village indeed.'

Sue changed the subject, but not entirely. 'I can't understand Mrs Greville. Suddenly she's as nice as pie. She's keen to take on some village girls as waitresses for some function she's planning – asked who I could recommend.'

'So you said Lindi and Lucy! Thanks a bunch!'

She looked at me blankly.

'I've not seen Lindi since the Tregothnan business' I explained. 'And barmaids, even lazy inept ones like Lindi, don't grow on trees round here. Though you'd have thought some of the young married women would be glad of the work.'

'Not if it impugns their husbands' ability to provide for them. Twenty-first century this may be elsewhere, Josie, but Hardy would recognise some of the folk round here. No, we're too far west, aren't we? That man who wrote that book about Exmoor.'

'R D Blackmore,' I supplied, catching a glimmer of surprise in her eyes. 'Not part of my OU course, but I did a lot of reading when Tony was doing bird. Plenty of time, of course.' It had kept us together, reading the same books: we'd think of each other while we were reading, and as a bonus we had something to talk about, not always easy with men doing stretches like his. OK, you had family news, but I saw as little of my in-laws as I decently could, and there was gossip about friends, but many of his were also doing time and were therefore pretty lean pickings. So there could have been horrible silences like at other tables in the visitors' room. Instead, we'd talk about Scott or Dickens or George Eliot. It always struck me that with a decent education, Tony could have made as much money doing a legitimate job as being a villain. Well, no. But enough.

Since Sue obviously couldn't think of anything to say, I got to my feet and summoned Lucy.

Her face was transformed into a series of O's when she

reached out her pie. As well it might. Between us, we'd done a very professional job. I was going to have to be very strict with myself and inhospitable towards Sue, who was plainly slavering.

I looked at my watch. 'I'll keep an eye on the place now. Before you go, is there any chance you could do a couple of extra hours tomorrow and on Sunday? I know it's usually the day you cook the family lunch but –'

'No reason why they shouldn't have family supper instead,' Lucy observed stoutly. 'What time do you want me, Mrs Welford?'

'Potato peeling starts as soon as morning service is over,' I said, grinning at Sue, 'for those who ring bells. You'll be without Mr Thomas, remember.'

Lucy nodded. 'Mrs Greville said as how she'd be along. But she's as much use as a chocolate – ' she obviously didn't want to use my usual crude analogy ' – chocolate tea pot, with that back of hers.'

'You'll find that pie dish just fits into that round wicker basket hanging behind the back door. Slip a tea towel in it for insulation first: there. And here's one to cover it.'

Lucy looked nonplussed.

Sue twigged. 'Put your jacket hood up and you'll look like little Red Riding Hood off to feed Grandma.'

'But –'

'You made it, Lucy. I can't possibly eat any – not with my diet. All that butter! And it'd be nice for the family to see the whole masterpiece, not just a chunk of it. No, no argument. Pop along, now. Got your torch?'

She flourished the weighty specimen I'd pressed on her when she'd started work here.

I patted her on the shoulder. 'No talking to strange men.'

She turned. 'That'd mean most of the village, then!' And she was gone.

'And not a word of this beyond these walls,' I said, my index finger an inch from Sue's nose.

'*Do good by stealth*,' she agreed 'It's not a bad maxim. But it wouldn't do you any harm in the village if your kindness were known.'

'The mood they're in they'd see it for what it may well be – bribery. Or they'd think the pie was full of eye of bat and toe of newt.'

'Bribery?'

'Keeping her sweet.'

'Is it?'

It was hard to bluster when Sue turned her eyes full on you. 'I never had a daughter. I wouldn't have chosen one quite like Lucy. But it's nice to have someone to teach the tricks of the trade to.'

'You mean take her on in your kitchen?' Did she sound pleased or reproachful?

'One day I mean take her on as my manager. Got a wonderful head for figures, she has. And a good grasp of situations. If I want anyone in my *kitchen* at the moment it's Tom. I suppose no gossip's reached you?'

'I'm afraid it has. Well, about Tom's girl's pregnancy. Sharon, isn't that her name? Seems the father's not Tom, but Sharon's dear old dad.'

I reeled. 'I knew he beat her up. I didn't know – oh, my God. So where's Sharon now?'

'No one knows for sure. Half the village hope she's having an abortion and that Tom's standing by her; the other half say he's well shot of her and he shouldn't have got involved with a girl from such a harum-scarum family in the first place.'

'And you?'

She fidgeted. 'In an ideal world she'd keep the baby and Tom would still stand by her. But would you take that on? I'm not sure I would. All the genetic risks…'

'Incest! You can't imagine it, can you – a man doing that to his own daughter.'

'Best if he stuck to sheep. Oh, yes: you must have heard the joke that begins, "Me Lud, the plaintiff was quietly grazing in a field…"' She collapsed in heaving, choking sobs of laughter.

This was a side of Sue I'd never seen before. Maybe that half-bottle of lunchtime wine brought it out.

Whatever it was, she seemed scared by its intensity, and imme-

diately gathered her things together as a preliminary to leaving. I
didn't argue: I hadn't eaten and was suddenly tired. But her final
words revived me.

'I suppose I couldn't ask a big favour? I know you're not down
to do the flowers tomorrow, but with the floods I can't rely on
the usual ladies –'

'No problem. There shouldn't be much to do anyway – we
started afresh last week, didn't we, so it'll be mostly dead-heading and filling in gaps.'

She shook her head shyly but firmly. 'I'll bring in plenty of
fresh ones. Josie – make it look a bit special if you can.'

'The best I can. But Sue, God'll forgive a few tired blooms.'

'It's not God I'm worried about. It's the other ladies. And –
well…' She shifted like a schoolgirl about to meet the pop star of
her dreams. 'Well, the new dean's going to drop in unannounced,
you see.'

Was that the real reason for her visit tonight?

Grinning broadly, I said, 'I love the concept of unannounced
visits being known in advance!'

'I know his secretary, you see, and –'

'Sue, it'll look as good as I can make it look. But for real
expertise what about Mrs Coyne or –'

Her jaw jutted. 'I want it to look like church flowers, not a
huge bag of hundreds and thousands.'

'Mrs Greville?'

'It's you I've asked, Josie. Get in there and sock it to them.' So
it wasn't just the dean she was worrying about. She was trying to
rehabilitate me. I wasn't at all sure that pushing me forward
would endear me to anyone, but at least her heart was in the right
place. On impulse I hugged her.

She was rather too obviously taken aback. Her exit was almost
an escape. Well, I didn't rate Nick's chances highly if that was
how she regarded physical contact. Waving just in case she looked
back, I stood in the open doorway for several minutes, breathing
in the clean, newly washed air. And presenting a lovely target,
Tony's voice observed dryly in my right ear.

Saturday was a good day for passing trade, so my day started very early laying in supplies of fresh meat and vegetables. Shortly after eight, Sue and I arrived at the church simultaneously, me cheerful and bustling, her nervy and cautious, as if I'd made a pass at her last night, not just offered a sisterly gesture. She dropped the flowers and, gabbling something about a wedding at one of her other churches, bolted back to her filthy, condensation-filled car, that accident in the making. Nick'd better be back soon and have the guts to do something.

I'd always enjoyed my own company – a good job, in all the circumstances. So the empty building held no terrors, not when I'd shoved the latch down good and hard so I'd get plenty of warning of any visitors. And bullies though there were in the village, I'd bet that most of them would have an atavistic respect for the building that would prevent them doing any violence in it.

In the silence, the damp rising almost palpably from the old stone, I could identify with those nuns who did even the most humdrum task for the greater glory of God. AMGD, or something like that. I worked quickly, true, as my fingers turned blue, but all the more confidently for having no one looking over my shoulder. I couldn't believe a few well-placed carnations and ferns would make up for any damage I might have done with my traveller's tongue, but maybe it was a form of reparation, an act of contrition. And I was in a place that spoke of a millennium of forgiveness.

There were two altars, the main one and one in the tiny Lady Chapel, both jealously guarded provinces. I did them first, risking Mrs Coyne's fury as I simply removed her displays and replaced them with very simple ones of my own, white freesias, carnations and gypsophila. The first time I'd been invited, I was just back from Madeira and had brought a huge pack of exotic flowers. In the gloom of the church, they'd simply looked like bad plastic ones. So now I knew better. I couldn't claim Constance Spry skills, but maybe the bishop couldn't either. Next to the embrasures and sills, which I filled with slimmed down versions of last week's, augmented by Mrs Coyne's collection. And finally I swept up, wishing that T S Eliot hadn't been so smugly patronising about the scrubbers and sweepers of

Canterbury Cathedral.

Accustomed to the dim light, I was almost blinded by the brilliant sunshine I found outside. Not a bad day for a walk today,
provided I bore in mind that the ground would be waterlogged.
And provided the lunchtime crowd dissipated while there was
still enough light – every encroaching dusk reminded me that
soon the clocks would go back, and my explorations would be
sadly limited. Maybe I should wait till afternoon to collect my
paper. And maybe I shouldn't. Whenever I'd havered, Tony had
always quoted an old Midlands maxim to me: 'Faint heart never
shagged a pig.' Only the word wasn't shagged. OK, from what
Sue had said, antics with animals were more in the villagers' line
than mine, but I took his posthumous point. No, I wasn't surprised he hadn't communed with me back there in the church –
that wasn't his way at all. The more profane the place the better
for old Tony.

The shop was seething with enough customers to bring a smile
to Molly's face, which even my presence didn't dim. Seizing the
moment, I gathered some of the items I'd had to forego the previous day, and was gratified to find my *Guardian* waiting for me
as I approached the till. So what had yesterday been about? A
warning? Or did I owe it to the good offices of Lucy and Sue,
busily putting it about that I was a Good Thing, and not connected with that there Nasty Grockle, Nick Thomas? Or had
Molly put the fear of God into everyone, lest they damage her
business?

Lunchtime flew by, with no regulars but plenty of walkers and
other weekenders: one by one they polished off the day's specials, which would have to be replaced in time for the evening,
just in case anyone turned up. So that was my afternoon gone.
Unless I could risk a couple of short cuts, making individual portions of pie filling, ready to be topped with pastry should anyone
ask for one. Lamb curry wouldn't take long to prepare and would
benefit from a nice long simmer; if no one came, it would taste
even better a day or even two later. Yes…

All the same, it was nearer four than three by the time I'd

loaded the dishwasher and washed the pans, and if I was going to push anything forward I'd better do it by car. There shouldn't be any activity at the rendering plant at the weekend, surely, which meant I could case it in safety. I waited only to fax a couple of employment agencies about replacement bar staff before pulling on my outdoor gear.

It wasn't much to look at, not from the hillside that provided the only vantage point, just a small complex of factory buildings with a couple of tall chimneys, sore thumbs in the otherwise lush countryside. You'd have thought such an ugly place ought to be in an industrial estate in the middle of the Black Country, until the wind blew, that is. Then it became all too clear why you couldn't site it anywhere near centres of population. Local residents would soon twig that the place wasn't making fine perfumes, for instance, and even the knowledge that so many animal by-products used by the beauty industry and even medicine had to be extracted in smelly dumps like this would hardly reconcile them to its presence.

Close too the stench was far worse, as you'd expect. But there were confident signs on its high, wire mesh gates, set twenty or so yards back from the lane on a tarmac apron, announcing it was Wetherall Industries, and plenty of hard-standing inside for lorries, with a couple of what looked like office buildings to the right. There were several huge cylindrical vats beyond these. There were also, more gruesomely, a set of skips from which protruded what looked horribly like animal limbs. Yes, even as I snapped away with my neat little camera, I acknowledged that I was operating on double standards, but then most of us do. I was happy to prepare chicken, lamb, beef, pork and any other recognisable animal that came my way, but to see the waste parts jumbled up in death like that turned my stomach. I told myself we'd all be vegetarians if we had to kill our own meat, but was soon cramming calorie laden mints into my own as fast as I could fish them out of the glove-box. So that was the sort of place Food Standards Agency officers like Nick had to deal with: far from sneering at him as a coward, I should be taking my hat off to him.

Putting the car quickly into gear, I had one last look. If it had been inspected, it must be all right, mustn't it? And for the first time I was pleased to acknowledge that it really was none of my business if it wasn't.

Or was it? As I pulled away, a tarpaulin-covered lorry bore down on me, trapping me. Two dogs the size of donkeys leapt from the cab as the driver scrambled down. I covered the camera with the OS map, plonking my index finger on what I hoped would be a local beauty spot.

Winding down the window only about three inches – I didn't like the look of any of the party, four or two-legged – I smiled vacuously. 'Took a wrong turning,' I said to the man, who might well not have heard about the throaty growls of his colleagues.

He kicked the dogs aside and leaned both forearms on the top of my car, peering down at me.

'Ah. And where might you be heading for?'

'They says there's a nice church in Treborough.'

'Do they indeed? Well, you won't find it here, will you?' Halitosis and sweat. A far from heady mix. Thank God for the mints.

'Quite. I took a wrong turn about five miles back, I reckon.'

'Ah.'

He stood back far enough for me to embark on a three point turn, but so close that what with his feet and his lorry it seemed more like ninety-nine. The dogs provided more mobile hazards. At last I squeezed between the hedge and the side of his lorry, close enough for the matter oozing from the sides to drip on my paintwork. If I stopped to clean it off I'd either be eaten alive or be sick. Someone had told me that if the gap was wide enough you could get through it at sixty as easily as six miles an hour. I didn't make sixty, but I didn't hang about. I might have had the guts to stop and write down the lorry's number – might – but somehow a flap of tarpaulin had managed to cover it. Pity there was nothing to cover mine.

Maybe I'd make the other special for tonight something wholesomely vegetarian.

Chapter Fourteen

Because Sue had to officiate at so many other churches, the times of the services were rotated. If we had eight o'clock communion one week, next week it would be an eleven o'clock service, the following one evensong. Normally I had to skip eleven o'clock services, time being of the essence when you had lunches to cook and serve. But today I felt I had to support Sue in the presence of the new dean and was up before seven to prepare vegetables and everything else. Thank goodness roasts – pork, beef and a couple of huge free-range local chickens - looked after themselves nicely. I'd made the veggie option a stir-fry I'd prepare to order. Puddings? Well, no problem, thanks to microwaves and an interesting cheese board that was already gaining a reputation across the district. All the same, my mind was more on logistics than on Sue's not very inspired sermon. The flowers looked good, even though I says it as shouldn't, in Tony's phrase. I had hard stares from Mrs Coyne and a rather haughty, amused one from Mrs Greville, but since I was out of that church like a greyhound out of a trap, no one had a chance to say anything. Lucy came panting along five minutes later, not, as she knew, to peel spuds, but to meet and greet and take orders. I felt like a puppet, dancing back between the kitchen and the bar, cursing the law that prevented Lucy pulling a pint.

And people kept on coming. It was nearly five before I could wave the last guest away, locking the door behind them and leaning on it wondering how I'd done it.

'The bugger of it is,' I said to Lucy, who'd just kicked off her shoes, and was unloading the dishwasher, 'that there's hardly anything worth giving you for your tea.'

'Friday's pie,' she said. 'Yesterday I gave them that cheese and potato pie you taught me how to make. But all that carbohydrate, Mrs Welford: and they wanted it with chips!'

'And you gave them –?'

'Big bags of carrots going cheap at Jem and Molly's,' she grinned, though her face was as pale and drawn as I'd seen it.

Without speaking I pushed the last portion of damson tart

towards her. 'Sit! Go on: I don't want you fainting.' Sinking opposite her, I helped myself to a nibble of cheese and a stick of celery. My shoes joined hers. At least I could have a slop of wine. Thank goodness I didn't do Sunday evening meals. With luck, the locals would continue with their cold shoulder treatment and I could have a night off. A night off and a very early night.

Sure I was simply going through the motions, I went to open the snug door and switch on the porch light. As I did so, this huge four by four pulled up.

'Nick!' I began, only to have to add 'Ola!' as the TV reporter almost fell into my arms.

'Josie darling,' she said, 'I told them you wouldn't let us down.' The silver monster disgorged another four young people. 'I suppose you wouldn't have a table for five?' She must have read my face. 'But we've come all the way from Exeter – go on, I'm sure you can rustle something up for us?'

'Of course I can,' I beamed, working out permutations as I shook hands – yes, it seemed we were on that sort of terms – with her mates. 'But it'll have to be table d'hôte, not à la carte.' And this time they'd bloody well pay for their wine. At any price I chose.

We were all best buddies by the time the meal was cooked, Nicola insisting, when she realised I was on my own again, on my sitting at the table and eating with them. Starters had been defrostables. For the main course I had to scurry round a bit. At one point I thought I heard someone knock at the back door, but I was too busy to do more than check the back window – no, no sign of anyone, in a car or out of one. So I turned my attention back to the stove. I reheated the lamb curry, then knocked together a variety of other rapid curries – one for green beans, another for kidney beans, and a creamy, possibly inauthentic but nonetheless delicious chicken, all courtesy of my Indian and Pakistani friends from Brum. A huge bowl of plain Basmati rice and there we were. And they all drank easy-to-top-up-lager, bless them.

Sweet: my own private rumtopf, summer fruits macerated in rum and sugar for the last three months, with Devon cream ice cream. My famous cheese board appeared next, though it was scarcely touched, then coffee. Since Nicola had been making a big thing about not drinking and driving, I didn't mention liqueurs. I'd like to add I didn't mention a bill, but I'm afraid I did. I knew what such a meal would have cost in Ladypool Road, the heart of Brum's curry district, and doubled it. Even then it seemed cheap – after all, I was using top class ingredients. So I added a bit more, and then shoved on the drinks bill. To my embarrassment, they then insisted on paying for my share, too. One of them was going to design me a website as soon as the restaurant was up and running; another had a mate who'd do a feature for *Somerset Life*. There was talk of a spot on one of the local news magazine programmes. If I'd known about all that, I would have fed them for free.

Or doubled the bill again, on the grounds they could afford it.

As they left, I touched my finger to my lips – the village was already asleep. And they tiptoed out like lambs, each one hugging and kissing me as they left.

What a night. One of the very best ever.

I'd even brazen out the accusations of the heaps of dirty plates. OK, I loaded the dishwasher, but wash up I couldn't. Twenty years ago, I'd have managed the extra effort. Not now. I forced myself to pad barefoot to the back door, just to make sure it was locked.

And found a puddle of blood, with more steadily oozing underneath.

If I opened that door, whatever was the other side would fall on top of me. I might have been paralysed.

The blood continued to trickle. The pool got larger.

Staring fascinated wasn't going to do any good. Someone might be lying there dying.

I couldn't bear the thought of warm blood on my bare feet. Couldn't. What if I just dialled 999 and hoped rescue would come in time?

I could look if it didn't fall into my hallway. I could. Of course I could. And if it didn't get on my shoes, which I crammed on willy-nilly.

And it couldn't get on my shoes, couldn't fall on top of me if

I went out through the front door and all the way round the pub. So that's what I did. Clutching my mobile in one hand, my heaviest torch in the other.

However fast asleep I'd been, even that first deep sleep from which you can never rouse anyone, whatever their nightmare, screams like mine would have woken me. I'm sure they would. Because I hollered and hollered, till at last it penetrated even my hysterical brain that no one was taking the blindest bit of notice. I might have been an on-heat vixen calling for a mate for all the windows that shot open, all the lights clicked on. So I staggered back and locked myself back in. God in heaven, all the meat I'd cut up, why had I had to go all girly? Time for deep breaths, a deep drink and the application of some common sense.

One hand clutching a stiff whisky, the other thumbed 999. 'Police. Police, please.'

It seemed aeons before a man with a Devon burr thicker than this evening's cream answered. 'Officer,' I gabbled. 'I need help now. Someone – someone's tipped a load of offal all over my doorstep. Intestines. Lungs. Liver. The lot. And a gallon or two of blood.'

'Is the person alive or dead?'

'It's not a person. It's animal remains.'

'And is the animal in need of immediate veterinary assistance?'

'No.'

'So there's no one in danger, and no animal in danger. Now, if you think that's an emergency, madam, I can get a vehicle to you. But I don't think it'll be in the half hour we try to reach rural emergencies in, because there's been a major incident elsewhere in the county. All our mobiles are involved with that.'

Mobiles. I had a sweet vision of those airblown things people string over babies' cots. Any moment I'd start laughing and might not be able to stop. 'All right,' I said quickly. 'Why don't you put me down for a morning visit. I'll leave the evidence where it is.'

Which is what I did. OK, I rolled newspaper into a sausage I shoved up against the door. That reduced the blood flow.

And then, not even bothering to sink the rest of that malt, I literally crawled upstairs and fell into my bed.

Chapter Fifteen

I might have been flippant in my request for police help first thing next morning, but someone was taking it seriously. I'd hardly finished what would have to pass for breakfast – all last night's calories were already congregating round my belly – when someone applied a remorseless digit to my doorbell. The front one. I flung it open to greet a silver four by four as monstrous as Nick's and a couple of miserable looking men who could only have been plain clothes policemen. Two of them, one round Nick Thomas's age, the other a lad looking scarcely older than Lucy, showed their IDs as one.

'DCI Mike Evans,' said the older one, a Cornish burr to his voice. He might once have been a carrot head, but the colour had faded to rust. With his pale skin, he was weathered rather than tanned, and you could have passed him in a supermarket without giving him a second glance. For my money, that dozy stolidity was a front. His eyes, blue, if you had a romantic tendency, as a summer sky, narrowed as the smell of the guts wafted along the dogleg of corridor, but he didn't remark on it. 'And this is Detective Sergeant Scott Short.'

Scott Short. Whatever had his parents been thinking if? He was dressed so sharply he'd have to be careful not to cut himself when he pulled his trousers on, and his hair was fashionably spiked. Was it coming from the Smoke that gave him his swagger, a metropolitan amongst all us bumpkins? Whatever it was, I didn't take to him, especially when I showed them into my lovely living room and he appraised it with a pronounced sneer. A man for Habitat beech and beiges, no doubt. And a weekly manicure. Interesting.

I was very impressed that they'd taken my incident so seriously, and was about to tell them so.

But Evans coughed portentously, and began, 'You may be aware that Mr Fred Tregothnan has been reported missing.'

I swear I felt Tony's hand on my shoulder, pressing me down, warning me not to say anything yet about my incident. I almost patted it reassuringly. 'There's still no sign of him?' I asked, pouring both of them some of my excellent coffee and adding more fuel to an already bright and warming fire. 'This must be very worrying for his family.' I was as well aware as they that he did-n't have any, but I was hardly going to let on I knew him so well.

'Indeed,' agreed Evans.

It was clear they were waiting for me to say something. The question was, what? And how? I wasn't going to go all weepy on this pair: I didn't think Evans would buy it, anyway. What about wrong-footing them altogether with news of the red stream and the shed so illicitly fenced off? I could keep Nick out of the story, but that might backfire if it later came out that we'd explored it together. Blast the man for pushing off precisely when he was needed here. But that might be why he'd gone. After all, he had had a row with Fred – perhaps he had actually had something to do with his disappearance.

No: Nick was a victim if ever I saw one, not a murderer.

But rats turned vicious if cornered – what about mice?

Clearly the less I said about Nick and our activities the better.

Time to be the dumb blonde, then. Dumb as in silent. I put on my listening landlady face, a half smile and slightly tilted head, as if I was interested, just like a kindly counsellor. And waited.

Yes! It was Scott who broke first. 'You had a disagreement with Mr Tregothnan.'

'I did. He goosed one of my employees. Lindi Taylor. Sexual assault, in other words. I told one of your colleagues in Taunton.'

'Ms Taylor denies all knowledge of the incident. So do all the other people in the bar at the time. And she says that when you spoke to Mr Tregothnan, you threatened to kill him.'

All the years I'd practised, I'd never been able to stop myself going pale when I was accused of anything. In the discreet light-ing of my living room, the change might not be detectable; if I flushed afterwards, they might have thought it was my age and my hormones. Certainly my voice would give nothing away: Tony had coached me for far too many long hours. 'No, of course I didn't. Nothing like as tame. I cursed his soul to eternal perdi-tion and one or two variants of that. Although in general I don't swear, when I curse, constable, I curse good and proper. I wouldn't bother with a mere death threat, believe me.' Was that why I'd been cold-shouldered in the shop on Friday morning? Because they genuinely thought I'd done him in?

Or because they felt guilty for shoving the blame on to me?

Evans managed a wry smile; Scott blinked.

'Is there anyone else he might have argued with?' Evans asked.

'Being a landlady's rather like being a priest,' I said. 'You hear and see things you can't repeat.'

'Is that a yes or a no?' Scott demanded.

'I know he had disputes with a number of people, but I never heard a death threat. I think he was owed money – but I gather that's the usual scenario for vets in these hard days for farmers. His paperwork would show that.'

'And where would that be?'

I allowed myself a raised brows blink. 'Why ask me? I have enough trouble with my own paperwork, let alone anyone else's.'

'You were seen leaving his house, Mrs Welford.'

Hell's bells! Was there anywhere this village that didn't conceal eyes?

I smiled smoothly. 'Yes. With the Reverend Sue Clayton. I'm sure she's told you. When we heard Fred hadn't turned up for surgery we thought someone ought to check he wasn't lying ill in his house. So we used his spare key to gain access. We didn't find him. And – I'm also sure she's told you – she hunted for his address book and so on but couldn't find them. So we gave up. I presume she contacted you?'

'Were you with Ms Clayton all the time?'

'I left her downstairs while I went to check upstairs.'

'So she could have removed items without your knowing.'

'Or I without her knowing. But I didn't. And Sue's not that sort of woman –'

'What sort, Mrs Welford?'

'The sort to be anything less than a hundred per cent honest. If she'd taken anything, it would have been for safekeeping. She'd probably even have asked me whether she should. And she'd certainly have told you.'

'So we can't impugn *her* honesty. What about *yours*, Mrs

Welford?'

I took a calculated risk. If they wanted to check up on me they'd find out soon enough, so I produced an embarrassed smile. 'This won't go any further, will it? I mean, I have a reputation in the village –'

Short gave a crack of laughter. Evans frowned him down.

'You're implying I have a reputation for something I don't know about, Mr Short?' I opened indignant eyes wide. 'Whatever that may be – and I trust you'll enlighten me – I'm sure it's not for what I am. I'm the widow of a man who at one point was the most wanted man in England. I was his child bride, and he was in prison for some twenty-five of the thirty years I was married to him. Tony Welford. Ended his days in Long Lartin for a heist that went wrong. Maximum security prison,' I added, as if Short were a kindergarten kid who needed things spelling out. 'Suffice to say my own record is immaculate, or I'd hardly have got an alcohol licence, would I? And yes, the authorities do know about Tony.' Had someone's sister or cousin or aunt seen the confidential documentation and split? May they rot if they had. It was only then it occurred to me who could easily have dropped it out – so why hadn't I immediately suspected Nick Thomas? 'So what do they say about me in the village?'

'That you're –' Short stopped dead. I kept my eyes full on him. He flushed scarlet. 'A witch,' he mumbled.

'Twaddle and bilge,' I said, drawing a grin from Evans. 'Mind you, I wouldn't mind being one, not just at the moment. All my staff have mysteriously disappeared, gentlemen. I could magic them back again. Abracadabra!'

'Why should they have disappeared?'

'Given the choice, would you work for a witch?' I asked as lightly as if I didn't care.

'No notice?'

I shook my head.

'No word since?'

Another shake. When I was young, my hair had been long and heavy and silky enough to flop from side to side when I did that. It had made me feel a million dollars. Then I'd reached the age when long hair doesn't work – mutton pretending to be lamb, and looking all the worse for trying. The hairdresser actually picked up a lock for me to keep, but I slung it down when he wasn't looking. No point in clinging on to a past life.

'How are you managing?' Evans looked genuinely interested.

'Not much business this last week, what with the rain. You may have seen me on the TV news on Friday, talking with passion about the problems of the poor farmers and tradespeople round here. No? Your heart would have bled. In any case, I planned for a fairly fallow period while the restaurant was being set up. A few sulking rustics won't kill me. Could that be what happened to Fred Tregothnan?' I speculated aloud, almost as if I were talking to Nick. 'Vets don't earn that much, do they, in rural practices? Far more money in overfed city pets. Some folk take things hard – he might have topped himself.'

'The possibility isn't lost on us, Mrs Welford. Very well.' Evans pulled himself to his feet, not quite suppressing a wince as his knees straightened. 'Thank you for your time. And for the excellent coffee. Is that what you'll be serving in your new restaurant?'

It struck me that the news of the pub's transformation hadn't come to him as any surprise. He'd obviously done his homework – or simply listened to villagers all too ready to fill him in on the news. I outlined the plans briefly, leading them down the stairs – to the back door this time.

'Now you're here, Mr Evans,' I said, pointing to the stinking ooze, 'perhaps you could tell me what you're going to do about that.'

Scott Short took one look and spewed, all over my feet. Well, he'd go far in the police, wouldn't he?

'It must be the shock, poor lad,' I said kindly, kicking off my shoes all the same, and wondering how he'd take it if I stripped off my spattered stockings. The trouble with vomit is that the tiniest spec stinks for ever, and makes me want to heave in sympathy.

Despite his gabble of apologies, Short goggled – hadn't he ever seen woman wearing stockings for anything except seduction? I wasn't about to give him a lecture on the causes and prevention of vaginal thrush, however. Hopping from one foot to the other, I flung the offending items on to the floor. 'I'm sorry – I shall have to go and wash this off.' What else would Tony have considered the bidet was meant for except feet?

I left plenty of time, while drying between my toes and pulling on fresh stockings, for them to ponder more calmly my unexpected gift. I pondered from afar, amid the smells of lavender and rose. Entrails. Intestines. Guts. A lot of them. Never having seen the innards of a cow or whatever, I'd no idea how much to expect. Had I had the contents of one beast or more? No, I hadn't actually counted the hearts or lungs or livers, any of which could have appeared on my menu later that week – if I'd had any idea of their provenance, of course.

Of course, I had a damned good idea where they might have come from. The animals I'd seen being delivered to the makeshift slaughterhouse. Pity I'd resolved not to implicate Nick by reporting it – at this stage anyway. The first question they'd now have to ask, of course, was who might have it in for me. Well, I had a good alternative theory, which came out equally pat when, pale about the gills himself, poor kid, Short sat on my sofa again, knees tightly together as if he was afraid I might flash my suspenders at him. After a good swallow, he managed to stutter out a direct question. Evans, meanwhile, was barking into his phone.

'As a matter of fact there is one person who might have a grudge against me – the sort of grudge you might express that way. Trouble is, I don't know his name.'

Short groped for his superior expression, missing horribly.

'Look, have another of these biscuits – they'll settle that poor stomach of yours. The man was my meat supplier till quite recently. You might say I inherited him when I took over the pub. But I only ever contacted him through a third party. You need to ask Mr Bulcombe, the guy who runs the campsite recently under several feet of water: he'd know. It was he who did the deals.'

Short wrote assiduously.

Evans, over his head, asked, 'Why did you stop getting your meat from him?' He snapped his phone shut as if to emphasise the question.

'No paperwork' I told him. 'See, I told you what a law-abiding citizen I was compared with my late husband.' I swallowed hard, not entirely for show. 'No matter how many times I asked, an invoice, a receipt would always come next time – honest, Mrs Welford. And then I did a spot of research about BSE and how it can affect humans and decided to go organic instead. Apart from anything else, it'll add cachet to the restaurant when it opens.'

Evans joined Short on the sofa, leaning forward to ask, ' Did you have any reason to believe that the meat you were buying might be infected?'

'None at all. Like I said, all I wanted was nice legitimate paper-work for my nice legitimate business. And when it didn't appear, I changed to a supplier who practically bakes his beasts birthday cakes he knows them so well. And he knows the slaughterhouse, too,' I added, wondering if they were bright enough to take the bait.

'Why did you do the research?' Short asked, surprising me.

'I just happened to be surfing the Web one day and saw an item on this young man with – what to they call it? CJD? And I took it from there.'

'But why?'

'Serendipity,' I said, still preferring to keep Nick out of this.

'And do you reckon,' Evans jumped in, 'that it was serendipity that brought all that – that *matter* – to your doorstep?'

I sensed a trap. 'Like I said, ask Reg Bulcombe.'

'Is this Mr Bulcombe's handwriting?' He flourished a scrap of paper torn from an exercise book.

'I'll need my reading glasses. Could you pass me my bag? Thanks. There.' I read the words aloud. '*You nozy bastared, I warned you to clear out or you're lanlady'll get a nasty surprise.*' Where did this come from?'

'Someone had tucked it under a windscreen wiper.'

Hell and damnation! OK, some of Nick's activities might have to come into the open. But fancy him just clearing off like that, in that cowardly, supine way, without a word to me! I'd have stood up to whoever it was, you bet I would. I supposed I should say something. 'Yours?' As he nodded, I mused, 'So all that wasn't meant for me!' I ought to feel happier than I did.

'Only indirectly. So who would the nosy bastard be?'

'I can only think it must be my temporary lodger. Nick Thomas. But why they should leave a note on your car...' I feigned innocence. 'Ah, I suppose you wouldn't drive a dirty great gas-guzzling four-wheel drive? Silver? That'll be it, then. They thought it was his.'

'So why should they wish to get rid of him?'

'I'd tell you to ask him yourself, but he's left a phone message saying he's working in the South East for a bit. He's some sort of civil servant,' I added carelessly, leaning back and crossing my legs above the knee. How much had Sue, not to mention the villagers, said about him?

Whatever the effect on Short, Evans didn't buy my ignorance. 'What sort?'

'I'm sure he'll tell you when you talk to him. He's definitely coming back, he says.' The men exchanged glances – so they did know about him. To clarify, I added, 'He's paying me to keep his room. He's based in Taunton, mostly.'

'And has now conveniently decamped.' I couldn't tell who Evans was more irritated with, Nick or me.

'I'd have thought,' I objected, for both our sakes, 'that you need to talk less to Mr Thomas than to the guy who threatened him, wouldn't you? And I don't know Mr Bulcombe's writing, but I'd say whoever wrote it spelt the way he speaks, and that certainly doesn't rule him out.' To mark a change of subject, I recrossed my legs. 'What are you proposing to do with my gift? I take it whoever it was committed some sort of offence to dump it there? It's not exactly good for public health or the environment.'

'I've already arranged for its disposal,' he said stiffly. 'And here are a couple of industrial cleaners we sometimes have to use.' He flicked two business cards. 'The caravan site, you said.'

'Yes, just down the road here. While you're at it, you could even ask him why his field's flooded and nowhere else is. No, better not. Because he'll know who tipped you off. I saw him loading waders and shovel into his car the other day and we exchanged a couple of sentences. I think he must have gone off to reorganise a watercourse. The stream next to the post office virtually dried up while the caravan field flooded, you see. Now the stream's running as usual, and the field's conveniently recovered.'

'That'll be for his insurance company to sort out,' Short said, his face lifting with relief: someone else would get to do the paperwork. 'I'm sure they'd be grateful for a tip-off too.'

How much else should I reveal? Damn and blast Nick.

I checked my watch. 'I'm afraid I have a pub to run, gentlemen.' And a call to make to my insurance company, for the cost of cleaning and a fresh carpet and a spot of redecoration.

'You reckon you'll have any customers?' Evans demanded, taking the hint and getting to his feet.

I looked him frankly in the eye. 'To a large extent that depends on you. If you let it be known that there's actually no sign of Mr Thomas, they may come flooding back, keen to show me all is forgiven. On the other hand, they might not like me either. We shall see.'

'We shall indeed. Now, the council should get that lot clear by nightfall.'

'Nightfall!' I squeaked.

'You might try soft-soaping them. The men might even hose the place down if you slip them a fiver.' He took a step forward. 'I reckon it's Mr Thomas they're after – don't take kindly to strangers, round here.'

I looked him straight in the eye. 'What are you and I, Mr Evans, if not strangers?' Perhaps that was why I'd told him more than I'd meant; perhaps that was why I'd formed that unlikely alliance with Nick – because however much they might need someone to run their waterhole, the villagers certainly didn't want an incomer like me to do it, no, nor any other incomers around the place either. If they were feuding with me, I'd make my alliances where I could.

Like any good hostess, I saw my visitors out – through the main pub door, that is – walking courteously with them to their car. It was actually a twin of the first one Nick had tried, gross in

the bodywork with huge wheels and, no doubt, a full comple-
ment of bells and whistles within. I wasn't the only one to have
taken umbrage. Someone had taken a set of keys to the paintwork
and slashed all the tyres. But I didn't think it was the aesthetics
of the thing or the harm it did to the environment that had
offended them. 'You're right,' I said quietly, while the men
sounded off. 'The villagers don't like strangers.'

Monday always was a slack pub day, closed at lunchtime and open just for drinks in the evening. No, not my idea: the previous landlord's. He'd needed time to breathe occasionally too. But there wouldn't be much breathing till they'd lugged the guts to another place. The phrase was irritatingly familiar, more irritatingly elusive when I tried to track it down. Maybe it'd come to me if I drove into Taunton to clear my head. Actually to check with the employment people about possible bar staff: they should have had time by now to respond to my fax. There were a couple of possibles, both, fortunately, with their own transport. I'd try the first on Tuesday lunchtime, the other on Tuesday evening, I said. Hang WeightWatchers, just this once. There was no fee to forfeit, since I was on their Gold Standard: I never lost less than my target, and often lost more. Apart from the first vulnerable weeks, I'd never hung round for the pep talk and socialising. My own scales told me I'd lost another couple of pounds, and that would have to do. So I set off briskly to collect my photos and have the current lot developed. As before, negatives and a set of prints would go to Piers.

And I – would go to Birmingham.

No, not so mad. The industrial cleaners couldn't make it till tomorrow morning, though the council had promised to remove the waste by the end of the day. And I couldn't face a day and night of ever-increasing pong. I had to go somewhere, and why not Birmingham, my home town and proud possessor of the central library which Prince Charles had described as a place better suited to burning books than to storing them? And if the library's archive failed, then I could always go to the offices of the local papers and ask to see their back numbers. I hadn't packed an overnight bag, of course, but had no intention of wasting time going back to get it. A spot of retail therapy in a city with decent shops was called for, and, the way the city was changing, a bit of sightseeing. Selfridge's, the new Bull Ring – here I come.

I never liked going back, as a matter of fact. Too many memories. OK, there were good ones as well as bad, but my philosophy

has always been that you should always move forward, never
back. And, despite myself, I'd become a countrywoman. The traffic, the fumes – I felt totally bombarded. And it wasn't just traffic noise – it was people noise too. Unwilling to fight through
roads I'd once laughed at, I checked in at a hotel in suburban
Edgbaston and caught a bus. Not a single passenger seemed to be
sitting silently or even talking quietly to a neighbour. Every conversation was at maximum volume, with the odd one not joining
in adding to the mêleé with overloud personal stereos. No wonder someone was smoking pot to calm their nerves – I wouldn't
have minded a spliff myself. But not in a bus plastered with no
smoking notices. I looked around – no, no furtive fags cupped in
hands. Except one in the driver's.

At least none of the librarians were smoking, not visibly at
least. I made my way to the sixth floor. What I remembered,
probably wrongly, as a silent place of study, now seemed to be a
dating agency for kids for all the ethnic backgrounds under the
sun, their voices rising like those of the flocks of starlings that
had once ruled the city centre. I could be an old codger and
remind the librarians of what seemed like baby-sitting duties. Or
I could concentrate hard on what I was putting through the
microfiche and maybe I wouldn't hear.

There was a lot to concentrate on in 80s Birmingham – race,
politics, pollution, unemployment. But nothing seemed to fit the
bill. Not until I came across the magic headline, *KINGS HEATH
SIEGE.* Hallo, hallo, hallo, as Dixon of Dock Green might have
said.

Kings Heath was not one of my regular stamping grounds
though in fact not all that far from Bartley Green, the suburb that
Tony had for some reason made his base. Bartley Green included
a reservoir where nice people sailed little boats and a lot of high-
rise council flats, latterly home to a lot of cheap-skate drug-deal-
ers Tony wouldn't have given the time of day to. We'd had a top
floor flat in one of them. Don't ask me why he was taking up
cheap accommodation meant for the poor and homeless when we
were spectacularly neither. Tony could have afforded to buy the
whole block, several times over. Well, he owned enough overseas,

ones he'd always meant to use as bolt holes when the Law got after him. None of them was in his name, of course, and it would have taken more dedicated forensic accountants than the West Midlands Police had ever had at their disposal to trace them back to him. They were in quite different names now, many quite legitimately since I'd sold them and bought other things, including my education. Not to mention my pub and my flying lessons, of course.

My memories of Kings Heath were mainly of streets and streets of Victorian terrace housing, some better than others. There was some more recent stuff, and one or two grander Victorian houses, many now multi-occupied, of course.

Once upon a time, mentally ill people had routinely been crammed away in remote institutions, long ago even used as objects of upper-class amusement. Under Thatcher, two initiatives changed this. One was a realisation that in many cases this was plainly unsuitable for many, unnecessary, even. Another was a more pragmatic need for health authorities to clear old institutions to sell them and raise funds. So it became fashionable to turf out institutionalised folk and call it care in the community. Fine if there'd been any care in place and readily available. There were a number of highly publicised cases where innocent men and women were killed by mentally ill people who really should have been locked away for life – but whose hospitals were now bijou housing. One case was in Birmingham: it was all coming back to me now, courtesy the fuzzy pictures now on the pages I was now scanning.

A kind and loving young man had been returned to the community and popped into a Victorian bed-sit. He'd decided that his pregnant sixteen-year-old girlfriend was carrying the Antichrist. He proposed to stab her to death and crucify the foetus. Fellow lodgers overheard her screams and his rantings, and called the police.

The evening, but not the lunchtime, edition carried the story, which seemed to be ongoing. For some reason there'd been some delay in bringing in the officers used to dealing with what rapidly turned into a siege. I knew that by that stage police had actually started to train teams – one of Tony's less likeable associates had been talked out of shooting his mother-in-law, though I hadn't liked her much either. And there were certainly armed response units in the force, because they'd started to arrive suspiciously promptly at bank hold-ups and the like. But on this particular day ordinary local officers were involved. Maybe there simply wasn't time to bring the experts in. Who knows?

The following day's lunchtime edition carried the grim news. Someone had taken the decision to rush the young man, who'd slit the girl's abdomen in front of them. As she lay dying, the young man turned on the officers, some of whom had also suffered terrible injuries. At last a sharpshooter had arrived and the man was killed. No police names were given. All this in a quiet and uninteresting suburb, known to people like me more for the number of charity shops on its high street than for anything else. What I needed now was the report of the inquest, which would no doubt appear in greater detail in the *Evening Mail*'s more sober morning stable mate, the *Birmingham Post*.

'You want it *now*?' the librarian asked. 'We'll be closing in five minutes.'

And so they would. Doesn't time fly when you're enjoying yourself? And, damn it, I couldn't come back for more. I'd got a pub to run, remember, and a new bar-person to try out. So I had to be on the M5, scene of all those lovely Midlands traffic jams, by five at the latest. Hell and damnation. But at least I could take advantage of Birmingham's culinary excellence. Not for nothing did the natives regard it as the curry capital not just of the UK but also of Europe.

The industrial cleaners did a wonderful job, inside and out, and I rewarded them with on the house food. The new barman, an affable young man from Southampton called Robin, clearly thought it an unusual way to run a pub, but handed across pie and chips and engaged both them and the other customers – passing trade to a man – in pleasant football chitchat. So why did I have reservations about him?

'A motorcycle's a pretty vulnerable form of transport,' I said awkwardly. I didn't want to spell out my fears about tripwires and attack by four by fours.

'Very green,' he countered. 'And cheap.'

'All the floods we've had –'

'The rain's easing off. And I really need the work.'

I took a deep breath. 'The village doesn't always take to grockles – I've had a bit of trouble myself. Hence the cleaners.' I explained. 'Though I think the entrails were meant for one of my guests, not me.'

'I noticed the vacancies sign. It could do with a bit of a clean up.'

'It could do with taking down. Until the refurbishment's over, anyway. The furniture and décor's out of the ark.'

He looked wistful. 'I suppose there's no chance of accommodation?'

'Thrown in?'

'I could pay.'

'Not much on the wages I advertised at. And you can see from today there's not much in tips. None from the locals, should they deign to turn up.'

He put down the glass he was polishing and regarded me steadily. 'Why don't you tell me straight I don't get the job? And could you tell me why?'

It was hard to lie to such clear grey eyes. And perhaps it was better for us both to be quite honest. 'I think you'd be brilliant and I'd throw in accommodation for free. But I'm afraid for you, Robin. Seriously afraid.'

'Will you be afraid for the person you're interviewing this evening?'

The answer was that the evening's candidate – Dec, a shaven-headed Irishman in his forties – could have used his head to knock in nails and never even blinked. And he smoked more than an unswept chimney. It might have been prissy to object when he was to work in a room where you could have cured kippers on the leftovers of previous cigarettes and pipes still floating in the atmosphere. But I did. And I didn't like the way he hummed silently and kept time with his clicking fingers to a tune I couldn't hear. As for his communication skills, there was little chance for him to practise, the only ones in the bar being a party of French tourists who preferred Lucy's tortured attempts at their tongue to attempting to break through the language barrier. Was it that that made matters tense between her and Dec? No, Dec was almost certainly off my list. Was it back to Robin?

Or should I rethink the whole thing? Should I try once more in the village? I could ask Sue to exert some pressure. Yes, and put her in an awkward position. A toss up between Robin, whom I liked, and a Neanderthal I didn't. One for the ethicists, that.

'I'll get back in touch with you as soon as I've seen everyone else,' I told Dec lamely.

'Suit yourself. Not much custom, is there? Hardly worth having anyone else except that cute kid working here.'

'If Lucy were eighteen, I wouldn't have anyone else. But since she can't serve drinks – ' I stopped short, looking at him closely.

He became so blasé I knew what the spat must have been about.

'You didn't make her, did you?'

'Oh, she offered – said you let her.'

Which, in view of the chicken pie, I didn't believe. So Robin it would have to be.

He seemed over the moon when I phoned him.

'You won't be welcomed in the village, remember. And being sent to Coventry may not be the worst you get. Think guts, Robin.'

'I'll be fine,' he said. 'And you'll let me have cheap accommodation?'

'I told you, I'll throw it in for free. So long as you promise me to lock your motorbike away every moment you're not using it. I'll clear one of the outbuildings for you.'

'No. That'll be my job. Least I can do.'

'See you tomorrow then.'

Wouldn't it be nice to have fallen on my feet?

Especially when the following morning's post – oh, not the official one, the sort that left parcels anonymously on the doorstep – was a polythene bag, a label round its neck, full of bulls' eyes.

Yes. Eyes from bulls.

Chapter Seventeen

No doubt about this one. Not for Nick or Robin. The label made that clear. For Mrs Josie Welford, The White Heart, Kings Duncombe. Damn it, you'd have thought he'd have got the spelling right. All he'd have to do was look up and see the sign. Or maybe he couldn't spell, like the author of the note on the detectives' vehicle. Or maybe he wasn't from the village, though at least he'd spelt that right. Maybe he was an outsider and someone had told him to take the eyes to the interfering bitch at the pub and he'd heard the name as *heart*, not *hart*. It was as good a theory as any: you got cross with someone and picked up the phone and gave your orders. That was the way Tony worked. You didn't do your dirty work yourself; you got someone else to do it. The lower orders. 'See it it,' he'd say. And if anyone queried anything, he'd snap, 'Just see to it, I said.'

You'd think that after all this time I'd give up aching to hear his voice. I tried replacing it with someone else's voice. Mrs Coyne's. I'd have loved King Duncombe's Mr Big to be Mrs Coyne. Such a nice Dickensian name for a money-grubbing villain. The money-grubbing villain round here was supposed to be Mr Luke Greville, however, son and heir of the lady who'd poached my bar staff from me. Interesting, that. The owner of the land from which the pink water rose. And much other land round here. She wouldn't by any chance own the land on which the dodgy slaughterhouse sat, or the rending plant? It was worth checking out. I might even float the idea to DCI Evans when I phoned him to tell him about my gift. I could always invite him round and dish them up as a Middle-Eastern delicacy. No, that was sheep, wasn't it? And I couldn't see him sitting cross-legged on my floor while, houri-like, I served him. Lucy'd make a better houri, of course. I wondered how she'd get on with Robin. Which reminded me – I'd better clear at least a space for his motorbike, if not the whole outhouse, which, as he'd said, he could always tackle himself if business were slack. Correction: when business was slack.

The eyes could wait till I'd changed into my gardening clothes and got a spade with which to carry them. Hell! How stupid could I get? I'd dressed fowl, paunched rabbits, gutted fish. I wasn't going to let a few dead orbs faze me. I picked up the bag, carrying it as if it contained no more than a dozen eggs, and deposited in the food preparation sink in the pub kitchen. I phoned through a message for DCI Evans. And only then did I get changed and prepare to tackle that outhouse.

People left keys under flowerpots down here. They didn't lock things like sheds. Or rather, not till Aidan, the ducky one of the bell ringers, brought his latest squeeze down here, a rent boy with kleptomaniac tendencies. The boy went, and Aidan stayed, now with what looked like a long-term partner, and the system went back to normal. As far as I knew, there wasn't a key for the door. And if there had been, the frame was so warped a good heave would have got you inside anyway. I'd buy a big padlock and chain next time I went into Taunton.

Propping the door wide open – no one had ever got round to installing lights – I surveyed the scene. A little of the mess was mine – one day I really ought to return those packing cases to the removal firm and get my deposit back. Most, however, had been bequeathed to me, as it were, by generations of previous land-lords. There were garden implements I didn't even know how to use, and nets and seed boxes and twine and my gardening gloves and —

I moved closer. A notebook? An A4 notebook, card covers and cloth spine. Where the hell had that come from? And why was it nestling under my gloves? I lifted a corner. Accounts. Not mine. Without a closer look I was only guessing. And I wasn't going to take a closer look, because I didn't want my dabs and my DNA all over the missing vet's property. I had to face it. Someone was framing me. And even as my mind raced, a salient fact obtruded: I'd phoned the police and they might well be on their way.

Now what?

Whoever had put it there had wanted it to be found, and not by me. By the police. So if I left it there I'd be incriminated; if I moved it, I'd be writing my arrest warrant, because, as sure as God made little apples, they'd have grassed me up.

Leaving everything exactly as it was, I withdrew, closing the door behind me. The fewer signs of disturbance the better – forensic scientists would be able to check, for instance, on how many pairs of feet had walked in that aeons old dust. But then I started second-guessing: if someone wanted to entrap me, they might well come in again and disturb what I was now beginning to think of as a crime scene. Bar sitting on my now pristine back-door step, how could I preserve it? I was upstairs and back, clutching my trusty camera before you could say Fox Talbot.

And then I phoned the police again. Urgent, I said. Dead urgent.

So I could hardly ask them to stop on the way and collect my paper from the shop.

Hell, I could understand why people wanted a fag with their coffee. It gave the hands and mouth something to do. My substitute was the ballpoint I held to my lips while I was doing the crossword. The easy one, of course. There were days when I congratulated myself on having done two clues in the serious one, the one Tony had always done. I used to clip a week's supply for him so he wouldn't have to spend his cash on buying papers he could read in the prison library. And no, he never got a chance to do the crossword in the library *Guardian* – one of the screws spotted how much it meant to him and started filling it out himself. Fast. As if he were Mensa level. One day Tony got to look at it – the bastard had filled in letters at random. The whole exercise had been just to get under Tony's fingernails.

So who was framing me? Who'd planted Fred Tregothnan's account ledger? I needed to work out how much to say to the police, who'd be sure to ask me. It was a bit subtle for Reg Bulcombe, though he'd have enjoyed the guts and eyes game. The person in charge of the ad hoc slaughterhouse? It couldn't have been Nick, having obscure revenge for never having traced Tony's fortune? There'd been no call from him since he'd bolted, after all. No, I didn't buy that. What did worry me was a pair of images I couldn't get out of my mind – Sue rifling Fred's desk, and Sue clutching her raincoat together as she left the cottage. Not Sue. Surely not Sue. I'd much rather blame the Mr Big who favoured me with offal – and that certainly wouldn't be Sue's style. And it was the obvious theory. I'd been sniffing round his enterprises, seen by what I suspected were at least two of his associates, however far down the pecking order they might be. Even the lowliest driver had eyes and ears he might find it profitable to put at his employer's disposal.

The question came back to the identity of the man at the top. And whether his minions might even include the detectives even now pulling up outside the pub. Tony had managed to suborn several in the course of his long career: the now defunct West Midlands Serious Crimes Squad hadn't get their bad reputation for corruption for nothing.

These two Somerset cops weren't fools. This time they came in a much humbler vehicle and they parked in the back yard. But were they honest and decent and above corruption? Before I answered the door, I tucked my camera well out of sight.

'Do you want to see my gift?' I asked as I gestured them in through the nice clean rear hall. 'Actually, maybe DS Short should stay here. We don't want a repeat of yesterday.'

Scarlet to the ears, he mumbled and chuntered.

'The nearest loo's that Portaloo there,' I said, cutting him short. 'Come this way, Mr Evans. This is the pub kitchen, as you can see. When you're ready, the better coffee is upstairs.'

Evans looked rather more revolted by the eyes than by the intestinal ooze. Short didn't even attempt to look, merely holding open an evidence bag for Evans, who, with finicky fingers, slipped off the address label.

'Is there – where would you – er –?'

'There's a trade refuse bin out there. You can't miss it. Or if you prefer, I'll get my chef to deal with it. Me,' I added, as Evans opened his mouth. 'But while we're down here, there's something else I want you to see.' Still not sure whether I was doing the right thing, I led the way to the outhouse, pulling open the door but gesturing them to stay back. Even I could see my trail of wet prints across the otherwise dry floor, to the bench and back again.

Short thought it was time for a spot of bravado. 'Opening up a museum of country life, are you?'

Evans muttered something. Short blushed.

'I think you might want to be the curator,' I said quite kindly. 'You see where my footsteps lead. To that bench, with my gardening gloves on it. Can you see what's underneath? A sort of large exercise book? It looks to me as if it's Fred Tregothnan's missing accounts, gentlemen. And, before you ask, I've no idea how it got there.'

The men looked at it, each other and then at me.

'Why did you leave it there?'

'What would you have thought if I'd suddenly "found" it?' I asked, my fingers making little quotation marks for them. 'You'd have thought it was all a bit too convenient, wouldn't you? So I left it there for you. You'll find my prints on the corner where I lifted it up. There shouldn't be any others. Because, as I told you, I've never seen it before.'

'Some people would say it was weird for you to be taking so many precautions – an admission of guilt, say?' Short chipped in. '*The lady doth protest too much,* and all that.'

Hamlet! And of course that was where the phrase *lugging the guts* came from too. Well done, the OU.

As for Short, I lifted a silent but expressive eyebrow. 'I'm a woman living on my own, Sergeant. Someone is sending me fairly unsubtle hints.'

'I thought they were for your civil service friend.'

'The guest in my pub. But today's gift was certainly for me, wasn't it, Chief Inspector?' I risked a twinkle of amusement at his underling's expense. 'It's all right,' I added to Short, 'the label's not bloodstained.'

He looked at me and bolted for the Portaloo.

'Is he ever going to make it?' I asked, serious as an elderly aunt. 'I mean, you have to see some nasty sights in the force, don't you? Or is he all right with human corpses?'

He gave a snort of laughter. 'Maybe he could do with some of that excellent coffee of yours. See you upstairs!' he yelled at the Portaloo.

'And leave your shoes on the door step,' I added. 'No, not you, Chief Inspector. But I'd be grateful if you'd wipe them thoroughly, this yard being as muddy as it is.'

Seeing me remove mine, he followed suit. He had nice feet, from what I could see. And his personal hygiene was adequate – a risk you always run in such situations.

He leaned against my kitchen wall, an ironic smile on his face. 'Shoes, stockings – what else are you going to remove, Josie? Sorry, only joking! Honestly! I'm sorry, Mrs Welford. That was quite out of order.'

'Yes, it was.' I nodded curtly. But was tickled pink. So they used that damned expression in real life, not just on fictional police programmes. 'Are you all right, son?' I asked over his shoulder. 'Would you like some brandy in your coffee?'

Short shook his head. Despite myself I felt sorry for him, and at infinite risk to my diet fished in the freezer for some home-made rock buns. I defrosted a few and set them on a plate. 'Go on. Help yourself. And you, too, Chief Inspector. To a cake.'

He obligingly choked. Short didn't know what the hell was going on.

I gestured them through to the living room, leaving the cakes on the table next to Short. Excusing himself, Evans stepped into the hall, where I could hear him using his mobile phone. Scene of crime team, eh? I wasn't at all sure how I felt about that. But I suppose that that was why I'd preserved the scene.

'You're not going to get the accounts book?' I prompted when he returned.

'You've been careful with it, Mrs Welford: I can't imagine you'd want us to be any less so.'

'But I wouldn't necessarily expect you to take my precautions seriously.'

'I couldn't take them any other way, circumstances being what they are.'

I didn't know whether to be relieved or scared. 'You sound as if you're preparing for a murder case.' I suppressed a nervous smile, still more a nervous giggle. Tony would have been proud of me. So would any one of his counsel.

Evans was equally serious. 'Have you, Mrs Welford, any reason to believe we're not?'

Chapter Eighteen

It was time to get Nick Thomas back. I'd managed perfectly well without him, true, and he might actually prove an added hazard. But if he stayed away, there was little doubt that Evans and Short would want to bring him back. Always better to return under one's own steam than be dragged kicking and screaming: that was my motto. Plus, apart from being my wheels should I need a quick getaway, Nick had a right to be sniffing round that rendering plant, if and when I could at last get it into his thick skull that he should.

The question was, how could I get hold of him?

There was dear old 1471, of course, provided that his was the last call to my number. And I couldn't remember any others. But – Sod's Law – someone who had withheld their number, some double-glazing salesperson, no doubt, had tried on Sunday evening, when I'd been too busy juggling for the media even to notice.

Directory Enquiries? For a mobile?

The Food Standards Agency? There wasn't a local number in the phone book. Even if I phoned the London headquarters number (even one of the new phone number call centres should have that, even one in Mumbai!) I couldn't see them dishing out an employee's phone number to a casual enquirer – even I wouldn't divulge personal information and I didn't have all sorts of civil service regulations to enforce a privacy code. My best hope was to tell the appropriate person there was an urgent personal problem. Getting through to the said appropriate person would probably be like flying to Mars, and I might get as lost as the poor UK Beagle spacecraft.

I did. I got passed to so many people I felt like Jonny Wilkinson's winning Rugby ball. But no cups, world or otherwise, for me – I just got dropped into some black hole with canned music and, when I'd heard the tape three times, I dropped the handset back so hard I might have damaged it. No, a quick shake confirmed it was all right.

Plonking my bum down on the stairs, I sat inhaling the smell of disinfectant and picked a hangnail that had had the cheek to appear, despite my regular expensive manicure. No, not acrylic nails, nothing like that – imagine them in a kitchen – just a decent tidying up of the cuticles and a massage. Drat it. And – this was clearly not my day – one of the workmen had left something behind on the tatty hall table my predecessor had left behind. Some sort of ring file.

I heaved myself to my feet – this prolonged damp weather and the lack of decent exercise recently had got to my joints. No, it wasn't a workman's file, not unless one of his kids went to the local school. One of Lucy's. The poor kid had left her homework here! But I wouldn't have to leg it down to the school, pronto: there was nothing in it but two sheets of paper. The first, in her thickest felt tip, carried the legend

THE WHITE HART
GUEST REGISTER

The second comprised several columns, the headings of which were NAME, CAR REGISTRATION NUMBER, ADDRESS, PHONE NUMBER. In the columns, in what was presumably Nick's writing, was all the information I needed. He'd given his office address in Taunton and in addition to the phone line there, his mobile number. I could picture Lucy, head bowed, mouth slightly open (all that smoke in the bar gave her catarrh), doing her best writing and then standing over Nick while he solemnly did her bidding.

I could have hugged them both. Though when I found Nick had switched his phone off I'd have preferred to box his ears. However, even he would surely respond to the message I left: *Get your arse down here now. And for God's sake phone if you can't.* Words to that effect, anyway.

A glance at my watch told me it was time to get lunch preparations underway. No time even to nip to the shop for my *Guardian*. There'd be blood for supper if they didn't keep it for me.

Trying to hide behind the walkers, whose packs and boots seemed larger than ever, a couple of locals lurked on their regular settle.

Not Reg Bulcombe, that would have been too much to hope for, but some of his cronies. They engaged in tentative conversation with Robin, who'd done no more than dump his gear in the first available bedroom – he said he'd make a more informed choice when he had time – and don an apron. I'd have preferred him to arrive a little earlier, but couldn't fault him on his management of the bar itself. He was happy to gather dirty plates as well as glasses, and recommended specials with as much gusto as if he'd actually tasted them.

'So why can't I use the outhouse for my bike yet?' he asked as he dropped a selection of empty soup bowls by the dishwasher.

'That missing vet I told you about – some of his property's turned up in there and –'

'In your shed! That's weird.'

'Not as weird as the postal delivery I had this morning.' I explained. 'Robin, I'd be much happier if you told me to stick my job and went back to the wicked city. You'd be safer on Death Row than out here.'

He shook his head. 'I really need the money, Mrs W. And if you told the DSS I've left the job voluntarily, I'd lose my dole.'

'I don't grass,' I snapped.

'But the agency might. Come on, the locals know I'm just a temp. They haven't any axe to grind with me, surely.'

'Not unless it's guilt by association, I suppose,' I conceded, reluctant to get rid of a potential asset. 'But promise me you'll be more careful than makes sense. No buzzing around the back lanes at night after work. Or even after dark. Come on, let's go and check out those bedrooms. I'd have thought the big one at the back.'

This time his look was amused. 'So I can watch what the police get up to and hear if anyone does try to get into the shed.'

I grinned. 'Exactly.'

But the window rattled, the curtains hardly closed and it was clear he'd be much better off where he was.

As luck would have it the SOCOs arrived just as I was setting out for my post-prandial stroll. Much as I'd have liked to hang around watching, I still went for the walk: I hoped it would give me an air of disinterested innocence. Actually, I'd have preferred a real zap through the village. The faster the feet, the faster the calories flee. But looking furtive was not on my agenda, and I took care to meet and greet as many folk as I could. Pensioners with tartan trolleys, mothers with pushchairs, none was spared the warmth of my smile. Or the news that I was trying out a temporary barman, just for a few days until Lindi could come back. OK, Robin was worth a dozen Lindis, at first glance, at least. But her value as a hauler in of locals was beyond pearls.

My newspaper sat in solitary state behind the counter. As Jem passed it to me, he leaned forward to say something confidentially. But a gang of school kids exploded into the shop and he had to abandon me to ride shotgun. Clearly I'd have to come at a quieter time tomorrow.

Meanwhile, my journey wouldn't be wasted. Sue Clayton was just getting out of her car, parked with the front nearside wheel squashed halfway on to the kerb. We exchanged waves, though she didn't seem particularly keen to see me. Then, she never did. For my part I cursed under my breath. Sue and I needed to have a long conversation involving hunched up raincoats, Fred Tregothnan's desk and my shed. And the village street wasn't the best place for it. On the other hand, the grapevine being what it was, the whole village would know about the activities in my shed and the reason for them, so I might as well confront her now.

Before I could open my mouth, she was all over me with a jolliness that I was sure masked a deep anxiety.

'I meant to phone you! Have you heard from Nick? Will he be back in time for practice tomorrow? We really can't do without him, you know.'

'I'll let you do as soon as I hear anything,' I said, equivocally. Hoping my deep breath wouldn't show, I continued, 'Sue, when we checked Fred's house to see if he was ill or something … I suppose …' How could you accuse a woman of God of theft and planting evidence? 'Did you see anything at all that … You know, the police are turning my place upside down at this very moment.' It didn't need her face to tell me I wasn't making a very good fist of this. I tried an outright lie. 'I'm afraid they may try to plant something and if you saw it when we were there, I'll be able to say I've got a witness that –'

'No, you won't. You could have gone back any time yourself once I'd shown you where the key was.'

I didn't know if she was simply being logical or if she was telling me I was on my own. So where did that leave me? Could I snitch on her?

'Have they checked your place yet?' I ventured.

'Why should they?'

'Why should they be checking mine?' But I couldn't keep it up. 'Sue, just put my mind at rest. When you came out of Fred's house you were clutching your coat round you as if you were trying to hide something. Were you? And no, I've not breathed a word to the filth.'

'How dare you! I was trying to keep warm and dry, Josie Welford! It was raining – remember?'

I held up a pacifying hand. 'OK, OK. That's what I wanted to hear. And I believe you. It's just that we need to sing from the same hymn sheet, Sue, and be careful not to incriminate each other with a careless word. Which is why, I promise you, I've not said a word to Evans and Short.'

She wasn't completely mollified, I could see that. But she said, 'You're right. *Careless talk costs lives*, and all that. But you're not a very good liar, Josie – you know why they're checking your place, don't you?'

A couple of kids came bounding up, daft as red setters on speed, hotly followed by their mothers, who simply sailed into the conversation as if I wasn't there. And there too was Lindi – talk about being saved by the belle.

I didn't try calling after her; I simply outpaced her, then slowed to fall into step.

'Are you feeling better?' I said, just as kindly as if she'd been laid low with flu.

Her eyes opened so wide I was afraid she might bolt. But not in those shoes. 'I'm fine,' she muttered.

'Good. Now, I wanted to assure you, Lindi, that as sure you feel up to it, you can come back to work any time you want.'

Maybe I projected my voice a little: I wasn't averse to the odd witness. 'This Fred Tregothnan business must have been very upsetting for you. Now, you'll have heard I've got a new barman, but he's only temporary. He knows that. Now you know it.' I gave the sort of reassuring smile the nurse gives as she's about to shove a hypodermic into your bum.

She had to respond somehow, of course. And you could see from the little furrows about her forehead and mouth that she'd put her brain into gear. 'Um, I've – well, you see, Mrs Welford ...' The clutch slipped a little. She tried again. 'Mrs ... Well, there's someone else offered me a job. And it's a bit better paid, see.'

'And is it as many hours?'

'Well, no.'

'Could you not work for us both? I'm sure we could make the hours fit in if we tried.' Mrs Greville would scarcely be entertaining every lunchtime and every evening.

She was wavering.

'And you're due a pay rise. Another couple of months and you'd have been entitled to sick and holiday pay.' Clear as if he was standing beside me, I could hear Tony's voice: *Play on people's greed. That's the way to get them on your side. But don't push too hard.* Smiling, I added, 'Now as soon as you feel up to it, just let me know. Look after yourself, now.' There. Soon she'd have woven a comfortable myth that she was a poor soul with tender sensibilities, and would be back with me. With luck, that is.

They'd only brought in one of those mobile home sized caravans, so big it almost dwarfed the White Hart. All right, I exaggerate. But it really didn't enhance the beauty of the place. Any moment now the TV cameras would roll in and Nicola and her chums would be interviewing me as a possible murder suspect. Great.

I made a show of opening up, and made sure everything was ready to roll in the kitchen. And hey presto, customers arrived. No, not the normal clientele – in your dreams! Forensic scientists and police officers. Hungry, all of them. It might have had something to do with the discount I offered on the specials, of course, but I felt sorry for them with nothing but the official issue of sandwiches and coffee to keep them warm on what was becoming a pretty cold night. It wasn't cold enough to keep away the locals, however: there was another pair on the settle this evening. You could almost feel the draught from their ears as the grockles talked shop. It didn't go unnoticed, of course; I could hardly keep a straight face when a couple of them, not older than Lucy, it seemed, started discussing in penetrating voices a case in which a man's head had come off as soon as the SOCO had touched it.

'All on your own?' Evans put his head round the kitchen door.

'For a few minutes. I didn't think it would do either of them any harm if Robin walked young Lucy home. They've both worked their socks off.'

'And you?'

'I've worked my shoes off, but that's all.' The floor felt pleasantly cool as I padded round. 'Well, am I going to have to bake myself a cake with a file inside? Hey, I am, aren't I?' I sat down rather harder than my lower back liked.

'We may want a DNA sample.'

'The old gob swab? OK. But why?' There was a bottle of wine within reach. I poured a couple of glasses and pushed one across to him.

Almost absentmindedly, he picked it up and drank.

'Come on, Mr Evans: you want a swab to eliminate me or to put me in the frame. Which is it?'

I'd hardly fainted with surprise when Evans wriggled out of replying, and then, having sunk the wine far more quickly than it deserved, made his excuses and left. He took, I'm glad to say, his entire crew with him and left my yard in its original state. It was clear he'd rather I found somewhere else to store the motorbike, but finally, taking my point about an employer's duty of care and the vulnerability of motorbikes, taped off a limited area for Robin's use. I locked the door, but knew it'd take hardly more than a gentle push to open it.

'Home, sweet home,' I remarked to Robin as he strolled up, having taken just about the right amount of time on escort duty.

He heaved the bike into the shed, and, cocking an eye at me, produced a thick chain for its rear wheel, just as if he was parking in a public place. I nodded my approval.

'She's a nice kid, that Lucy,' he said as he came back into the pub, closing the door behind him. 'I take it you use all these locks?'

'And the bolts,' I agreed. 'So long as you remember she is just a kid. Or could she be the Queen of Sheba and it wouldn't matter a toss to you?'

'Nothing like being direct, I suppose,' he said, taking a step back.

'Nothing. I don't care the click of my fingers about your sexual orientation, Robin, so long as it's for adults. But my late husband once shared a cell with a paedophile who regaled him with his adventures and it rather put me off.'

'So if I were a paedophile you wouldn't employ me!'

'Sure I would, if you'd had treatment and were no longer practising. I just wouldn't ask you to walk Lucy home, that's all. Of course,' I added over my shoulder as I set off upstairs, 'this may be a case of shutting the stable door. I should have asked before. But I've been a mite busy.'

He didn't follow but turned towards the kitchen. 'Hey, you've tidied up in here.'

'My job as chef,' I said.

'I've worked in some bars in my time,' he said, closing the door and following me, 'where the boss worked hard. But you beat the lot, Mrs W.'

I shook my head. 'I had support staff tonight. You and Lucy. You should have seen me the other night. Sunday. We were supposed to be closed, but ...' I gave him an edited version. We shared a laugh. But as he went off to his new room and I unlocked my door, I called him back. 'Young Robin, you never answered my question. Which end of the ballroom do you dance?'

'I like to wear the tails, not lift them. But young Lucy's safe from me. I might not say the same of a real looker I passed in the village. Blonde? You know...' He gestured.

'Flashing her tits even in this weather? That's our Lindi, Robin.'

'You couldn't introduce me, I suppose. What have I said?'

'She's the girl you're replacing. Trouble is, if she comes back to work here, you may be surplus to requirements.'

'Is she coming back?'

Closing the door on myself – no point in letting all that nice warm air out – I turned back to him. 'As a bar worker, she's a waste of space – not worth your little finger. But she pulls in the locals. She's currently being used in some game I don't know the rules of. Probably she doesn't either. So if she comes back, it could be a good sign as well as being good for business. Who knows, I may be able to afford both of you if trade really picks up. After all, I'm happy to manage without an extra chef, which would save enough for your wages.'

He nodded. 'It'd save even more if you paid my wages direct, and not to the agency.'

'Let's cross bridges like that when we get to them. At the moment you've got a wage and a free room. And I've got a damned good barman. Whatever forces removed Lindi in the first place may not let her return. Leave the ifs and maybes till tomorrow. I eat breakfast about eight in my kitchen. You're welcome to join me. Otherwise, you can forage in the main kitchen or get cereal or whatever from the shop. No dirty dishes or plates in your room, ever, by the way: we have a mouse problem. As from tomorrow, work starts at eleven thirty for twelve o'clock open-ing. I'd be grateful if you'd check the food deliveries I'm expect-ing. I mean check – they can be dozy bastards. OK? Sleep well. And if you smoke, don't burn the place down.'

Before I even reached for the Laphroaig, I checked the answer-phone. No. Nothing from Nick. Bugger him. What the hell was he playing at? I phoned again, pushing a nail back painfully in the process: it was a good job for him I didn't break it. This time the message was clearer. 'If you don't contact me I shall spill every single bean about our activities to the police. And I won't be able to keep your name out of it. And they'll want you to explain why you didn't go straight to them with information and asked me not to. Get back to me. OK?'

Thursday morning made me realise I'd have to go for a walk, weather or not. My knees and hips, the parts I'd put so much pressure on in my overblown days, were aching enough to wake me up on a day I'd much rather have slept in. Or it might have been the moan of the wind or the smash of rain against the win-dow. Yes, the weather was back. The sort my joints liked least.

The nearest to a ball I could manage these days, I pulled the duvet right over my head. I'd stay put. No. I wouldn't lie on the floor and stretch until my joints and muscles squeaked, I would-n't haul myself up by scrabbling on to all fours and then heaving myself vertical. I wouldn't turn the shower on maximum and spray each ache in turn. I wouldn't have a miserable low calorie good-for-me breakfast and most of all I wouldn't open the front door – or the back – to find what the latest offering might be. No.

Except I needed a wee. And once up I might as well stretch. Well, it'd take the poor back altogether too much effort to lie down again. And then the shower would be a real boon. As for breakfast, I had to start the day with something, and might have to prepare food for Robin, too.

And then I'd have to check what lay beyond the doors.

It wasn't often I put my head down and howled, there being not a lot of point in it when there wasn't an audience to leap into action comforting me and offering me consolation and maybe consoling goodies. I'd cried far more when Tony was at home than when he was doing his time. So why was I standing there in the shower with tears pouring down my face, snot mingling with the shower gel? The last way I wanted to greet my latest employee was with bloodshot eyes. No one would know how the meat treatment was getting to me. In fact, today I'd bloody well do something I should have done when the donations started coming. I'd wring from Reg Bulcombe the name of his meat supplier and go and challenge him straight.

'It's all done by arrangement, see,' the old bastard whined, trying to inch back into his cottage. It wouldn't have done him any good, since my foot was already in place.

'I don't see. Any more than I ever saw any paperwork, Reg Bulcombe. But I do see offal appearing on my doorstep with irritating regularity and –'

'You don't know it's him,' he put in, too quickly. 'You never seen him.'

'And never saw the men on the moon, but I know they were there. Evidence, Reg. Circumstantial, I grant you. So you're going to take me to see Mr X and I'm going to tell him to his face to stop messing me around. Otherwise,' I added limpidly, 'you can tell him I've got friends who'll stop him for me.' Mistake. I meant some of Tony's lads, who smashed kneecaps as easily as I shelled peas. But the way his cunning little eyes narrowed he might well have thought I meant Robin and Nick. Would it do them harm or give them street cred?

'You mean now?'

'Why not? We wouldn't want him to go to the trouble of baking a cake for us, would we?'

I waited while he fetched a Barbour I could smell from two yards, and then watched while he locked his front door. Locked. Not the sort of thing folk did round here, remember. He headed for his utility truck.

'Uh, uh. My car.' Even though I'd want the interior valeted before I next used it.

I couldn't read his look. 'Likely you'll get stuck in that.'

'Good job I've got you to push!' I laughed as if I were only joking. I wasn't. Letting him in, I started the engine, rolling down my window not just to clear the condensation but to let out the rich pong of his jacket and boots. So where were we bound? Some remote farm, moss growing on the thatched roof, or a classy country house *à la* Greville?

Neither made any attempt to break the silence. I didn't know what he was thinking, of course, except, judging by the way he cracked his knuckles from time to time, they weren't thoughts full of sweetness and light. I was puzzling over why he'd come so quietly, why he hadn't insisted on phoning ahead. Puzzling, and making damned sure I remembered every twist and turn in an exceedingly twisting and turning road. I might know the area well; he knew it like the back of that gnarled and tattooed hand. And I suspected he was leading me in circles. No, I'd never been up this particular lane, I was certain of that. Lane? Track, more like, the sort they use on car rally special stages, usually on Forestry Commission Land. I was plunging into woods now – deciduous, not coniferous. So in addition to the mud washed down from the steep banks, there was a thick overlay of nicely rotting leaves. The car didn't like it at all: I was hard pressed to maintain traction.

Suddenly he pointed. 'Over there. Pull in over there.'

I braked and pulled the car into a small clearing. Hell. There was no house, no car, to pull in for. My plan had backfired horribly, hadn't it? Especially my little quip about him pulling me out of mud. Even as I tried to reverse whence I'd come, my wheels spun helplessly. Forward, backward – I dug myself deeper in.

Cackling with laughter, Bulcombe heaved himself out. For a big man, he was surprisingly lithe. He was free of the mud and up a steep bank like a goat, merging into the woodland and disappearing.

My mobile announced it couldn't get a signal. What a surprise. Almost laughing at the ease with which I'd been taken in, I decided to do the obvious thing – walk. I teetered round to the tailgate to dig out my spare walking boots. As I bent to tie the first, I sensed rather than saw movement. There was a rush.

'I think I'll take that!' he crowed, grabbing my spare boot.

Mistake. Big mistake, Reg, as Tony could have told you. You never gave advance warning, even a second's. At least, not to someone whose reactions have been speeded by anger. Not to anyone carefully coached in the principles of retaliation first, as I had by Tony's minder.

Reg screamed twice, once as I made him drop the boot, a second time as I kicked him in the balls. I was tempted to go for a third when I saw my boot upside down in the mud, but mature reflection told me he couldn't have meant to drop it that way up. Or could he? Even as I reached for it, he kicked it from me. OK, he'd asked for it. I turned him over and smashed his head down into the mud. Retrieving the boot, I shoved my foot into it. I'd even started lacing it when I realised something was wrong. His arms were flailing, dreadful muffled grunts bubbling in his chest. The bugger was only drowning in the mud.

I yanked him up and turned him on his side. Recovery position, that was the term. He sank down, his mouth soon level with the ooze. Another yank, so this time he was supported by the car bumper. Damn and blast him – if I knew my back, I'd pay for all this lifting. Yes, he was breathing again. Any moment he'd throw up and I didn't intend to minister to him. So I tipped his head forward so I could lock the tailgate and, removing an in-car OS map and anything of immediate value, locked up and, without the proverbial backward glance, set off whence I'd come. As soon as I could I started picking up landmarks to work out what I pompously, but possibly accurately, called my coordinates. A church here, a stream there. Yes. I should be able to guide the AA rescue truck after lunch. No time before. If I was to get back in time to cook lunch. I'd have to send Robin into Taunton with a list of things vital for the evening. Even as I steamed along I reviewed the contents of freezers and cupboards and worked out menus – after all, you couldn't carry all that much on a motorbike, not his sort.

The recovery people thought it would be altogether easier if I went in the cabin with them. I couldn't argue. Robin had been delighted with the extra responsibility, no doubt seeing it was a step closer to a permanent job. He even offered to start preparing vegetables, an offer I immediately accepted. So here I was with Des and Pete, bumbling along lanes so narrow we could have reached out and touched the sides.

'Just stop here a moment,' I said at last. 'I just want to make sure we're in the right lane.'

We were. There were my recent wheel tracks, and the clear imprints of some very irate walking boots. But a couple of turns later, when we should be turning off, the tracks stopped abruptly. Weird.

'We need to back up,' I said apologetically. 'Must have missed a turn.'

Des trundled us back. And forward. And back again. In the fast falling mist, we couldn't see what had happened to the car. I had to give Reg marks for trying. He – and to judge by the footprints – several cronies – had given up trying to move the car. Instead they'd yanked a great pile of young trees across the entrance to the clearing.

Des put it succinctly. 'Looks as if someone doesn't want you to get that back in a hurry.'

Pete was already out, pulling on tough gloves and wrestling with the wood spaghetti. Someone had added odds and ends of barbed wire, damn them.

'And of course,' I panted, joining in as soon as Des had thrown me a spare pair of gauntlets, 'even if we get rid of all this, there's a good chance the car still won't come unstuck.'

'It'll come all right,' he said, with quiet confidence.

And it did, ten minutes later, with a plop straight from a children's comic. It was so foul with mud that I agreed the safest thing was to take it straight to a garage so that the underneath could be checked.

Which was how I now came to have a hire car. Which I pulled up nose to nose in the back yard with a four-wheel drive that looked vaguely familiar.

No, they all looked the same, didn't they, these big silver-finished monsters? I bent to lock my titchy little job – nothing as sexy as a zapper – braced myself for an hour of real cooking pressure, and marched in.

Chapter Twenty

'There you are!' Lucy sounded as exasperated as if I were one of her siblings, late after school. 'We're rushed off our feet and there's no one except us to cook. Robin's doing his best but he can't be in two places at once. Though,' she added, pulling herself together with a ghost of a grin, 'you seem to manage it.'

I dropped my jacket and bag on top of my walking shoes and donned my pinnie. A quick – OK, thorough – scrub of the hands and I was ready. 'Get me up to speed,' I said, leafing through the orders. 'Most of these are specials, so we should be able to knock them off in no time. Start up the deep fryer.'

'It's on. And Robin prepared a load of potatoes this afternoon.'

'Chip them then. Now, chicken, lamb steaks – moussaka? How the hell did we get an order for moussaka?'

'It's on the specials board.' She looked as scared as if she'd written it up in error herself.

I sniffed. 'And I'd say it's in the oven. Well done, Robin.'

'Bloody butcher delivered lamb mince, not beef,' Robin said, erupting through the service door with another order. 'He'd really cocked up – it was all really weird cuts and joints I didn't recognise. When I said I wouldn't pay, he threatened to take everything away. I said fine, but leave the lamb, which I did pay for, because moussaka's one thing I can do well. And, hey presto, when I did the supermarket run, there was an offer on aubergines and mushrooms.'

My organic butcher messing up? I'd have thought he was one person I could have relied on. Unless someone had phoned through a false order. Not impossible when I thought about the Portaloos. But I didn't have time to worry about that now. 'Good lad. But why all this activity?' I wondered aloud. 'It's Thursday. Bell ringing night. There's usually no activity at all till nearly ten and then there's a rush on pints.'

'Half the village seems to be here. All the regulars are back,' Lucy said.

'We'll worry about this later,' I said. For 'we' read 'I'. 'OK, team: you're working wonders. You know where you are. Just tell me what I can do that'll be most useful. When there's a break, we'll take a breather and regroup. OK? No arguing, I mean it.'

Robin blinked. 'Could you – would you mind manning the bar?'

I didn't even correct his sexist language.

If I was front of house, as it were, I wasn't going to appear like a river-cooled hippopotamus. Somehow I'd managed to get mud in my ears, up my trousers and even my sweatshirt, as well as more obvious targets. I stripped down in two minutes flat, dived under the shower and was back grabbing clothes before I was properly dry. The first top I reached happened to show my décolletage, so I added a glittery necklace. OK, it was your classic barmaid look, so just to improve the shining hour I added frosted eye shadow and particularly glossy lipstick. The hair was rapidly becoming a disaster so I mussed it vigorously and went wild with the spray. Diamanté mules completed the ensemble. Tony would have smacked my bum and told me I looked a right trollop.

Perhaps I did. After all, something about me made Reg Bulcombe drop his pint glass. Literally. It must have been almost full, too. The fire simply died, and wet ashes splattered all over his feet and those of his cronies. Magic.

It was worth the effort of fetching first the broom and shovel and then the mop and bucket – all that power walking over hill and dale had found me out more than I cared to admit. One or two of the more brazen men stuck out their legs so I could mop the worst off their boots and jeans. Reg Bulcombe, to catcalls and jeers, none of them mine, strode out and would have slammed the door behind him, I'm sure, had he not run smack into Nick Thomas.

No, I didn't drop the mop. I nodded him to a table and carried on with what I was doing. Dumping the regulation Wet Floor easel near the epicentre of the erstwhile flood, I scanned the floor for further splashes. The floor and customers. One woman, a smartish townee about my own age, was vainly mopping her tights. Her escort didn't know whether to laugh with the others or get outraged in a suitably alpha-male way.

'Why don't you come up to my private bathroom?' I whispered discreetly.

There'd be some tights somewhere in one of my drawers, much cheaper than the free meal I probably ought to be offering.

'I got the impression,' Nick said mildly, over a mug of my finest organic drinking chocolate, not the normal tipple for the bar but one we could all share, 'that something upset our Reg.'

He'd got back in time for bell ringing, he said, but found it cancelled. Well, it would be. Reg had called a celebration of my humiliation. Yes, in my own bar. Lucy had got wind of this, and, to my eternal gratitude, sacrificed her one evening of self-indulgence to help Robin, hoping the two of them could wing it. Without the men and Lucy, and with Mrs Greville mysteriously absent too, there'd been nothing for it but for Aidan to call off the session. He'd given Nick half an hour of private coaching, that was all, which pleased Nick because his jauntering around the countryside had made his stomach play up and he needed food. All this came out in a rush, as if he were a naughty school kid trying to fend off a bollocking he knew was due to him.

As if I'd given him cause! I had raised one eyebrow as I'd taken his order, and he might well have perceived it as ironic and even accusing. But I'd said nothing I wouldn't have said to my other customers, nor that I wouldn't have wanted overheard. I suppose you might say I'd rather kept him in suspense, a state that pleased me since it gave me my preferred upper hand.

'Upset?' I pulled a face as Lucy and Robin tittered.

Robin licked a chocolately moustache, put down his empty mug and coughed delicately. He and Lucy had already heard all about my day, it was late and it was more than time for Lucy to be home – after all, it was a school day tomorrow and since she hadn't had time to do any homework tonight she'd no doubt have to be up at the crack of dawn to deal with it.

I nodded, getting up to shoo them out, stopping Lucy only to stow the remainder of the excellent moussaka in my favourite basket for her to carry home. 'You've both worked wonders,' I said for the umpteenth time. Fishing in my pinnie pocket, I pressed a twenty-pound note into her palm and another into

Robin's. 'For you, not the taxman. Nor anyone else,' I added to Lucy.

Not that she'd take any notice. I waved them off. The yard was still blessedly free of offal.

'Robin seems a decent kid,' Nick began as I returned to the snug to find a skin growing over my chocolate.

Excellent. I dipped my little finger in to swish it out and relish it. The best part, in my opinion. And it always makes grown men shudder, for some reason.

'A real find,' I agreed. 'He's only supposed to be a barman, but he turned his hand to everything this evening.'

We could have gone on like this all night, two middle-aged folk having a pleasant meaningless chat. That's probably what Nick wanted. At least until he could decently yawn and back out gracefully, escaping before breakfast the following morning because of pressure of work.

I'd got too much adrenaline still sloshing round my veins to be able to sleep. Besides which, I went nowhere until Robin got back in. Should we talk about the news item I'd found in Brum or the goings on down here? Or, as Robin slammed the back door and audibly bolted it, should I let Nick off the hook? After all, there was nothing to be done about anything till tomorrow afternoon. Friday morning was chopper lesson morning and nothing would make me miss that. And there was no doubt he'd be on tenterhooks until I had said something. Perhaps I'd just leave it at that.

Almost.

'Tell you what, Copper,' I said, pulling myself out of the chair, to which my limbs seemed anchored, 'you and I need to have a good long talk. I'll call into your office at about two tomorrow, shall I?'

There's nothing like a good shag and a flying lesson to make you feel good about yourself, not unless it's a good shag and a flying lesson preceded by a good tally on the bathroom scales. All my rushing round and my forgetting to eat yesterday had helped the scales ignore the hot chocolate and enabled me to award myself a gold star in the form of lunch at the Castle after a swift gob-swab

– DNA sample to you – at Taunton nick. The food was designer scrumptious – the sort of thing I'd got in mind for the White Hart when everything was up and running. More scrumptious even than Piers, the smell of whose sweat and aftershave still lingered enough for me to feel sexy all over again.

There was an impressive pile of files on Nick's desk when I announced myself. I usually wanted to strangle him or protect him in equal measure; today I wanted to shake him into some sort of action.

'I thought you were joking,' he said weakly. 'I've got masses to do. There's this bastard buying condemned meat, cleaning it up and selling it to decent little restaurants as bona fide chicken.'

'Decent little restaurants should check their sources,' I said tartly, 'as you know. Which is how my little adventure started. Since you've been away I've had a couple of generous gifts, a police car's been trashed, and my own car was kidnapped. Fred Tregothnan's accounts have materialised in my shed. So far I've said nothing to the police in case it implicated you in things you'd rather keep out of. But sooner or later someone will be asking you what you and Fred were talking about when you had your little *contretemps* a couple of weeks ago. And I shall have to tell the police about my expeditions.'

Gutted. It wasn't a term I liked but it suited Nick's expression. Instead of talking to him I might have filleted out his spine and other inconvenient bones.

Perhaps if I'd had children I'd have got rid of this inconvenient maternal streak. As it was my urge to shake the shit out of him was rapidly being replaced by a desire to make all better.

Enough of that.

'Did you kill him?' I asked brutally. Probably the same tone he'd used countless times himself, actually. Including to my Tony. 'Come on, Nick. *Did you kill him?* Was that why you wouldn't so much as come with me when I was looking round that abattoir? Why you've stayed away from the rendering plant? Because you killed him in one and disposed of him in the other?'

I'd never seen thought processes so slow. Even saying the words had rung bells for me. Now, very slowly, they seemed to be making a similar tune in Nick's skull.

'No,' he said, almost reluctantly. 'But that might be what's happened to him. There's no evidence, though, is there, that he's dead? Anything like blood at the house to make it a crime scene? And where's his car? You don't get rid of things like that without leaving some trace.'

Shrugging, I replied, 'Minor problem.' I spread my fingers. 'Motive. Opportunity. If you don't have them, who does?'

'You told the police about the accounts,' he said. 'Pity. That's the first place I'd look.'

'In which case the Avon and Somerset Constabulary are no doubt getting a warrant even as we speak. How comforting. It means it's not you or me. Possibly.' I leaned forward on the desk, glad I was wearing a businesslike polo neck: flashing my boobs wasn't on the menu at the moment. 'You haven't answered one of my questions yet, Nick. Possibly the most important one. Why were you arguing with him?'

'I can't remember.'

I almost believed him; DCI Evans certainly wouldn't. 'Not good enough. The villagers are grassoholics: they can't resist snitching. Some kind soul told the police they saw Sue and me leaving Tregothnan's house –'

'Sue?'

'She knew where the key was. We went to check he wasn't lying ill in the bathroom or somewhere –'

'You went for a good snoop!'

I smiled sunnily. At least he was less torpid.

'So those accounts weren't planted at all! You nicked them and thought better of it!'

'Nope. If anyone took anything I'm afraid it might have been Sue, though you are not, repeat not, going to tell the police.' I explained. 'Forget it. I shouldn't have mentioned it. Yes, we went for a good snoop. It's a very weird house, Nick. Not the house of a professional man with no one to spend money on except himself.'

'As bad as a mobile home on a flooded field?' he asked bitterly.

'I presume you've got a sock under a bed somewhere. Full of

your lump sum, with your police pension keeping it topped up. You could buy tomorrow. On the other hand, he was self-employed and things have been bad for farmers ever since the year of Foot and Mouth. So he might not have had much money to flash around.'

'Women?'

'He was a flirt and a groper but if he had a proper adult relationship with a woman I'd be surprised. His mother kept her claws in him for years. But at least he inherited the house – he's never had to buy his own. Tatty Land Rover. Clothes the Oxfam shop'd turn its nose up at. Where did his money go?'

'And if he had and then lost money, what did he do to replace it?' Nick was a changed man. He was visibly straighter, more alert. 'That's the question.'

'Exactly. And almost as important as the one I asked you. What were you arguing about, the two of you? You have to remember. And tell me.' Suddenly all sorts of stupid words were pouring from my mouth. Words like, 'So we can sort this out together.'

Taunton isn't so very far from Porlock. Porlock's a tiny place in Somerset, a Person from which interrupted Coleridge in the middle of that gorgeous poem, *Kubla Khan*. Tony and I – yes, we talked poetry as well as novels – used to joke that the stately pleasure domes referred to the breasts of a woman like me. Correction: like I was then. Not any more, of course. From the sublime to the pendulous.

It was a person from not Porlock but Taunton who interrupted Nick and me now. DCI Mike Evans, as it happens. At least he was the sort of man who phoned to find if it was convenient to interview a fellow professional. Or simply to make sure he was there to interview, Nick being the elusive man he was.

'I told you he was on to you,' I said, gathering my bag and coat. 'And it'd do neither of us any good if I was found here. For God's sake, Nick, get your memory back. Or find a psychiatrist with an explanation for your amnesia that'll stand up in court.'

I went back to the White Hart by way of the farm supplying my meat, ready to tear them limb from organic limb. But as always, I went in quietly enough, ready to hear their explanation for the weird order.

Which was sickeningly familiar. The phone call from someone working for me.

I managed a rueful smile. 'I'm afraid F Drake doesn't exist. Except in history, of course, when he was knighted. We've both been taken for a ride. What can you let me have now, to take away for tonight and the weekend? I'll work out a proper order for next week and fax it through to you. In fact,' I added grimly, 'let's agree a password, shall we? Any communication from me that doesn't carry this password, ignore. Bartley Green.'

'What if you're in a hurry and forget it?' Abigail asked.

'You could phone me to check? Now, if you're offering pork as well as beef …'

Given his dodgy stomach and his encounter with DCI Evans, Nick tucked into the pork with coriander seed and spiced rice with amazing gusto. So did everyone else who ordered it from the specials board.

Robin approved, too. 'It's always nice to have a staple that looks after itself and doesn't need individual cooking, isn't it?' he said, dropping an order for very pricey fillet steak on the counter. 'Not like this. Very rare, he said, not just rare. Blue?'

'Bleu,' I agreed. 'You might want to recommend one of my reserve bins of red to go with this. Sidle up as if you're doing him a special favour.'

'Am I?'

'At that price he'd certainly like to think so. Vegetables or salad? Come on, Robin, you need to make it absolutely clear with each order. And fries or sautés.'

A house full of foodies, and hardly any beer-drinking locals. Well, that was what I wanted. Theoretically. But I'd have welcomed a chat with some of the locals, now folk hero Reg Bulcombe was the butt of their humour. Possibly. I surveyed my domain with satisfaction, however. Three couples were already waiting for tables, and I'd had to turn a party of five away on the grounds they'd have to wait so long I couldn't guarantee them a full menu. But they booked for the following week, perhaps encouraged by the promise of a bottle of wine on the house.

Not from one of the reserve bins, however.

Robin, having politely shooed Nick upstairs to drink his coffee in my sitting room, was just seating the second of the waiting couples when Lucy erupted into the kitchen. 'Mrs W – it's only Mrs Greville. With a party of six. Won't take no for an answer. Even slipped me a fiver to make it all right.' She handed it over with hardly more than a swallow.

I patted her shoulder: nice to know she trusted me to make it up to her. 'My job to turn her away, not yours,' I said. 'Keep an eye on that pasta, there's a good girl – one more minute, and drain it. Table number seven.'

I don't think Caro Greville recognised me in my chef's outfit. The clogs seemed to exercise a particular fascination, or perhaps she simply didn't want to meet my eye.

'I'm most terribly sorry, Caro,' I said, burying my Brummie vowels as deep as I could, 'but you can see we're absolutely full, with people still waiting.'

'Surely you can –' she gestured, as if wafting away a few hapless diners. This side of her, new to me, was no doubt the one that Sue knew and loathed.

'Nothing till ten thirty at the earliest,' I said with firm regret. 'And the choice will be very limited. As I'm sure you know, I get fresh produce daily: I've simply run out. But if you come tomorrow I can put your little advance payment towards the meal.' I smiled. 'Robin!' A Roman empress wouldn't have summoned a minion with more authority. 'See if you can book in Mrs Greville and her party on another occasion, would you? Unless, of course,' I added slyly, 'you'd all be happy with sausage, eggs and chips? All organic, of course. Even the baked beans if you'd fancy those?'

So she couldn't say I hadn't tried to oblige. One or two of her entourage thought it might be awfully jolly to slum, but none wanted to wait even for that. Where they thought they'd get a meal in this part of the world at this time of night goodness knew – anywhere halfway decent was always fully booked on a Friday, and I didn't think they'd fancy a motorway service centre, with or without Tom's cooking.

In a re-run of the previous evening, the team sat down, shoes cast off, and drank chocolate.

'Guess who I saw earlier,' Lucy yawned. 'Lindi. She said to say hello.'

'The tits?' Robin gestured.

'The same. Say hello back if you see her.'

Lucy shifted in her chair. 'She said she wasn't very busy at Mrs Greville's and she was wondering if you could offer her any hours, now she's better. Funny, I never heard she was ill.'

I smothered a grin. 'What do you two think? Do we need an extra pair of hands?'

Robin looked anywhere but at me. 'We can manage.'

'We could manage better with someone doing the washing up,' I said. 'It'd mean Lucy got more homework done, and could fit in her bell ringing. No, no – I just mean you'd go back to the hours you used to work, that's all. And I've no intention of getting rid of you, Robin, either: I owe you both.'

'Lindi, washing up? You've got to be joking, Mrs W!'

'Not entirely, Lucy. Someone's got to do it – which reminds me, I think the dishwasher's just switched off – and why should it be either of you? Or, come to think of it, me? She'll get a bit of a Cinderella complex, but I shall let her out into the bar too often for her to be a real martyr. Let's go and empty that machine, then it's more than time for bed.'

As before, Robin escorted Lucy home. As before, he was back in reasonable time, and as before, he locked up carefully.

I shouted goodnight from the kitchen. He popped his head round the door. 'Leave it, Mrs W. It'll still be there in the morning. I'll sort it while you get the shopping in – or vice versa, whichever you prefer.'

'It's like going to bed on a quarrel,' I muttered.

'You sound like my mum,' he said. He looked as if he meant to say more, but he shut his mouth firmly and flapping a hand, disappeared.

Nice kid. I flapped mine and heaved myself up to bed. Would the scales notice if I helped myself to a knob of cheese?

They would. Especially after the drinking chocolate.

The stairs creaked in agreement as I toiled up.

My flat was in darkness, but the door unlocked. I froze, ready to call Robin. Then I remembered that Nick had been relegated up here with his coffee. The chances were he'd simply fallen asleep. So I padded through to the living room, ready to startle him awake.

He was far from awake, standing in the window. 'No lights!' he snapped.

I joined him, falling over the Persian rug as my eyes adjusted. That's another thing about ageing: your eyes slow down too. He pointed. Forget the lock: very, very quietly, someone was pulling on the outhouse door. A man. A big man. No idea who: he'd pulled an anorak hood up and drawn it tight. The door responded.

'Camera!' Nick said, holding out a hand as if I'd have it ready.

This time it was an occasional table I tripped over. And the rug on the way back. 'Here.'

'Time exposure? Don't want to risk flash. Put it on the sill so it won't shake so much. Look, he's switching on a torch. Go, Josie.'

Josie went. I took four or five, all of him bending over Robin's bike. Still couldn't place the face, damn it.

'Computer enhancement,' Nick murmured. 'I'd say he'd been working on Robin's brakes.'

'Let's stop him, then. Now!' I was out of the flat and opening Robin's door before I knew it. Robin was stark naked, dealing with a zit on his nose. 'Get your shoes on. Your bike!'

I was out of the back door and across that yard before I knew it, hurling myself with all my might at the still preoccupied stranger. Four stone, nearer five, I might have lost, but I was still no lightweight. I'd smother the bugger into submission if necessary.

I might have been a flea for all the notice he took. He tipped me off and pulled the bike down on top of me. It slammed down on my hip, driving the other into the concrete floor. By now I could hear running footsteps – what the hell was the matter with my menfolk? – but I also heard the roar of a powerful diesel engine. No lights, of course. Except several blue flashes. Nick and the damned camera. A farewell kick at my shins and the stranger was gone, the car or van or whatever reversing with the sort of shriek from the tyres you expect on a kiddies' movie.

By the time Robin, now sporting underpants, and Nick got to me, I realised the bike was hurting me quite badly. But I didn't think it had broken anything – I should be thankful for my excess upholstery, not to mention the angle I was trapped at. All concern and solicitousness, they lifted the machine. I lay where I was, panting. 'Did you get the number?' I barked.

'No lights. And I think they'd taped over the plates,' Robin said, kneeling and dabbing at my knee, bleeding through laddered stockings.

'I'll get an ambulance,' Nick said.

'What the hell do I need an ambulance for?'

'Internal injuries. Stay with her, Robin.'

'Internal buggery. Just get me to my feet, nice and gently mind. Shit! I'm too old for this lark.'

And Robin was too young. And as for Nick – what sort of a man stands taking photographs when he could be practising a spot of citizen's arrest on my intruder?

'A man who has some hard evidence,' he said, applying a tea towel full of crushed ice to my bum. 'Unlike you and your hard fall. All you've got is bruises. We'll have something for Evans and Co to go on, now. Whereas you – you're lucky not to have been killed.'

'I wouldn't have so much as a scratch if you two had joined me.'

Robin wrung his hands.

'OK, it's hard to be brave with no knickers on. Go to bed, kid. The police'll no doubt want to talk to you in the morning.'

'I'm not sure,' he said, managing a snarl, 'that I want to talk to them. Seems to me everyone's talked enough. I want to get the shit that did that to my bike. And to you.'

I allowed Nick to catch my eye.

'She's right, son,' he said. 'Nothing to be done now. I'll call the police first thing. Are you sure you want more whisky, Josie?' he added, as Robin, giving the same hand flap as before, shrugged himself off to bed.

I heaved myself upright. 'I'll tell you what I want. I want more whisky and I want the truth from you, Copper. What is there between your damned ears?'

Anyone taking that tone with me would have regretted it. Nick merely poured a good three fingers of whisky into my glass and sighed. 'I don't now about you but I'm ready for bed. A two hundred and fifty mile drive yesterday, a full day's work today, including a visit from your friend DCI Evans, and now this. We'll talk in the morning.'

I went for the bait, of course. 'Evans? What's he got to say?'

He poured himself the merest taste of malt. 'Tell you what he reminded me of. One of those little dogs you see in the park, squaring up to a big one, legs all tightly braced.'

Not the sort of observation I'd have expected from Nick. He

was more perceptive than I'd thought. Though if anyone was going to be aggressive I'd have expected it to be him, not Evans. Wrong, Josie: Nick was passive-aggressive, wasn't he? The sort of man who wore people down by sheer inertia. The sort who was so afraid of doing something wrong he ended up doing nothing at all. And what had caused it? Something, I'd bet a week's anti-ageing treatments, to do with that Kings Heath siege.

'And, once you'd squared up to each other, did you have a useful conversation? About your altercation with Tregothnan?'

'Altercation! That's a very long word for a very short exchange of words.'

This time I wasn't drawn. 'Which were about?'

He sank the last of his whisky, all two drops of it, and pressed his hand to his stomach.

'Something that puts you in the frame?' I pursued. Perhaps lightening up would be more effective. 'If I've got to make a file in a cake, I need to know in advance.'

He responded blank-faced. 'I don't suppose you'd know a good solicitor in the area?'

'Conveyancing? Or d'you want to make a Will?' I eased into a more comfortable position. 'Criminal? There's a hotshot in Exeter Tony used to swear by when he was based in Brum.'

He flinched. The thought of being on the same side of the law as a man he'd helped put away, no doubt.

'And you'll have to be a damned sight more open and frank with him than you have been with me,' I said. 'Or, presumably, with Evans. Oh, for God's sake, man, I'm on your side. We're in whatever it is together. Victims. Like young Robin could have been if you hadn't spotted our intruder. If you're going to be accused of anything, you've been set up. By the folk behind Chummie tonight. While you're still at liberty to sniff around, start sniffing. Bring one of your FSA mates along …'

'They're all tied up with this contaminated meat scam. Where I should have been, but for your delicate, diplomatic phone messages.'

'I'll have to learn to text,' I said affably. 'OK. You have right of entry by virtue of your job. Enter. Tomorrow's your day off –

No?'

'Very flexible hours in the FSA. I ought –'

'You ought to check out that abattoir. You ought to check out that rendering plant. And tell you what, just to make sure you do, as well as in the interests of safety, of course, I'll come along as your driver.'

Chapter Twenty-Two

The only way to get out bed was to tip the duvet and a couple of pillows on to the floor and roll on top of them. Not pleasant for the poor old body, which was in a miserable state. The hips and shoulders were the worst, bruises with colouring so dense and subtle it would have been wonderful on a scarf or top. The knees. Hmm. It looked like a trousers day today. And tomorrow. And the foreseeable future.

Stiff wasn't the word. Overnight, despite the daily stretches I always did my best with, I'd turned into a crippled old lady. I heaved myself upright and headed for the bathroom, catching sight of myself in the mirrors on the wardrobe. Hell! What on earth did I look like! Neanderthal woman! Reduce me to this sort of shuffle, would they? Not bloody likely. Or any other sort of rather more colourful likely. No, not so much as a wince or a sigh would I permit myself. A lot of swear words under my breath, and maybe a few scorchers out loud in private. But nothing to give the game away to bystanders interested or otherwise.

So it was back on to the floor for stretches, which were hell. Showering afterwards was interesting because usually I liked to douse myself with the hottest water I could stand to ease the frame. Today I craved icy jets. In all, I treated myself to a sort of ice cream and hot chocolate sauce shower. I won't begin to describe towelling dry and dressing. Suffice to say it would have been more sensible not to add to my general discomfort by biting my lips and raising blood blisters.

Somewhere at the back of the medicine cupboard there should be some painkillers I'd been prescribed when my joints started to play up. They were as old as my diet, which I'd embarked on to save the joints another way, and I'd never taken more than half a dozen. My reasoning had been that if it was the weight causing the problem, than the constant reminder of exactly why I had to lose it wouldn't be a bad thing. My only concession had been to take lots of Omega oils to protect the poor old cartilages while I was exercising the obesity away. However, I might just pop a couple of pills now.

Warning. May cause drowsiness.
If affected, do not DRIVE or OPERATE MACHINERY.
AVOID ALCOHOL

And this was the morning I was supposed to be Nick's getaway driver. Hell several times over. Well, as Tony used to say, always to my great irritation, what can't be cured must be endured. There was something else Tony used to say, too, that I also said now. Aloud. Bother that for a game of soldiers. One shouldn't make me fall asleep at the wheel, and I never drank till I'd finished cooking.

A sad little group inspected Robin's bike. The brake hoses had been slackened, not fully removed, so, Robin said, you'd just notice gradual loss as the fluid oozed away.

'That's not so bad, then?' I said hopefully.

You could see me plummet in his estimation. 'Hills like these round here?' he snorted. 'Blind corners?'

'Plus you might simply have interrupted him,' Nick put in.

'Nah. If he'd emptied the system, I'd have noticed a great pool of fluid, wouldn't I?' He straightened, looking at his watch. 'Did the copper give any idea what time he'd be round? 'Cos someone's got to go to the shops.'

A hundred Brownie points, Robin.

To my amazement – and then suspicion – Nick offered, provided we equipped him with a complete and detailed list.

'Brilliant!' I began. 'No. Hang on. They know you drive a gas-guzzler. You ought to check that over too. They don't know about my little hired roller skate – yet. I'll go. It'll be quicker. After all, you want to talk to the police about those photos in my camera.'

Not to mention explain to them why he was the one behind the camera, and I was very much in front of it. That was one hook I didn't mean to let him off, even if it did mean missing a bit of the action as I set off in the weak but welcome autumn sun.

As it happened, all I'd missed, as I discovered when I tried to lug all my shopping bags from the tinny-mobile, was a long wait. Short, but not Evans, arrived almost as I did, with a young woman also in sad plain clothes whose haircut yelled grunge-dyke. It was she – DC Grace Wendover – who trotted over to help me unload the car.

'That's very kind of you.'

''S'all right. My gran's got a bad back too.'

Gran! So much for a helping hand. I might just deserve another pain pill, this one for my wounded ego.

'No, you can't take it away,' Robin said flatly. 'I need it. You can do your fingerprinting here.'

'In any case,' Nick added, 'I'd be very surprised if you found prints. And if there are any, they almost certainly won't be on file.'

Short jumped as if the bike had spoken.

So did I, I must admit. What had happened to make him suddenly assertive?

'If my reading of the situation's correct, we're dealing with amateurs here. Small-time farmers driven to crimes they wouldn't normally commit. Oh, you can throw any number of books at them when you catch them. But in a community like this, you'll have trouble doing that.'

'Though Reg Bulcombe's no longer the flavour of the month he was,' I observed. 'Not since he put out the snug fire.' I explained about the kidnapping of my car and his reaction to my unexpected return.

Wendover cackled. 'You walked all that way and still did your evening shift? That's woman power for you. Was that when you hurt your back?'

'It's not my back that hurts. I sustained injuries –' I widened my eyes to emphasise the jargon '– when the guy tampering with the brakes pulled the bike on top of me. I fell on my side, so what the bike didn't do to my shoulders, hips and knee, the shed floor did. No, you can't look. Not till I've worked out admission charges to the exhibition. Beats anything at St Ives Tate,' I concluded.

Short, no doubt fearing I had the same disregard for trousers as for stockings, spluttered something about an FME.

'Police surgeon,' Nick translated.

Since he'd spoken, it was to him I addressed the next question – and yes, it was purely as a diversion. It would save me having to spell out my intentions about a medical examination, either in Taunton nick or in A and E somewhere. 'Was your ... vehicle ... all right, Nick? Or had it had the treatment accorded to DCI Evans' the other day?'

'Looked all right,' he declared.

'I'd like to check it over,' Short said, evidently deciding it was time to make his mark.

We all looked. No. Perfect. So why did Robin yelp?

Damn and blast the knees! The best I could do was lean slowly and ponderously from the hips, seeing little but a wall of other people's bodies.

I suddenly found Wendover's hand on my elbow, heaving me skywards. 'A home-made stinger. A stingers's what –'

'– you use to stop vehicles in car chases,' I finished for her. 'So Nick would drive over this device – '

'Devices – there's actually one in front of each wheel.'

'– and drive – what? nails? – into each tyre? Clever.'

'Pretty crude,' Short corrected me.

'But not immediately visible and very time-consuming. And ultimately expensive: tyres that size aren't exactly bargain base-ment,' Wendover observed, winking at me.

He shut up.

That was fine by me. A glance at my watch told me the morn-ing was three-quarters gone, and it was time to adjourn to the kitchen. So much for my putative morning's adventure with Nick.

The improved weather had brought out even more walkers than usual, so the lunchtime stretched well into the afternoon. The evening promised to be busy too, if the bookings diary was to be believed – Caro Greville and her party were scheduled to descend into pleb-land, and four other tables for four had already been taken. Even with Lucy and Robin's help, I'd have to spend the intervening time working flat out. Before I scrubbed and changed – getting into and out of trousers was a distinct white knuckle experience – I made a phone call. My hired tinny-mobile must disappear. Another hired vehicle must replace it.

'No delivery service?' I repeated incredulously. 'I think you'll find you're mistaken, young man. I'm sure when I tell Mr Harkness at your Head Office there's no delivery service, he'll say you're wrong. Now, what was your name? So I have all the details correct?'

A replacement would be with me at about six: the young man would drop it off himself and pick up the other one. And since I'd no idea if he was supposed to do it, still less whether a Mr Harkness existed (would he be related to Ena Harkness, a rose in my garden?) I'd give him a meal voucher for two at the White Hart.

All went very well till about eleven, when the last diners had left, mostly leaving the kids large tips, and I was ready to collapse with a mixture of pain and exhaustion. I'd eschewed the most recent dose of painkillers on the grounds I'd rather sink an extremely large malt. Nick had wandered into the kitchen with an offer of help, welcome because I'd got behind with the washing up and didn't want to inflict any extra on poor Lucy and Robin, both asleep on their feet by the look of them. I'd hoped and indeed prayed that Lindi might make a welcome return, but there'd been no miracle. How we'd cope if this boom continued, goodness knew.

The accident was my fault. No doubt about that. I'd left a couple of pans to soak on the top of the hob. Trouble is, I'd forgotten to turn off the gas under one of them. So the water Robin tipped into the sink was, if not boiling, hot enough to scald him when he plunged his hands into it.

He screamed, dancing about the kitchen in pain. Lucy screamed too, shouting, 'Do something, do something!' to Nick, who was nearest.

He did. He reached for his mobile phone.

Elbowing him aside, I grabbed Robin and shoved his hands under the cold tap, turned on to its maximum. When he tried to pull away, howling that the cold was worse than the hot, I gripped all the harder, trying not to notice that we were both getting soaked in the process.

'What the hell are you doing?' I yelled at Nick over my shoulder, as soon as I had a moment.

'Trying to raise an ambulance.'

I think I shut the phone on his fingers. 'At this time of night? On a boozy Saturday? It'll take for ever. If he needs treatment, we take him to A and E. Why don't you go and check that at least one of our vehicles is roadworthy? Take Lucy with you, for God's sake. In fact, take her home. Robin, who told you to turn off that tap?' Shaking Lucy gently, I said, right into her face, 'He's going to be fine. There won't be so much as a blister. I promise. The best thing you can do is stop crying and go home to bed. The next best is try and roust Lindi out tomorrow so we've got an extra pair of hands for the lunchtime rush.'

'It's Evensong tomorrow,' she said, accepting the jacket Nick was trying to slip over her shoulders. 'So I can come early.'

'Come early and bring Lindi. Here – don't forget tonight's earnings.' I passed her her share of the tips, wrapped up in an extra fiver. 'Say goodnight to Robin and be off with you. Nick'll see you to your door. Won't you?'

Neither argued.

I turned off the tap. The kitchen was suddenly and blessedly calm. I found a clean tea towel and patted Robin's ice cold hands as tenderly as if they were a new born baby's. The skin was just as undamaged.

He spread the fingers, turning his hands front to back and front again. 'Looks like I made a bit of a fuss about nothing,' he said.

'You had an accident – entirely my fault – that could have been very nasty. I remembered that dodge when a kettle of boiling water landed on my hand, not in the teapot.'

'How on earth –?'

'Because someone poured it there,' I said flatly. Yes, back in the days when Tony thought it necessary to ask one of his lads to keep an eye on me. After that he thought it necessary to ask someone to keep an eye on that lad. He didn't stay in the team long. 'Now, do you think we should get you to casualty? Because your solicitor will want a medical report.'

'Solicitor? Medical report? What *are* you on about, Mrs W?'

'Compensation. Industrial injury. Health and safety at work.'

'Like I shouldn't check how hot water is before shoving both my mitts in it? Look. All I've got is a set of cleaner fingernails than I've had all day, and you're telling me to sue you? Thanks but no thanks, Mrs W. If you've got some nice slathery hand cream, I might not say no, but otherwise I'll finish off here and –'

'Just leave it to me, Robin. And what I can't do tonight, we'll do tomorrow.'

'With the delectable Lindi! Can't wait.' He rubbed his hands together with a vigour that did indeed suggest he'd come to no permanent harm. 'How old did you say she was?'

'Nineteen going on old as the hills. Here – don't forget your share of the tips.'

'Cheers. One thing, we've got an extra hour in bed tonight, haven't we?'

'Eh?'

'Clocks going back and all that. Don't forget to change your heater clocks and all that.'

'Would have. Thanks, Robin. I owe you.'

'But not for these.' He flapped his hands.

'OK. Let's get you that hand cream…'

I was giving the work surface a final swab when Nick bustled back in, twirling his car keys with an indefinable air of self-importance.

'OK, let's get moving then.'

'Where the hell have you been?'

'You told me to take Lucy home and check the car.'

'And it's taken you this long?'

'I – er – We got talking.'

I picked up a handy meat knife. 'Copper, you touch one hair of that kid's head and we'll find a use for this. OK?'

He raised his hands in surrender. 'But where's Robin?'

'Tucked up with his teddy bear, I should imagine. It's a good job he doesn't need to go to A and E, isn't it? Because he could have walked by now, the time it took you and Lucy to have your little talk. And, while we're on the subject, what the hell d'you think you were doing, pithering with your mobile in a black spot when you should have been using your police first aid? Don't kid me you're not trained. You just can't hack real life any more can you? Photos here, cameras there – you can do life at second hand. But something here –' I placed a furious fingertip on his forehead '– means you're as shackled as I was by that gin trap. And what are you doing to get out? Zilch, as far as I can see. Now, get out of my kitchen. I've work to do. And I don't need someone reading from a textbook to tell me how to do it. Go on. Now. For once, man, just shift your Pygmalion arse.'

I'd always wanted less flesh. Now I'd have been grateful for a bit more between the bruises so I could lie down in comfort. For the first part of the night the (large) tot of malt did indeed anaesthetise me, but later on I had to reach for more painkillers. They might have done their job, but it seemed their remit didn't include returning me to sleep. There was no way I was going to be able to enjoy the extra hour.

Not unless I got up and took advantage of everyone else's lie-in. It was a double-edged sword, of course. If there weren't many people around, they'd be all the more noticeable, and though the new hire car was as anonymous as I'd wished, the very fact that it was strange might attract attention. And I'd be going on my own, with not even the dubious comfort of Nick as back-up. To the abattoir, of course. Inside this time, now I hadn't got Nick nannying round to prevent me.

It would have been nice to trip nimbly down the stairs, spurred on by determination. I was spurred on, all right, don't doubt it for a moment. But in my state tripping was more likely to be the arse over tip sort that results in hospitalisation. One foot at a time; one step at a time.

I must have been mad. How had I kept going yesterday if I was as bad as this? Answer: either I hadn't been as bad as this, or, and this was the more likely explanation, there was nothing like being self-employed to keep you going when others would simply keel over. Not to mention employing other people: these kids needed me on my feet so they could earn their pay.

There. Talked out of my Glorious Adventure. But it was a lovely crisp morning, with a light frost to pick up the colours nicely, so I wouldn't surrender to the suddenly strong call of bed. I'd walk, even if I had to will each foot in front of the other. I'd walk – all the way round the village, just for the hell of it. See what I could see; whom I could see. Take a few photos. Just what got me my reputation for being nosy. Why not? I slipped in a film to replace the one Short had taken away yesterday.

Who was out and about this fine morning, apart from me? And

no, they wouldn't look at me with concern and ask how I was. No way. Well, they wouldn't. It was nothing to do with my erect carriage and serene air. The streets were deserted.

Quite independently, it seemed, my feet took me toward Fred Tregothnan's house. I'd be crazy to try to get in, now the police knew about the connection between us. In any case, the police would have removed the key left under the plant pot. Or Sue would.

Someone had. But only very recently. There was still a little dry patch on the earth where the key had lain. I could see from where I stood that the back door was ajar. Should I assist it to open a little further? Why not?

Because I was a vulnerable old lady, that's why not.

Like hell I was.

But though I could do slow and dignified, I couldn't sprint, cut it how I would. So I'd better resort to a Nick trick. I'd use the camera.

Great idea. Whoever was in there would stand still and let me take a mug shot?

'Just what the blazes do you think you're doing?'

'I might ask the same of you, Nick Thomas,' I hissed, hoping I hadn't actually cried out with pain when I'd tensed. 'But before we exchange explanations of how and why and when, let's deal with our current problem. There's someone inside Fred's house. Look: you can see where the key was and the door's open.'

'And what do you propose to do? Sail in and do a spot of citizen's arrest?'

I bit my lip to keep back a moan about my bruises slowing me down. 'Now I've got reinforcements, why not? You still look like a policeman – you'd do it more convincingly than me.'

He went grey. 'No ID.'

'Don't need it for citizen's arrest. All right,' I said eventually, knowing by now there were better occupations than banging your head on a brick wall, 'why don't you simply go and ring the front or the surgery bell and tell whoever answers that the back door's open and you're Neighbourhood Watch concerned about security. If he's pukka he'll thank you. If he'd not, the chances are he'll bolt out of this door and I'll take his photo. And scarper,' I added hopefully.

He opened his mouth and shut it again.

'What are we waiting for? I'll holler if I need any help. And you, of course, can do the same if you need me.'

Shrugging he shoved his hands in his pockets and headed not to the front door but to the surgery, quite a good move because I could keep an eye on him, and possibly on whoever opened the door. I could see him peering in, covering his eyes against the reflection. Giving up, he headed for the front. His knock would have awakened the dead.

It certainly flushed out the intruder. Not a Burglar Bill type at all. Not a kid robbing the place just to get a few quid for his next fix. A man in his forties, slim but well set up, wearing a black polo neck and designer jeans setting his figure off to perfection. His haircut was as expensive as mine. If we'd met at a party, I'd have made a beeline for him. As it was, I just hoped he hadn't heard the shutter or the whir of the motor drive. I'd shot from the stomach rather than eye level, so goodness knew what I'd get. But it meant all I had to do was tuck the camera under my capacious jacket and stroll away, apparently intent on being the first customer in the shop.

Actually I was using the window like a rear-view mirror. Nick was walking towards me from one direction, Mr Chic from another. To my surprise, Nick tucked his arm in mine, and kissed the top of my head, turning me away from Mr Chic and back towards the White Hart as if we were a couple staying there for a dirty weekend. We heard footsteps behind us for a few yards, but then came the slam of a car door, and an impressive engine starting first pull. Nick fished out a ball-point and wrote on the back of his hand. 'You get out of practice. Or maybe it's these double letters to start with,' he said, which I interpreted as an apology for not getting it all.

'There are photos of all the cars in the street in my camera,' I said. 'Now, shall we go back and check he's locked up? I'd hate anyone off the street just to walk in, wouldn't you?'

'You just don't get it, do you?' Not much of the dirty-weekender left now. 'You can't go waltzing into someone else's house.'

'I might just want to stop anyone else doing just that,' I retorted. 'And hand over the key to young Short.'

'And you might want to fly to the moon,' he said, nonetheless turning as I did and falling into step with me.

In the event, he needn't have bothered. Mr Chic had purloined the key.

'So you make a habit of prowling round the village when every decent citizen is still asleep in bed?' DC Wendover asked dourly: at a guess it was her day off.

'At my age it's hard to adjust one's internal clock,' I said limpidly. 'I'm sure that's why Mr Thomas went for a walk, too.'

Nick produced the most open smile I'd ever seen on his face. 'As a matter of fact I forgot to put my clock back. I just assumed it was time to get my paper. When Mrs Welford saw me she called me over and told me that Tregothnan's back door was open.' I approved his slight reorganisation of the sequence of events. 'When we discovered that the key had been recently removed from its hiding place under the plant pot, we thought we ought to check if the intruder was still in the house.'

'You didn't simply go in and check?' Wendover might have told us to pull the other leg.

'Unarmed civilians, with no authority?' Nick shook his head as if neither of us could even have conceived of such an idea.

'All right. Now, I wonder if you'd know the face again. I can get some mug shots sent down line on to this.' She patted a nifty little laptop.

With the air of producing an exhausted rabbit from a rather battered hat, I passed over my camera.

She raised his eyebrows in disbelief. 'Who are you, Patrick Lichfield or someone?'

'Other women carry handbags,' I said. 'I carry this.' It would have been a good moment to tell her about other photos of interest, those safely in Piers' care, but I never like to over-egg my puddings. Which reminded me, Robin and Lucy's help notwithstanding, it was time I was in the kitchen.

I never forgot a face. Never. On the other hand, I rarely thought I'd recognised people I didn't. So why did I have this nagging feeling that I'd met Mr Chic when I was quite sure I hadn't? Tony always claimed he did his best thinking when his mind was actually on something else, so I left the Chic problem simmering at the back of my mind while the front half was very definitely preoccupied with today's cooking. A glance at the reservations file, now Robin's province, told me that I was booked solid. I hated turning people away, but it looked as if we'd have no option. I'd have been terribly tempted to press Nick into service as a temporary waiter, to speed up the through-put, but he'd taken himself off to his room with a sandwich and the Sunday papers he'd had to go out again to buy, saying he'd rather eat *en famille* with me this evening when things were quieter. Yes, I'd invited him, largely to free up a table now.

I was just about to blast Lucy for being late on a day she knew we'd be frantic when I noticed she hadn't come alone. Lindi had sidled in behind her, looking as coy as a girl with that sort of décolletage can ever be said to look.

'Are you sure you're up to this?' I asked, all concerned mother hen. 'Because we're flat out from the word go. Start laying the tables, will you, Lucy? I'll keep Lindi in here with me for a bit.' Not for anything would I let Lindi loose on Robin till all their chores were done.

The racing round, the bending, the reaching must have been like a particularly aerobics session: they certainly ruined my hair and eased my stiffness. I was entitled to a long, scented bath and a nap, revelling in the knowledge that there was no meals service tonight. Much as I loved the work, it was possible to have too much of a good thing.

I was standing by my living room window taking my earrings off – funny how when you're tired your lobes ache – when I realised Nick's monster-mobile was missing. A tap on his door suggested that he was missing too. Put it another way, a grown man had decided to go for a drive.

So why was I alarmed enough to turn off the bath?

All those things I'd said to him about being useless – had he decided to be thoroughly quixotic? Without a getaway driver?

Before I even had time to think, I was stumbling down the stairs at something approaching my usual pace. And then had to go back again: I'd forgotten my camera. It took me valuable minutes to realise it had disappeared. Nick. I kicked myself all the way back to the hire car. It was intact and still immaculate – what were its chances of being that way when I'd finished with it?

OK. Where would he have gone? The campsite? The abattoir? The rending plant? Fortunately all the options were in roughly the same direction.

I didn't pull into the campsite: slowing down was sufficient to tell me that Reg Bulcombe's pick-up was safely parked. But I wasn't reassured. Tony had always told me to listen to what my instincts were telling me – my Gippo second sight, he'd called it uneasily, both proud of my ability and nervous of it. Well, it had been me that warned him he was overreaching himself, and look where he'd ended up.

The new car was more powerful than the first, but not up to my own. It responded well in lower gears, however, accelerating with some assurance when I asked it to. The late afternoon sun – very late, with the loss of that hour! – gave an air of glamour to the steep hills and now dark valleys. If only I'd got my camera. I kept going. Soon I killed the radio and opened my window. What the hell did I expect? Gunfire?

Not the furious baying of dogs. Faster than was safe in lanes like this, I headed for the abattoir, flinging the car into the approach lane with a swirl of gravel, quite stylish, really. Hitting Nick's four by four broadside on wouldn't have been stylish at all, so I controlled the skid, blessing the memory of Tony's mate Archie who'd taught me all his getaway skills.

I could hear the dogs, all right, my flesh creeping more with each deep-throated growl. But I couldn't see them. And I couldn't see Nick.

If only I'd got some sort of weapon. Nothing in the hire car, of course, and nothing in Nick's. Except for a fire extinguisher. Would that be any use? Anything had to be better than nothing when it came to dogs.

The main gates were still locked, so Nick hadn't got in that way. I followed the crushed grass round the perimeter fence, keeping my beadies open for more gin traps. But I was going away from the sound of the dogs. He must have gone all the way round, much as I was doing. To keep on going or double back? I pressed on. It was easier to spot traps this way. And to have both of us prostrate with our ankles broken wouldn't help at all.

Nick wasn't prostrate. He was suspended in mid air, caught on the barbed wire in silhouette against a fading scarlet and gold sunset. He flailed his legs violently to keep the dogs from tearing him down, quite unable to concentrate on freeing himself. I don't think he'd even registered my arrival. But the dogs had.

'If I lure them away,' I yelled, squinting up at him, 'can you slip out of that jacket and fall forward? Sort of somersault?' I added as I got his attention.

He peered through the fading light. 'Too far. Could break something.'

'Hmm. Like your neck. Any chance you could throw me your car keys?'

'Not a key. Stupid bit of plastic.'

'Whatever it is. Can you get at it? Here, boy. Nice doggie. There's some nice soft Josie meat here. Come on! Look. Nice bare wrist.' I snatched it back just in time. I'll swear I heard the snap of those damned teeth. Yes, they'd sliced my skin. The wire fence gave under their weight too much for me to try that dodge again. I ran a few more feet. But then I saw the glint of wire. I was back in gin trap territory. In deepening dusk.

Back to Nick. His hands were running with blood but he was holding something towards me, much as if he were proffering a dog biscuit. The movement unbalanced him. His foot was in jaw-range.

'Kick for God's sake,' I yelled. Then I remembered my secret weapon, and directed a good squirt between the eyes of the lead dog. 'Just hold on!'

In virtual darkness, as the interior light automatically faded, it took me valuable seconds to suss out how the card worked, but once started the vehicle responded like a Rolls Royce cum tank.

There. It smashed through undergrowth and traps alike, bucking and surging over whatever obstructed it. Hell, it was just like those TV adverts. I might almost be converted. Pulling as close to the netting as I could, I levered myself over into the passenger seat ignoring as best I could the protest of every fibre involved in the exercise.

Nick couldn't do it, could he? Ashen faced, he hung exactly as I'd left him.

'You can do it! Come on, Nick! Just roll! Pretend you're diving into a swimming pool. Think of the blue clear water. Ease yourself into it. Nice gentle roll! Think how warm and soft the water will be as it welcomes you.' What twaddle I was talking. Even the dogs' snarls sounded mocking. Well, sod them for a start. Let them bite on a bit more foam. Lasting side effects? I hoped not. They were only doing their job, after all. But I'd always rated humans above animals, and these had clearly tasted blood. Nick's yes, and near enough mine.

With a cry of utter despair, Nick rolled.

Abandoning the dogs to their fate, I sprinted round to break his fall if I had to. But the silver monster bore him up like a newly benign dragon. Twisting, he dropped his legs over my side, and slithered down, almost knocking me over. Clinging to each other like lovers, we managed to stay upright.

Somehow I was in the driving seat again. Nick was in beside me, slamming the door.

'Reverse? Where the hell's sodding reverse?' By chance I found it, and we hurtled backwards, Nick, not yet belted in, tossed around like a rag doll. I'd never mastered reversing fast, despite Archie's best efforts, and we weaved and rolled. Fortunately. As I pulled up alongside my hire car, I realised what the noise was I'd hardly registered: gunfire. How much a shield the four by four's door would be I'd no idea, any more than I could guess if the hire car would protect me. Or if Nick would be able to manage his monster. All I knew was if either of us failed to drive hell for leather away, no headlights, of course, we'd be gunned down. And if we left a car behind, it'd be totalled, one way or another. Nick must have realised the same. More agile than me, he was already in the driver's seat and pulling away as my car fired. We went off in the fastest convoy possible, both vehicles swinging from side to side as much with the force of acceleration as with the drivers' joint efforts to dodge bullets. How I avoided a huge truck bearing down on me, God alone knows. Maybe He acknowledged my breathless thanks by making its driver misjudge the bend and stuff his bumper into the bank. Let him worry about that: I was too busy concentrating on picking up the occasional glow of Nick's intermittent brake-lights. At last he judged it safe to use his lights; I'd have done the same if I'd known how mine worked. At least he'd spot any oncoming traffic first. Spot? Mow down, the pace he was going.

At last we reached the village, and its scatter of streetlights. He slowed to a sedate thirty. I found the light switch. There, two Sunday trippers by chance returning to base at the same time. We pulled up side by side. Even though he'd cut his lights and engine, the car wasn't still. Correction, Nick wasn't still. I heaved open his door to find him shaking so much he must be having a fit. He was. A fit of laughter. He roared, slapping his thighs and throwing his head back, tears pouring down his face.

'God, that was fun,' he gasped.

Maybe it was true what they said about women having no sense of humour. I'd always thought I could see the funny side of things. So maybe mine had simply gone AWOL. I certainly wasn't laughing at the sight of his shredded clothes and bloodstained flesh. Or at my own injured hand, now beginning to throb.

He was. Although he was trying to achieve and moreover keep a straight face, another little chuckle would force his lips apart and ring round the yard.

Arms akimbo, my own face entirely serious, I leaned forward, my face as close to his as my lack of inches and his bloody throne of a driving seat would permit. I said what I'd wanted to say ever since I saw him alone at that abattoir, as every single joint and muscle locked in spasms of pain as vicious as any dog's jaws. 'You idiot. You bloody stupid fool. Taking risks like that.' I was crying with pain. But then, as I recalled how silly he'd looked on that barbed wire, a rag doll blowing in the wind, I might have been laughing too.

And, come to think of it, by now Nick might be crying.

Chapter Twenty-Four

I stomped straight past Nick up the stairs and into his en suite bathroom, turning the taps on full. Shame I had to ruin the effect by going back down and returning with the cooking salt, which I shovelled in by the handful.

'That'll clean up the superficial cuts. Then we'll see if either of us needs A and E,' I said. 'I'll leave a pot of tea in your room. My sitting room in half an hour. OK?'

Because if he needed a cuppa and a hot bath, I did too. I'd added salt to the bathwater in the hope that it would act as a general antiseptic, but sloshed in lavender oil too, not just for the smell but also for its healing properties. Of course, I should have dashed off and sprinkled some in Nick's too, but that was one sort of room service I drew the line at. Until I could move again, at least. I now had a new crop of bruises, and running had taxed muscles that even the fiercest walking didn't trouble. But at least I only had one dog nip, one requiring a pretty small plaster, and my tetanus was bang up to date.

Nick would be in far worse state, I told myself as I hauled myself out, patting rather than rubbing myself dry. It was very tempting simply to sling on my dressing gown, but that might complicate matters and I compromised by digging out an old baggy velour tracksuit that added a stone to my appearance but chaffed nowhere. Moccasins completed the domesticated ensemble. Nick had clearly had the same reservations, denying any sexiness by wearing maroon socks with his dressing gown. Or perhaps he didn't realise how deeply unseductive socks were with a dressing-gown.

I sank to his feet with a first aid box in my hands. 'Are you up to date on your jabs?'

'For this job? Everything going a week before I started. What do you make of the cuts?'

'You bled like a stuck pig, but they're all superficial. I wouldn't have thought any of them needed stitches. I've got plenty of those butterfly things.'

'Flutter away!'

I bathed away blood still sluggishly oozing from a couple of cuts from his forehead. The pink water reminded me of the stream.

He must have noticed too. 'I'll get on to the water company tomorrow – pull a bit of rank,' he said, without my saying anything. 'See what Mrs Greville has to say about that.'

I put down the dressing strip I'd been about to apply. 'Mr Chic. He must be Mrs Greville's son. I knew he reminded me of someone. That's who! Luke Greville, MEP, no less.' No reason not to apply the strip. I got on with it. 'The one who got the order of the boot to Europe for doubtful scams. The family's involved with all this, Nick, you mark my words. I wonder why he didn't eat with the rest of them last night.'

Before he could say anything, there was a terrific banging on the front door. Nick was still fit enough to take the stairs two at a time. I followed more decorously, body resenting every step.

'Robin! What's the matter?' For he was too wild-eyed simply to have forgotten his key.

'It's Lindi! She's gone!' He almost fell into the hall.

Nick bent to gather him up. He was wearing passion killer knickers.

'Gone where?'

'I don't know! One minute we were walking along the road, you know, getting acquainted. Next she's not there. Literally disappeared from the pavement beside me. No idea where!'

Raising an ironic eyebrow, I caught Nick's eye. 'Just how were you getting acquainted?'

Robin had the grace to flush. 'How do you think?

'Was she enjoying the process as much as you were?' I asked. 'Or did she decide to do a bunk?'

'As it happens,' he said, sounding genuinely huffy, 'she was asking about videos we should get when I next had an evening off. And I was explaining I wasn't an evenings-off person and didn't she have to work too and we'd have to think of another time and turned – and there she was, gone.'

Neither of us laughed at the cliché. 'Come and show me where she disappeared,' I said, grabbing a jacket from by the back door.

Oh, and a torch. Six o'clock and it was pitch dark. 'We won't have any drinkers,' I flung at Nick over my shoulder, 'but in case we do maybe you ought to be dressed.'

The clear sunny day had given way to a clear icy night. Because we had so few streetlights, the stars always seemed larger and brighter than they did in Brum. Light pollution, wasn't that what they called it? Huddled into my jacket, head down, I set the briskest pace I could manage, Robin making little dashes forward and then back again to my side, like an excited puppy.

'Here. It was about here.' He stopped by one of the less attractive runs of Victorian cottages, what would be called a terrace in a city, complete with entries between blocks. Why anyone should have economised like this in a village goodness knows – unless, of course, they were tied to the Greville estate, at a time landowners thought the worst was good enough for their serfs. Yes, when the hymn writer produced those lines about the *Rich man in his castle*, saying it was right for a *poor man* to be *at his gate*. I stared, hands on hips. Two front doors opening on to the street, separated by a gated entry. Find the lady. Just like the card game.

'You tried knocking on all three?'

''Course I did.' He tried again, hard enough, as on my door, to waken the dead.

No response. Except from the church bells – not the full peal, with Nick *hors de combat* - which made us both jump like frightened dogs. Turning, I did the nearest I could to a scuttle. 'I know who to ask!' I said.

'Who?'

'Got to change. You and Nick cope with the bar. No food on Sundays. Ever. Or not till I come back from Evensong.'

'You're going to ask God, are you?' he asked as sarcastic as young Short would have been.

'Maybe. And certainly His representative in the village.'

Evensong wasn't my favourite service, because Sue simply didn't have the voice for it. To be honest, neither did most of the choir, though they now boasted a tenor who looked suspiciously like Mr Chic. Correction, Mr Greville. I wondered if he ingratiated himself with a spot of Morris dancing as well. He was hardly

Placido Domingo but did add a certain something. Lucy was singing her head off too, but while she might be a gutsy bell ringer, she'd never be another Charlotte Church. As we knelt for the first prayer, I had to bargain with the Almighty: if He wanted me down here, He'd have to make sure He could get me up again.

Sue's sermon reminded anyone listening that she used to be a junior-school teacher. I tried to work out why I'd come – after all, I could just as easily have hovered outside and pounced at the psychological moment. But there is, after all, something to be said for standing where feet had stood for hundreds of years – give or take a bit of Victorian prettification – expressing the same hopes and fears in more or less the same words.

It was Lucy I grabbed first afterwards, as she emerged from the vestry still stripping off her cassock, ready to dash home.

'Where'll Lindi be?'

She stopped dead. 'Thought you didn't want her tonight.'

'No more I do. But she literally disappeared from the street while Robin was chatting her up. By that run of terraced houses.'

'The ones with the entries? Well, she could be down any one of them. And there's a path down the back, connecting them all. So she could be anywhere,' She concluded helpfully. 'But I've got to go, I mean, really – ' She flashed a look at her watch and pulled a face.

'See you Tuesday,' I said, patting her arm as she fled.

I hung around making small talk with anyone prepared to talk to a publican. Mrs Greville lingered, nodding graciously at a flower display I seemed to have done years ago and telling me how nice it still looked. But she took very good care to tuck her arm into that of her chic son and propel him lickety-split out into the night, hardly even pausing to shake Sue's hand.

I joined the line of other worshippers ready to do just that, holding back so that I wouldn't be overheard murmuring that I'd love a word with her and why didn't she pop into the White Hart as soon as she was free. She looked more alarmed than enthusiastic, but agreed. Something about the set of her shoulders told me that a glass of wine rather better than she could afford might just hit the spot. Of course, it would mean throwing her and Nick together, and the length of time it took him to escort women home I might not see him till next weekend. But if that was what it took to worm information out of her, so be it.

Nick had managed to calm down Robin somewhat, possibly by assuring him that I'd come back with all the answers and possibly Lindi herself. His face fell like a child's.

'But Lucy's on to it. And I hope to enlist the services,' I said, realising the enormity of my pun only as I said it, 'of our vicar.' I carefully avoided Nick's eye – but he'd know what I expected of him. Which was not to get himself whipped up into a moral disquisition, as he had last time. 'She should be around any minute.'

'The sodding vicar! What's he got to do with anything?'

'She. And she knows more about this village than most outsiders. If anyone can help –'

'What about an insider?'

I nodded. 'I've tried the only really friendly native I know – Lucy. She said Lindi could be anywhere and I believed her.'

'Where does she live? So I can go and talk to her.'

He was well smitten, wasn't he? I only wished the object of his passion was more deserving.

'I don't think that'd be a good idea, Robin,' Nick chipped in. 'Her dad doesn't like her having anything to do with us grockles. When I walk her home, I have to stop thirty yards away. Don't you?'

'Well, yes. But this is an emergency! Surely he'd –'

'Lindi might have just not wanted to go out with you – have you considered that? Might prefer your room to your company and just be too shy to say it.'

I chortled derisively. 'Too shy! Our Lindi! I don't think so!'

Nick raised a warning finger. 'Hang on, Josie – Lindi would rather put up with Tregothnan's attentions than tell him off. Perhaps she just thought discretion was the better part of valour. Now what are you up to, young man?'

'I'm phoning the police!'

'And telling them what? That a lass who's not even your girlfriend ran away from you? Know what they'd do? Laugh their socks off. You wait to hear what Sue thinks – she's got a wise head on those shoulders of hers.'

Unforgivably I caught his eye and mouthed, 'Apart from when she's driving!'

We both sniggered, which did nothing for Robin. Fortunately there was soon a tap at the back door, Sue letting herself in, country-fashion, as I'd not yet had the privilege of doing anywhere in the village.

She flushed an unlovely shade of brick when she saw Nick and me together, but pulled herself together with commendable speed to address a still sulky Robin.

'Had you two had a row? Or had you come on too strong too quickly? You're sure? Well, when I get home I'll make a few phone calls.'

'Home? Why don't you join us here for a bite of supper? Use the phone in my living room while I cook.'

The poor woman seemed to have one layer of skin too few, the way her colour flooded and ebbed as she no doubt weighed up the merits of eating with Nick and sharing him with two others.

'I was going to stir-fry some very nice odds and ends of beef fillet,' I said, 'with mange tout and tamarind and ...'

'I'll show you where the phone is,' Nick interrupted me, risking a complicitous wink over his shoulder as he led her out.

'What's all that about?' Robin demanded.

'Private joke,' I said. 'Tell you what, if she comes up with the goods and you want to express your gratitude in the most appropriate way, you could valet her car, inside and out. She's always so busy doing things for others,' I embroidered, 'that she never has time for herself. Tell you what, why don't you lay up in my flat? It'll be nice and warm and less like work.'

Supper was a sadly flat affair, nothing, I suspect, to do with ambience or with the food, which was well up to standard, but perhaps because of our different hopes and fears. Sue confessed to having drawn several blanks, but – surprise, surprise – agreed with Nick that calling the police wouldn't be helpful.

'There's no point in exposing yourself to ridicule,' she said flatly. 'And it might do more harm than good if they did take you seriously and come sniffing round the village. No, no more wine, thanks. I've got to drive, remember.'

'Why not leave your car here overnight? It's only a step – OK, a longish stride! – to the rectory.' I let the bottle hover enticingly over her glass.

'I'll walk you back,' Robin said, unhelpfully. 'You never know, we might just see something. Someone. Whatever.'

The poor woman's eyes had flicked to Nick before she replied. 'No. Honestly. I've had enough,' she concluded ambiguously.

'Come on, you're over the limit already,' I said. 'How often do you let your hair down, Sue?'

I'm not sure what my motivation was. Nine-tenths of me really wanted her to enjoy life a bit more, and in my terms there was no better way of doing that than eating, drinking and enjoying good company. OK, in my terms the company might well have been solo, and the location private. But with luck I could keep Robin back to help wash up, and Nick could do the honours. After that it was up to them.

The other tenth was less laudable. I wanted to see if she'd give anything away about her activities in Tregothnan's house. The more I ran the picture over in my mind, the more I was convinced she was carrying something. If she'd had the keys to the surgery – perhaps they'd been in the bureau, even – she'd had time to let herself in and retrieve whatever it was while I was checking his mail. And then she'd hidden – whatever – under her coat and scuttled out. Did that mean it was she who'd planted his accounts in my shed? She might simply have wanted them to be found, not intending to incriminate me at all.

In the end I was hoist by my own alcohol. She drank it as if it were water and then simply fell asleep.

'Well,' Nick asked quietly, as her head sank on to her arms, 'this is going to take two of you. All right, two of us. Which car do you reckon, Josie? Hers and walk back, or mine and make her walk the walk tomorrow?'

'Whichever it'd be easiest to get her into and out of,' I sighed. 'Trouble is, neither of us is exactly legal.'

'OK,' he sighed, 'we'd better get enough coffee into her to wake her up and Robin and I can walk her home.'

'Why me? Can't you manage on your own?'

'I could but I'd rather not. Use your imagination, man!' Nick added roughly.

I'd just given everything a final wipe down when they returned, in mid-argument by the sound of things. But it turned out only to be about football. The three of us stood awkwardly in the kitchen, all of us ready for sleep but all of us edgy. The way Robin looked from Nick to me, he'd obviously deduced that the reason Nick hadn't wanted to be on his own with a drunken Sue was that he was afraid she'd jump him. OK, in her present state, crawl him. And perhaps he didn't want to be jumped by Sue because he wanted to jump me. As for me, both Piers and Morgan were great in the sack, and had either turned up offering what he did best, I'd still have wanted nothing more than a solitary duvet. So I yawned, very ostentatiously, looked at my watch and produced a genuine gasp. Tomorrow would, as always, be another day – but it had arrived already. And after a day as long as mine, any woman my age was entitled to be knackered.

Not that I'd ever admit to age or to being knackered. Ever. So I blew kisses impartially to both men and ran as lightly as I could up the stairs.

It was only after locking my door firmly that I collapsed ignominiously on the bed. And even then I had the bathos of having to lever myself up and take off the slap.

Chapter Twenty-Five

My internal clock still hadn't settled back into Greenwich Mean Time. So when my bruises and aches and pains nagged me awake, despite the painkillers, I stayed that way. The stretches were no more fun than I expected, but the results might have been a bit better. The shower definitely helped. OK. Face the day time. I told myself, forcing my walking pace into brisk mode and persuading my face into less of a grimace, more of a cheery grin, I'd be first in the queue for the shop.

Not today I wouldn't. Not by a long chalk. There was quite a knot of people half way along the street, and a babble of talk rising from them. Jeering? That was definitely jeering.

Well, if I could walk briskly, I could run. And run I did as soon as I got a hint of what was going on.

Almost before I knew it I was jostling and pushing through the other onlookers. And stripping off my coat and wrapping it round Lindi. Lindi, tied to one of the few lampposts with which the village was blessed, stripped to her undies and tarred and feathered. She was absolutely silent.

I don't know exactly what I yelled, but I yelled loud and long and pretty potently. By the time I'd finished, everyone had slunk away, all except one of Lucy's younger brothers, who shyly and awkwardly produced a knife. He was right: it was quicker to slice through the binder twine than to wrestle with knots. Then he legged it.

No, not cowardice – he'd got even more sense than I'd realised. Within seconds, before I could even start mopping Lindi clean, Lucy was running up with a sheet, which she wrapped round the still silent girl. 'Leave this to me. Get back home. Make sure that bloody Robin doesn't come poking his nose in.'

'But the tar –'

'Treacle. Just push off, Mrs W. Please.'

For once in my life I didn't argue, except a token bleat about school.

'Half term, isn't it? Please, Mrs W! If you go now, I'll phone you. OK?' She passed me my coat.

As I turned, aching with reluctance, she added, 'And don't you go calling the police either!'

'So do I have to obey?' I asked Nick, having decided not to wake the still sleeping Robin.

'Have you told the police everything about the abattoir and the rending plant?'

I shook my head, pushing away my coffee cup. 'Didn't want, to be honest, to dob you in. That's the modern term, isn't it?'

'How about the usual one, grassing up? Thanks. But it's widened our credibility gap.'

Our? 'Evans and Co already know about my Great Beef Battle – I thought a few questions from them might stem the flow of offal. They seem just to have changed to the direction – poor, poor Lindi.'

'Sleeping with the enemy – never really approved of.'

'So why's Lucy got away with it?'

He looked at me steadily. 'I should imagine Gay – God, what a name for the poor bugger! – knows which side his bread is buttered. You more or less feed his family, don't you? And no, Lucy didn't say anything about it. It was her efforts not to that put me on to it. But how long his buddies will let him get away with allowing her to continue, goodness knows.' He glanced at his watch. 'It's time I headed into work. I want to get the water people on to that stream diversion.'

'And its interesting colour.'

'Quite. And I think it's time I paid a visit to the rending plant.'

I shook my head emphatically. 'Not without back up, you don't. Get one of your FSA buddies to go with you. That should put the fear of God into them.'

'I'll see what I can do,' he replied, in that pseudo-ruminative way men have when they have no intention of taking sensible advice. He stood up. 'Time I was off.'

A glance passed between us. On my side it said, 'Look after yourself and don't take unnecessary risks.' I wasn't sure about his.

A morning wielding a duster and vac., ears cocked for the phone, lay ahead of me. If Lucy had said she'd phone me, she'd phone me. And I rather thought Sue owed me a call, too. When she did-n't phone, I tried her number, only to have to leave a message asking for an urgent response.

Nothing. Nothing till I broke for a cup of coffee at eleven. And then it was Nick, saying he'd put the fear of God into the water company, and, just to celebrate, contacted the county council about blocked footpaths.

'I told them that walking about in the open country was an integral part of my job,' he said.

'Good for you. What next?'

There was the tiniest pause while he worked out his lie. Or maybe not. 'Sorry. One of my colleagues from down the corridor returning my kettle. Any news of Lindi?'

'I thought you might be Lucy. Nothing from Sue, either. I'm so worked up I've taken to housework,' I added plaintively. But I wasn't so full of self-pity I hadn't noticed how he'd changed the subject. Nick was up to something, wasn't he?

'Mrs W?' A tousle-headed Robin put his head round the door.

I gestured to the phone. He nodded and disappeared again, presumably to get dressed.

He was an even better diversionary tactic than anything Nick could have thought up. In a low voice, I asked Nick's advice.

'You'll have to tell him if he asks. But I wouldn't volunteer anything,' he responded, putting down the phone.

No, he wouldn't, would he?

The best way to say nothing would be to be out. I had after all my morning paper to collect.

'If you want my advice,' Molly whispered, her eyes darting back and forth though the shop was completely empty, 'you'll cut your losses and clear out now. You've got planning permission and all. And with the renovations you've already done, you should get a really good price.'

'What if I don't want to go away?'

'What if this Lindi business won't go away? That's what you have to ask yourself. A matter of principle's one thing, Mrs W. A matter of life and death's another.'

'All I did was change my meat supplier!' I whispered. 'Local vegetables, local meat, local staff – that was what I wanted. And paperwork to go with it. That's what caused all this!'

She shook her head. 'You brought in outsiders to do your building work – bad mistake. It's been downhill from there, I'm afraid.'

I felt as if the floor was rocking. It was one thing hearing this from Lucy, another having it confirmed. 'I tried to get local builders – God knows I've done my best in everything, Molly.'

'I'm sure you have. Well, it was a struggle for us. But at least Jem's got relatives from round here. You take my advice, Josie – you cut your losses and go.'

I could hardly hold the newspaper she handed over.

'Don't you realise, you think you've tried to fit in, but others see it as shoving in where you're not wanted. The church – it takes years to get on the flower rota, and you're decorating the altar before you've been here five minutes. You might have thought you were being a good Samaritan offering Tom Dearborn accommodation: others see it as coming between father and daughter.'

'If the father's got the sort of relationship with his daughter that rumour says, then it ought to be Social Services and the Law coming between father and daughter!' Despite myself my voice rose.

In response, Molly's dropped to a sharp whisper. 'There you go again! People here don't see it like that.'

'What's happened to her? And to Tom?'

'Well, that's seen as your doing. Done a bolt. Goodness knows where. And neither of them with a feather to fly with. Her dad's off his head with worry.'

'Well, you can tell him that certainly wasn't my idea. My way they'd both have had a roof over their head, he'd have had a steady job and she'd have had her family – such as it is – and friends at hand.'

'No good getting on your high horse with me, Josie – I'm just the messenger. And look at the mess young Lindi's in.'

'Literally. Who's responsible for that – that outrage?'

'Shhh.'

'They're doing to her what they'd like to do to me – right? Only I'm not sleeping with the enemy, I am the enemy. But they can't be allowed to get away with such violence. Can't be!'

'And you're going to play your usual trick and bring in the police to sort them out? Not if you take my advice, Josie. Just leave well alone. And get the "For Sale" notice up by the end of the week. There. I can't put it plainer than that, can I? You're a decent woman, men friends apart, of course, they'll come to realise that. But you're not one of *them*. Here,' she added roughly, as the shop bell pinged, 'don't forget what you came for. And I'll put it in my ledger. No more papers from Saturday, then.'

I was on my knees by the drain, hoping there was nothing left to vomit, when I heard a man's voice. 'Not much of an advert for your own cooking, eh?'

By the time I'd scrabbled up, there was no one there. Well, I couldn't see anyone. But I'd have bet a lifetime's takings they'd see the mascara running down my cheeks and it'd be all round the village before lunchtime.

I thought about one of my Romany curses – but once I'd cursed Nick, and look how he'd ended up. I buttoned my lip.

The lunch trade was brisker than on your usual Monday, not just with walkers but also with quite a smattering of locals. These were almost certainly the men who'd tormented Lindi. So nine-tenths of me wanted to tip their tipples over their heads. The other tenth was still the little girl in the playground, betraying by not so much as a sniffle that she'd been tormented. I'm afraid pride won.

'Just get in there and do what you're paid to do,' I told Robin fiercely. 'And if I hear you asking after Lindi, I shall fire you on the spot. Publicly. Get it? We'll sort it out, don't you worry. But we'll do it my way.' Which just happened, today, to include a lax-ative in the cider of certain selected boozers.

They didn't include Lucy Gay's father, I noticed. Funny, the only thing that separated him from his booze was work, and there wasn't much of that going begging at this time of year. Perhaps he was still locked in argument with Lucy, who still hadn't phoned, any more than Sue had.

Despite my bright professional smiles and slick service, I was still screaming in my head. Whether it was hurt or fury, I didn't know. But as soon as I could decently hang up the Closed sign, I reached for the phone. Nick. If I was *persona non grata*, he must be positively at risk. And I had a nasty suspicion he was intending to put his head in the lion's mouth by heading out to the rendering plant with no protection. When I got no response from his office phone, my suspicions grew stronger. And all I got from his mobile was the sound of traffic and then white noise as he left range.

Grabbing my own mobile, my camera and even my walking stick, I yelled to Robin to stay put and answer any calls, either to the bar or to my private number. Without waiting for him to argue I was into the hire car, not without checking first it was still in once piece. Even as the adrenaline spurted and the blood pounded, I shivered as if someone was zipping a shroud over my head.

My response was as prosaic as they come. I pulled over to the phone box, still a village lifeline. Popping a tissue over the voice piece, I dialled 999.

'There's trouble out at Wetherall Enterprises,' I said, my voice as guttural as I could make it. 'Big trouble. And if you don't believe me, talk to DCI Mike Evans. He'll know what it's about.'

He wouldn't, of course, but he was bright enough to be interested.

At least I hoped he would. This cold dark shroud told me some one had to be.

Chapter Twenty-Six

Hell for leather. Not round these lanes. Not in a car I hardly knew. And not with a cattle-wagon coming towards me, more on my side of the lane than on his. Thank God for a fortuitous gateway.

Men drivers!

Hang on. Not the whole sex. But male lorry drivers. I'd had my fill of them recently, none of them just bad, more hostile. And there might well be more coming, like troubles, in battalions. If one came at me at this speed along a deep gully like this, the best I'd be able to do would be to slew the car across its path, the passenger side taking the worst of the impact. I hoped. Maybe then I'd be sufficiently protected to be able to crawl out of the wreck, even if that left me vulnerable to the lorry driver.

In the event, there was no need for all that ghoulish forward planning. I met no more lorries, nor any other vehicles.

But there was plenty of activity by the entrance to the rending plant, as I discovered when I cased the joint. Sorry about the lingo.

I'd tucked the rental car under as much cover as I could find, inching my way on foot the last fifty yards or so. The walking stick felt reassuring, but maybe it'd be more hindrance than help. What about ditching it now? Then I thought of the dogs in that compound, and though I imagined any animal here should be sated on marrow bones a-plenty, I'd prefer something in my hand apart from a camera.

It was the camera I used first. The short driveway was fully occupied by a tow-truck, winching a silver four-wheel drive. No, I couldn't see anyone in it. That didn't mean there wasn't. After all, if you're going to tow an ex-policeman's vehicle with him still in it, you're going to have to truss him first. Well, most ex-policemen. Nick was probably in one of his damned brown studies, wondering if he should breathe or not.

Plenty of photo opportunities, anyway. Thank goodness for telephoto lenses. I beat a strategic retreat while the Wetherall man – yes, his name was blazoned on his overalls – yelled final instructions. I couldn't pick up much, but I'd swear he said something about 'same place as before'.

It was time the police turned up, surely. OK, it was a largely rural force, and you couldn't expect them to turn out in their hundreds to a location as far from a town as this. But there should be some action. There should be someone to barge into that office building, where the Wetherall man had ambled, laughing loudly. No sign of any dogs.

Good job. He'd left the gate slightly ajar.

Ajar enough for someone my size to squeeze through without pushing on something that might squeak loudly enough to attract attention. The stick? Ditch it now? More in hope than expectation, I left it hanging where a passing cop might see it. Even one as slow as these seemed to be might see it as a Clue. OK, a passing Wetherall man might see it too, but by then I'd be committed one way or another.

Gagging, I reached for the peppermints.

It wasn't just the smell – correction, smells. Imagine the worst butcher's shop on the hottest day. There was that sort of sweet blood smell coming from huge open skips, grotesque with limbs waiting to be processed. Then there was the worst sort of rancid butter smell, no, nothing as wholesome as butter. Tallow, that was it. And curls of greasy smoke seeped from the chimneys dropping smuts you couldn't brush off.

Had the concentration camps been like this? Only a thousand times worse because when all was said and done, these were only animal remains.

Or were they?

If I wanted to dispose of a body, wouldn't I do it here? Had Fred Tregothnan's blood joined that in the vat over there? It was so full that when the wind blew, a little dribbled over the edge. Hence the puddle of gore below it. There was an even larger puddle under the neighbouring vat. Surely this must be why that stream was pink.

A few yards nearer the office were more open tanks, the source of the tallow smell. Several of these were leaking too. There were other, smaller tanks, these roughly sealed. Presumably they held matter that could be transformed into capsule casings or lipsticks and rated more care. Not enough in my book.

If it was here Fred had been – I sought for a word but could come up with nothing better than 'disposed of' – there'd never be any body for the police to find. As for his car, that might provide evidence, if it could ever be found. Perhaps I should have tailed the tow truck.

But finding a car's graveyard wasn't as important as preventing another disposal.

Could I hope that Nick was still alive? In the remote hope he was, I'd still need back-up to rescue him, and strain though my ears might there was still no sign of 'blues and twos', the flashing lights and sirens heralding the arrival of the police. Perhaps there was a different term these days: I could have done with Tony to tell me. I could have done with Tony beside me now.

Perhaps he was there. I could hear him say, 'Better get in there, gal,' as clear as if he were whispering in my ear. So get in I'd better.

There was nothing to prevent me. It was only an ordinary office, after all. So I pushed on the door, almost expecting a Cruella de Ville of a receptionist to halt me in my tracks.

I followed the sound of male voices. You don't expect West Country burrs ever to sound threatening – London accents, yes, or Liverpool. But there was something in the very blurred vowels and consonants that raised the hairs on the back of my neck. Yes, a dog can sound nastier when it growls than when it barks. Although one had now started to do just that. No, the bark broke into a snarl, quickly choked off. Someone was holding it on a tight leash.

To torment someone? These villagers liked that sort of pastime.

On impulse I dialled 999 again, leaving the call open. With luck, someone might pick up what was going on.

I inched closer, as close to the wall as I could, but needing to peer round the door to see.

Nick was just within my line of sight. He was pressed back against a wall, not yet handcuffed. But who need to be pinioned, when they had that dog for company? I couldn't risk a proper glance round the door, because the dog's ear had cocked and turned. Its humans were too busy discussing what to do with their prisoner and irritating the animal by sporadic jerks on its chain to notice. With luck.

To Nick's right, and my left, was the sort of desk I associated with the teacher's desk my school days, the solid oak sort now replaced by those dinky ones which even the teacher must have lest anything grown-up intimidates the kids. My teachers had sometimes left their drawers ajar, too, so you could see chalk and registers and bottles of ink. They certainly never crammed them with money. I'd not seen so much cash since Tony's heyday. Yes, literally wads of used notes, not just fivers, either. There must have been tens of thousands there.

One or two of my teachers had blotters or even jam-jars full of flowers brought by an anxious child or sycophantic parent. Much as some had needed them, they'd never had a collection of guns. There were a couple of modern ones, but most must have dated back to one of the world wars. Open boxes of bullets and cartridges jostled for space.

If only Nick had had a couple of minutes, he could have loaded one and shot his way out of the situation. I could. Tony had always made sure I could handle guns. But I was a matter of yards away, and Nick would have to take only two steps.

The obvious thing was for me to create a diversion, to give him long enough to act. But even if I sang the national anthem and tap-danced round the room, there was no guarantee Nick would do anything. Brown study man, Nick, remember. The last man to trust your life to in this situation.

If only I had a weapon myself, my walking stick for instance. Oh, yes. Fat lot of help that would be against two men and a dog. I'd have done better to bring some aniseed. OK, there was only one thing to do. It might take time but maybe they were enjoying themselves enough.

The problem would be if I didn't have the guts to do it. Actually, I had plenty of guts. And horns, and hooves and nice long bones. Tibias? Yes, one for the dog, one as a Stone Age weapon.

My stomach heaved as I selected them, and my fingers loathed the slime of the rotting flesh, but choose I did, yanking them from a skip with lower sides than most. And letting others fall with a nice echoing bang as I did it. I didn't even have time to swear. I was back in that office block as if I were running away from the danger, not towards it.

I even yelled, as I hoped Boadicca might have yelled. Just to make sure Nick knew what he ought to be doing if he got the chance.

First the scuffle of paws trying to get purchase on the office floor. Yes. I held the tibia's knee end forward, and managed, just as the dog leapt forward, to ram it down its throat. That left me with one to whirl about my head as I screamed and shouted. *For God's sake, Nick, take the hint!* If only there were a Tony inside his head too.

One man erupted into the passage, gun – small, modern version – at the ready. Just as he did so the bone slipped from my hand. It hit him on the temple: nothing to do with me, honestly.

As he thudded to the floor, the other man appeared. His gun wasn't just ready. It was held the way Tony had told me, steady and dangerous. And he wasn't going to mess around. I heard my voice pleading. I didn't want it to. But words just came out.

Pity? Compassion? No, he relished the moment. He smiled as his finger tightened on the trigger. I could see the joint whitening. This was it then. Oh, God, this was it. 'Tony,' I yelled.

And for a fraction of a second, he looked over my shoulder along the corridor.

Two gunshots, immensely loud in the confined space. Definitely two.

Blood exploded all over the wall. His, not mine. But it could just as easily have been mine too because his bullet buried itself in the ceiling inches from my head.

Nick. He'd come to his senses not even a second too late.

All Tony's training about staying cool and I started to whimper. The whimpering became sobs, just small ones at first, then great silly convulsions pushing their way from my diaphragm, or wherever sobs start from. They were so loud I didn't hear the police at first, or rather, didn't make sense of what they were saying. I couldn't have responded anyway: my legs had given way and I was huddled on the floor like a baby failing in its first steps. I couldn't even cover my face, my hands smelt so vile.

If only I was the sort of woman who could pass out.

But I couldn't. At last it dawned on me the police were telling me to lie down, so I did.

Only, a few moments later, to have Nick helping me up. It seemed we were both all right.

With all the filth and decay outside, I hadn't expected much of the loos, nor did I get it. But at least there was hot water and a bottle of dishwashing liquid, so in theory I could get most of the mess off my hands. But my nose insisted the stench remained, and I scrubbed and scrubbed, much as I'd have liked to see what was going on.

I emerged into the corridor to find it full of paramedics and armed policemen, most of whom were too busy with the dog and the injured men to notice me. There was no sign of Nick anywhere. So I wandered back into the office I'd only so far glimpsed a corner of. Yes, an Aladdin's cave of armaments and money, all prosaic and mundane, nothing like the stuff of fairy tales.

'Not a bad haul,' DCI Evans observed, putting out a restraining hand.

'Don't worry. I wouldn't touch any of it. Blood money.'

'Amazing thing, greed. A couple of years ago this was a perfectly legitimate plant – OK, it was doing unpleasant work, but as they say, someone's got to. See?' He pointed to certificates framed and tacked to the wall.

'They were even proud of the place. Same as I was of my first hygiene certificate.'

'They won't be getting many of those!' he snorted.

'Where's Nick?'

'In an ambulance. He seems to have had – some sort of a turn. They want to take him off to Exeter, but he won't go till he's spoken to you. Josie,' he added, as I headed for the door, 'go easy on him. He's not a pretty sight.'

'Go easy! He saved my life, Evans.' None of this first name business. Not yet. 'Which considering his past is possibly the bravest thing he's ever done. Like a man with shell shock going back to the trenches. That sort of brave.'

'How did you know?'

'A spot of research and a lot of guesswork. And you?'

'His personnel records. Seems there was an incident in some Birmingham suburb.'

'Kings Heath,' I supplied.

'Right. And this nutter decided to kill his girlfriend. The police were called –'

'Nick was first on the scene?'

'Right. Not trained for that sort of thing. Who is? You can reason with sane folks, but not –'

'Not someone who believes the girl's pregnant with the Antichrist and wants to crucify the foetus.'

'Quite. He did his best. There was even talk of a commendation. But he turned it down. And after that his career stopped in its tracks. You wouldn't know to see him now but he was a high-flyer, tipped for the very top.'

'I know. He put my husband away for life. I'd better go and talk to him.'

'Josie – he's not making a lot of sense.' He seemed about to add something, but thought better of it. 'I'll get someone to go with you.'

'You ask me, they'll section him,' the male paramedic was saying, his green overalls glowing in the still flashing lights of the ambulances and police vehicles crammed into the dusk-dark yard.

Over my dead body they'd section him. Sectioning meant losing your human rights. Drugs? ECT? I didn't know what they'd use, but I'd bet it wouldn't be as good as home cooking and home TLC.

I surged forward. 'Josie Welford,' I announced, as if the name should mean something. 'I'm here to talk to your patient. Mr Thomas. Is he sedated?' Without waiting for an answer – what did I know about any pharmaceuticals they might have shoved into his arm? – I stepped up into the ambulance, to find Nick in steady tears.

'Come on, let's get you out of those dirty things,' I said. One of the police or forensic team would have a spare paper suit, for goodness' sake, and it was better for anyone to be cold than be dirty and wet.

As if he were a child, he let me strip him off, mopping him with paper tissues and swathing him in a blanket. Why the hell had no one got round to this basic kindness? I yelled from the ambulance for a paper suit. One appeared as if by magic.

'And an evidence bag for his clothes,' I snapped. 'What planet are you people on? Come on, more blankets here.' Yes, I liked a bit of round-eyed, if tight-jawed, respect. 'Isn't it time we headed off to A and E? I'd like him checked over. Now. And one of you –' I summoned a PC with apparently little to do but hang round nattering to his mates '– tell DCI Evans where I'm going. We'll need to talk later. Here are my car keys. The car's parked outside the yard, a hundred yards to the south. Get someone to bring it to the hospital.' In my experience, if you assumed people would do things, they did.

I sat beside Nick on the long journey to Exeter, holding him till his sobs subsided and he fell into a silence I didn't dare break. From time to time the female paramedic checked his vital signs, largely, I suspected, because she liked to look busy and efficient.

'Any problems?' I prompted, nodding sagely when she reeled off a set of figures – I'd watched enough hospital dramas, after all.

'You saved my life, you know,' I told Nick at last. 'Without you I'd be dead. No doubt about it. None at all.'

There might have been a twitch of interest.

'It must have taken a lot of doing,' I continued, 'to pick up one of those guns and load it and fire it, knowing you'd got no time at all to do it.'

'It just came back. And it was easy. Wasn't so easy, seeing the girl die.'

'Girl?'

'The one attacking you.'

'It was a bloke, Nick. A bloke. One of the guys from the rending plant. The ones holding you prisoner. The one trying to kill me. And he didn't die.' Though I wouldn't give much for his chances.

'I think I must have had one of my blackouts. I saw it all this time, Josie. I was in the Kings Heath nick canteen, just eating a sarnie for lunch and watching the TV. There was this news programme about CCTV, with this guy sitting in front of a whole bank of them. And then the shout went up. This emergency. It was spitting distance from the station. There was procedure in place. The team was scrambled. But we got there first. It was supposed to be a watching brief. No action, just containment. But the guy heard us arrive. And he brought this girl down the stairs using her as a shield, we thought. Not that we had any guns, anyway – we were waiting for the Armed Response Unit. I had to do something. I was in charge, remember – the inspector. All the responsibility but none of the experience. That's the trouble with being a high flier. Well, I was being groomed for higher management, not a lifetime on the beat. That's what they said. So there I was, wet behind the ears, a couple of sergeants with twice my experience taking my orders. Supposedly. Orders. I couldn't have ordered a burger in McDonald's. So we all just stood there looking at him and this pregnant girl. And I started to tell him to put the knife down and let her go. And he moved his hand – I thought he was going to give me the knife. So I reached forward to take it. But he laughed, and shoved it into her belly. And all her guts – ' He started to sob again.

What should I do? I was like him all those years ago – quite out of my depth. Perhaps if I engaged his brain it would be easier for him.

'The first time I saw you black out was when you were in Comet or whatever. It looked as if you might be buying a TV. But you just stood there, frozen, clutching an electric kettle.'

'Don't remember it at all.'

'Or the first time you saw young Lucy in church? Apparently you gave everyone a wobbly.'

'Not that. Nor any of the brown studies you lambasted me for. I didn't mean to put you at risk, Josie – I'm sorry.'

I squeezed his hand. 'Forget it. Whoops!'

'Not the best thing to say in the circumstances,' he said, producing a pallid grin. 'I've felt that parts of me have been missing, Josie. Great chunks.'

'Post-traumatic stress disorder,' I intoned solemnly, 'I should imagine.'

He nodded. 'The police do things much better these days, apparently. You get properly de-briefed, offered support, that sort of thing. There's an ex-policeman who's a real expert in the subject living down here. I might just get in touch with him.'

'Sounds a good idea. Looks like we've arrived.'

'Where?'

'A and E in some Exeter hospital.'

'Why? We're both OK, aren't we?'

So he wasn't as up to speed as I'd hoped. 'Physically, yes. But they weren't at all sure about your – your mental state.'

He picked at his paper suit. 'I suppose I must have had another …moment.'

'A pretty major one, I'd say. Nick, there was talk of …hospital-ising…you.'

'Why? My God, I was that bad, was I? Did I hurt anyone? Apart from the guy I shot?'

'No,' I said carefully.

'In that case, they'll have to section me,' he said. 'I'm not going voluntarily, believe me.'

Now was not the time to talk about the paramedics' earlier theory. I stared down this one lest she shove in a helpful oar.

'I think you might need some therapy, though,' I ventured.

'Bucketfuls, I should imagine. But not as an in-patient, thank you very much. Will you wait for me?' he asked ambiguously.

'Of course. They might even want to cast their beadies over me, since I seem to have blood all over my clothes. I'm fairly sure it's not mine, though. And I shan't weep for the guy whose it probably is. How on earth do you do that job of yours, Nick? It fair turned my stomach, that yard. I might even become vegetarian for a bit.'

He threw his head back and laughed. 'You! Vegetarian! Oh, Josie – please don't. It'd tie your culinary hands far too tight.'

It was in this vein we continued to natter until we were parked in the waiting area of A and E. He was summoned almost immediately, thanks, no doubt, to the paramedics' reports. His hand fastened convulsively on mine. 'You won't let them section me!'

I returned the squeeze. 'Over my dead body! Whoops!'

So at least he went off laughing.

The sound rang out unnaturally in a place as cheerless as an undertaker's waiting room, and I choked my responding chortle immediately. What, more specifically who, was emitting such palpable misery?

'My God, Lucy! What are you doing here?' I darted over, hardly realising that there was a middle-aged woman sitting protectively beside her.

'Oh, Mrs W! It's Dad!' She turned to me her face so washed with tears it seemed to be melting.

I sat down, putting my left arm round her shoulder to pull her into my embrace. 'What's happened?' I waited while she collected herself. Some sort of drunken accident, no doubt. I always thought he shouldn't be trusted with anything more lethal than a can opener.

The woman – on reflection she probably wasn't even as old as I was, just more resigned to her years – shook her head in a minatory way.

Lucy ignored the warning. 'Blew himself up, didn't he?'

'"Blew himself up"? How?'

'Fertiliser, of course. Blew himself up. Didn't even have the sense to do it in the outhouse. Did it in the kitchen!' She sounded more outraged than distressed.

This time the woman spoke. 'You shouldn't be saying anything yet, Lucy. It's a legal matter now.'

I leaned across Lucy, extending my hand. 'Josie Welford. I'm a friend of Lucy's. She works for me at the White Hart. The village pub,' I added, still waiting for the woman to introduce herself and shake my hand.

Lucy beat her to it. 'This is Ms Barnet, Mrs W. She's supposed to be my social worker.'

Supposed to be? Something amiss there, by the sound of it. Time for a social smile as a flaccid paw barely touched mine. I responded by crunching its bones. Painfully. I was wrong, of course. I knew social workers had impossible jobs and that however they toiled against insuperable odds they were always blamed by the red-top press for all society's ills. But every single one detailed to me while Tony had been doing his bird had had the self-same handshake. I knew I was stereotyping, that I was prejudiced, that I was doing all the things I loathed myself for. I even knew I was getting angry with her so I didn't put my head against Lucy's and weep with her – not for her death-wish of a dad but for all that had happened this afternoon, to me and to a decent man I'd bullied into mortal danger. I swallowed and made myself smile.

'How do you do? How much are you allowed to tell me?' There, adult to adult, woman to woman.

She didn't respond. All she granted me was a thin-lipped sketch of a smile. 'It's all *sub judice*.'

'Lucy too?'

'Very much so.'

Lucy lifted her head. 'Too much so! She's only threatening me with Care, Josie. I mean, Mrs W.'

Another hug, this one even more maternal. 'You mean Josie. Come on, what's this about Care?' I gave it the same meaningful capital as she did.

'Care. All of us. Split up and shared between foster homes. All because I'm not old enough!' she raged.

'To be a responsible adult,' Ms Barnet explained. There was sufficient note of apology in her voice to make me soften towards her. 'In any case,' she continued, almost giving me a hint, 'the family home's in no fit state … If you could see the kitchen … And possible damage… We don't know the state of the structure…'

Almost a hint? Josie, you stupid woman, each and every one of these half-finished sentences is a hint! 'So whatever we mustn't talk about has made a good deal of mess. And the children can't stay at home?'

'No way.' The youthful cliché came oddly from that tired mouth.

'And we're too many for Auntie Pen down Falmouth way, or Uncle Dave in Sidmouth.'

Because we are too many. Where had I heard that before? Wherever it was, it tugged so angrily at my chest, I couldn't stop the words coming out. 'If it's a matter of room and an adult, I can offer both. I'm geared up for bed and breakfast accommodation, currently unused, and can offer myself and an ex-policeman as temporary guardians. I know you'll have to vet us properly. Oh, and there's a barman you'll need to look up too. Robin Somethingorother.' I slapped my forehead. 'Hang these senior moments! I'm getting quite hopeless with names.'

We talked practicalities nine to the dozen, me because I didn't want Lucy to have time to get emotional with gratitude and Ms Barnet, I suspected, because that was what she did best. OK, for another reason, too: Nick was being kept suspiciously long and I was having to work very hard at not storming up to the kid on reception and demanding instant access to him. It was far easier to think about turning the pub into a temporary orphanage – hell, it had better be temporary, or what would happen to my bijou restaurant? – than worrying about how to fight against the Mental Health Act on Nick's behalf, not to mention how to deal with Nick if he stayed on at the White Hart. The implications were beginning to overwhelm me. I dug in my pocket for a few coins, which I thrust at Lucy. 'Be an angel and find a machine. I reckon we all need a good fix of chocolate.'

She stood, gazing at me steadily, adult at irresponsible teenager. 'Me and Ms Barnet, maybe. But what about you, Josie? Shouldn't you be sticking to that diet of yours?'

Mike Evans, accompanied by a very subdued-looking Scott Short, waved away the chilled Villa Maria Reserve I was offering. Nick didn't, raising his glass in what seemed to be a general toast. He didn't make the mistake of singling me out: I'd made it clear that we had a lot to talk about before the word relationship even entered the general arena, let alone the bedroom. He would stay where he was, Robin too, provided the expedited vetting of his background threw up nothing untoward. The Gay family would be disposed in pairs – they were terrified by the thought of single rooms – either side of Lucy's room. She'd insisted that she would retain responsibility for the family, even to paying bills. She conceded that Nick might deal with her probably non-existent insurance matters, adding their file to his own. 'Don't know why I should bother you,' she'd said, 'seeing as I've had to do everything ever since Mum passed on.' She didn't add, but the implication was clear, that her father's death would actually mean she could carry one fewer burden. Back at the hospital Sue had suddenly evinced an interest in washing and ironing; after a moment's consideration, Lucy had accepted the offer, perhaps seeing it, as I was tempted to do, as conscience-salve.

For Sue hadn't arrived in Exeter till it was too late – for Mr Gay, at least. He'd done a very thorough job of blowing himself up, and it was truly a mercy he'd not survived long, even though Lucy would have loved him to receive the Last Rites. She might have refused confirmation for herself, and thought the kids' time better spent on homework than at Sunday school, but after the mess that her father had always been she'd wanted something as a full stop if not an opening to Eternal Life. And Sue had let her down. Her car, according to Sue herself. But Lucy had the same views of car maintenance as she did of family maintenance and I doubted if she'd bought the excuse any more than Nick had. A modern car not starting, indeed.

'When did she last have it serviced?' she'd muttered to me as we hung round in the hospital waiting area.

Sue, dragging me into the ladies', had been quite stern with me.

'Are you sure this...this hospitality...of yours isn't just an attempt to rehabilitate yourself in the village?' she'd asked in a stage whisper. 'Molly told me she'd had to spell things out to you this morning.'

'At the moment the only thing I care about is that the kids need to live where they've always lived,' I hissed back. 'As for the villagers, the narrow-minded –' I let out a stream of profanities that had shocked her as much as it would have shocked Tony. 'Bloody motes and sodding beams,' I concluded, my inventiveness having dried up.

Sue had swallowed and disappeared. It would be hard for her to get back from Exeter to the village, but just at the moment I didn't care. I'd make it up to her in the next Benefice Sunday collection.

Now from my living room we could just hear the sounds of Lucy organising the children into bed, her routine being even more rigid in view of their father's death. She'd locked the en suite bathrooms, not trusting any of the kids alone with water lest it overflow into the rooms below. I'd been more afraid of their drowning.

There was no noise from the bar, of course. Lucy had put up a large sign on the door: CLOSED – FAMILY BEREAVEMENT. I didn't comment. Everyone would know what she'd meant, after all.

So now it was just the four of us: the two police officers, Nick and me. I sensed we were all walking on conversational eggshells, but wasn't entirely sure why. To my mind, we'd not done a bad day's work between us.

Nick, disconcertingly relaxed, opened the batting. 'What I can't understand is why my predecessor said the rending plant – Wetherall's – was up to standard. I'd have closed down the place on the spot.'

Evans regarded him limpidly. 'Are you sure you've no idea, Mr Thomas?'

Nick shrugged, miming the passing of money.

'I'm sure you're right. Was any such approach made to you?'

'Not by the rending plant people. But Fred Tregothnan, the

missing vet, talked about...activities...which shouldn't be too closely looked into. I said I'd been as straight as a die all my life and didn't intend to change now.'

I nodded. 'Ah – that Friday morning conversation I saw you two having.'

Nick nodded. 'It was clear after that we weren't going to become best buddies. There was something else about the guy I didn't like, too – can't quite put my finger on it.'

'He put his finger on Lindi, all right. A whole handful of fingers. What's happened to her, by the way?' It was clear from the others' blank looks I was going to have to explain.

'You're talking twenty-first century England here! Jesus Christ!' Short exploded.

'You're talking about a community with roots older than we townees can imagine,' Nick corrected him.

Evans nodded. 'Quite: I wouldn't be surprised if that Ted Gay's funeral involved all sorts of things you don't get at the average crematorium.'

'Nothing too *outré*, I hope – I'm holding his wake here! I promised Lucy,' I added, aware of a frisson passing between the two officers.

Before I could say anything, Evans said, 'Maybe some sin-eating? It's where you get someone to eat some cake passed across the body. That way the corpse is absolved of its sins, which go to the one eating the cake. They used to do it up your way. Hereford, Forest of Dean, round there.'

Knowledgeable maybe, but geographically-challenged, certainly.

'Brummies,' Nick said with finality. 'Both of us. City folk.'

'This Lindi,' Short said, referring to his notes. 'You're sure you don't know what eventually happened to her?'

'Lucy'll know. She's probably smuggled her out of the county to a stray cousin in Newton Abbot or Ottery St Mary or some other polysyllabic place.' I got to my feet. And then sat down again. I didn't want to disturb the kids' bedtime and Lucy knew the police wanted to talk further to her.

'We'll need to interview her –' Short chimed in.

'Yes.' Evans agreed. 'Though I can't imagine she'd dare make a complaint. She's still got to live in the place when we've gone home. Assuming she ever comes back, of course.'

'I can give names,' I said. ' And those I can't name I can identify their faces.'

'But you've still got to live in the place too,' Evans said. 'Assuming you're going to. And I wouldn't blame you if you packed up and left tomorrow.' Again he seemed to change the subject with some abruptness.

Perhaps it was the booze, but I felt we were getting nowhere fast. If I was hungry, what was Nick's stomach doing? Grabbing my phone pad, I scrawled a checklist.

'OK. Now, that abattoir is illegal. Yes? So it'll be closed down?'

Hijacked, Evans had the grace to laugh. 'Yes. But may spring up again in another village at the back of beyond. It's a combination of ill-explained legislation and genuine hardship. Plus a desire to make money out of vulnerable people.' His voice hardened.

'In my book those who make money out of the vulnerable tend to be the rich and the most powerful,' Nick put in. 'Josie's had dealings with the landowning family round here – the Grevilles. Luke Greville, as I'm sure you recall, resigned with no explanation from one of the safest seats in the country and shot off to become an MEP. We also saw him emerging from Fred Tregothnan's house first thing on Sunday morning. The stream that runs through the village rises on his land. It ran pink the other week. Complaints to the water company from a member of the public failed to make any difference –'

Evans smiled grimly. 'Let me guess – Ms Josie Welford.'

'I prefer Mrs. I was married long enough.'

' – so I put my official hat on this morning and demanded action,' Nick concluded. 'I think after this afternoon we have a very good idea why the water turned pink. The rending plant was dealing with far more carcases than it was licensed for and spillage from those vats entered the water table.' He stared at the floor swallowing hard in what looked like an effort not to vomit.

He wasn't the only one trying to keep their stomach under

control. I chipped in quickly. 'Mrs Greville knew about the pink water because I mentioned it when I was helping arrange flowers in church. Almost before you could say "flood" I saw Reg Bulcombe in water gear heading off with a large spade. Within twenty-four hours the village stream was reduced to a mere trickle, despite the rain. What had been an ordinary steep path had become a torrent and – by coincidence! – the field on which Nick's mobile home was parked became a lake. His home – like the others – floated away. Unlike the others, his was stove in first.'

'So you're saying the Grevilles and a lout like Bulcombe are somehow connected!' To my amazement Short sounded outraged. Surely a young urban officer like him wouldn't still be a forelock-tugger!

'Since when did the rich hesitate to get their tenants to do their dirty work?' Nick again. 'I'd be knocking on the Grevilles' door first thing tomorrow. Sorry.'

Evans grinned. 'There may still be time this evening.' He shook a resigned head as he checked his watch. 'Funny – you'd think nothing of charging into a council maisonette at nine at night, but that long drive and that imposing front door demand a civilised hour.'

Short clearly didn't know what his boss was on about.

'Not to mention the fuss their brief would make,' Nick added, *sotto voce*.

'On to Wetherall, then, if I may,' I said, in full chair-of-meeting mode. 'I don't suppose we know who actually owns it?'

'It's a subsidiary of a Midlands based company registered in the Isle of Man. All of which may well be a tax dodge I'm not up to,' Nick began. A smile he'd not quite managed to suppress surfaced. 'I do know the name Luke Greville when I see it, however – and he's a major shareholder. As is his mother.'

'I'd hoped she'd be on the side of the angels,' I said. 'She's anti-hunting.'

Evans snorted. 'Not her! She's big in the Countryside Alliance. She was one of those promising civil disobedience if the government ever gets round to banning hunting.'

'So why should she bother to tell me she wasn't? I know, I know – so I'd think she was kosher. Silly me. And there I was sorry for her dog when she couldn't find Fred Tregothnan to treat it. OK. I know we touched on Fred Tregothnan, but there's no actual evidence that he did end his days at Wetherall, I suppose?'

Evans shook his head. 'Not yet. It can only be a presumption of death at this point. The SOCO team, poor buggers, will have to give it the going over of its life in the hope of finding human as opposed to animal tissue. I don't envy them the task, especially as I reckon it's hopeless. But before we close the case, I'd like a reason for him to disappear – and/or his vehicle.'

'You said you'd seen Mr Greville coming from Tregothnan's house,' Short said slowly, to be rewarded with the sort of stare you give a child you thought was asleep. 'Why were you there, Mrs Welford?'

I beamed. 'I was going to use the key under the flowerpot to let myself in. I wanted another sniff round. In his surgery in particular.'

Short spluttered but Evans held up a calming hand.

'There has to be some reason for the whole Tregothnan thing,' I continued. 'I know vets aren't well paid, but look at his house, for goodness' sake. No mortgage – it was his family home; not a penny spent on it in all the years he'd had it. He dresses like a tramp. His Land Rover's one that Noah sent to the scrapyard. What does he spend his money on?'

'So how would trespassing on Tregothnan's property have helped?' Short pursued.

'I was looking for evidence, same as you people. But sort of thinking sideways. Anyway, I gave up because Mr Greville pocketed the key when he left,' I added with a rueful smile. I had a nasty feeling I was going to have to involve Sue in all this.

'What would you have been looking for?' Evans had joined in.

Heavens, I was so hungry. What was the etiquette of producing sandwiches in what seemed to be a cross between a debriefing and parlour game? 'Gentlemen, if I don't eat soon, I shall drop. Why don't we adjourn till at very least I've made us a plate of sandwiches?'

Nick looked like a dog promised a muddy walk followed by a marrowbone. Even Short perked up. But Evans abandoned his laidback style and leaned forward, raising a warning finger. 'Just a minute, Mrs Welford. Answer my question, if you don't mind. What would you have been looking for? After all, you must have guessed that we'd take everything we thought relevant.'

'Yes,' I mused, 'like bank statements and so on. Truly, I was going to think on my feet. But I'd have looked where I couldn't before, because it was locked – the surgery. Things in locked cupboards.'

'Poisons!'

I shook my head. 'I was thinking more of restricted drugs – won't a vet use things like morphine? Pethidine?'

'Maybe even ketamine,' Evans mused. 'Are you thinking he was a user? Were there any signs?'

'Not physical ones, I don't think. No tracks up his arms, things like that. Not that I ever saw. But wouldn't he have to keep a record of what he bought and what he dispensed and make sure the two balanced?'

'Not physical?' Evans pressed.

'As a personality he was as inconsistent as they come. My theory, for what it's worth, is that someone found out he was popping whatever and blackmailed him. And because he was hard up he got involved with this bad meat brigade – I don't know, perhaps at one time they wanted him to forge paperwork, only to find people didn't care two hoots where the meat had come from so long as it looked and tasted good – and was cheap. But all this is supposition, isn't it? Since I couldn't get in for a fossick round.'

'You did before, though.'

'Yes. And scarpered like a guilty schoolgirl caught scrumping. OK if I get some food now? Soup? Or sandwiches? Or something more substantial? Go on, it'll be better than your canteen fare.'

While they considered, the phone rang. I answered. It was Sue, almost gibbering. 'Josie – Josie. About Fred. Do you think I ought to confess?'

Chapter Twenty-Nine

However much I hunched over the phone and cupped my hand round the mouthpiece, I wasn't going to stop Evans and Short hearing our conversation. Sue's phone volume was always moderate to loud; now she was stressed, it was *fortissimo*.

They'd probably hear the word 'confess' anyway. All the same, I urged her, 'Don't do anything without taking legal advice. Please.' Having no idea what else I could say, I cut the call. 'Sandwiches?' I repeated brightly.

But the three men were already on their feet. Evans and Short I could understand – but Nick?

'Someone has to be there for her,' he apologised quietly to me. 'Find her a solicitor and so on.'

'At least have a glass of milk before you go. Help yourself from the fridge.' Out loud I added, 'Sue's not going anywhere – you'd do better to accept my offer. Think ulcers,' I said darkly.

They were tempted, no doubt about that. But even as they dithered, there came the sound of a car driven fast, turning into the back yard. I think we all braced ourselves for the sound of metal on metal. None came. Someone banged furiously on my back door.

'That'll be Sue,' Nick said unnecessarily.

'She's come to see me, not the police – or you, Nick,' I said. 'You should let me speak to her first. On my own. You lot make yourselves scarce – oh, go and help Lucy read bedtime stories or something – until we've finished.' Impatiently I added, 'Oh, she won't get away from you. Think she'd take you on in a car chase? Well, she might,' I conceded, 'but I wouldn't bet on the outcome.'

I ushered Sue into the pub kitchen, dishevelled, her ponytail escaping its elastic band, a torn Tesco's carrier in her hand. Every bit as wan as Lucy, she didn't remark on the poor hospitality or the smell of wine on my breath, but did seem relieved when I asked nothing, simply filled the kettle and busied myself with coffee.

I heard movement behind me. She was opening the carrier.

'These were in Fred Tregothnan's surgery,' she said.

Only then did I turn, nodding at an A4 record book I presumed was his drugs ledger or whatever its official name. There was what looked like a receipts book, too, A5 or smaller.

It wasn't really my job to ask when she'd acquired them, though I'd have liked it to be. Her head hung as if she were one of Tony's gofers caught with his hands in an off-limits till. Perhaps it would do her good to get it all off her poor concave chest.

'Under your coat that morning in the rain?' I prompted, passing sugar and milk.

She nodded. 'I'd promised him, you see.'

Nodding her to a chair, I sat too. The table between us spoke of decades of hard use, and I loved it for each herb chopped, each apple peeled and turned into pie.

'Odd promise.'

'Not at all.' Her head shot up. 'I can't tell you why he wanted them concealed. The confessional.'

'I never realised –'

'The C of E permits; it doesn't insist.'

'OK. But he asked you to hear his confession.'

'Maybe it was more a confidential heart-to-heart. I don't know.'

But it would make a lot of difference in a court of law. And to her conscience.

'And you concealed them. But now you're giving them to me.'

'No. Not giving. Showing. You're a businesswoman. You must understand figures and things like that. Could you glance at them and see why – see if they give any hint why he might have disappeared?'

I sipped my coffee very slowly. Without thinking, I'd used the after-dinner roast and it was too strong and bitter on an empty stomach. Putting my hand on the books as if to keep them closed, I said hesitantly, 'I can't be bound by the same promise as you made. If I see he's been fiddling his books, I'd have to say something. And I think it's worse than fiddling his books. I suspect he's been taking illegal drugs and trying to square the entries.' From her wince I might have scored a direct hit. 'Is that what he was talking about, drug addiction?'

'You know I can't tell you.'

'It'd be the most likely thing anyone would want to confess. Or an addiction to hard porn, which a police geek would find on his hard disk in five seconds flat. But for either to be a problem, someone would have had to find out and be blackmailing him.'

Stony-faced, she stared at her coffee, as if she found it as unpalatable as the truth she was confronting.

'One thing I always found strange about Fred,' I continued, conversationally, but keeping to the past tense, as if to confirm I was sure he was dead, 'was his tendency to mix with the village lowlife. People like Ted Gay and the other fire-hoggers. The ones who made Nick Thomas's life such a misery. Fred was a professional man, after all. Middle-class. The sort who'd more naturally mix with GPs or teachers or clergymen, in the old days, anyway. Perhaps we're just less hierarchical now.'

'And you show me a GP or schoolmaster or clergyman for miles around. He loathes Aidan – I'm afraid he's really quite homophobic. And he seemed to take an immediate dislike to poor Nick.'

Poor Nick? But I wouldn't be sidetracked. 'So did he have any other friends?'

'How would I know?'

'He must have got…close…to you, even in your church capacity,' I inserted quickly, 'to make his confession. Or have his confidential heart-to-heart.' Maybe it was time to turn up the heat. 'I think he's dead. I don't think his body will ever be found, because I think he was disposed of in that rending plant where Nick and I were nearly killed. I'd dearly love to find who killed him.'

'In that case, why don't you ask the ones who attacked you?'

It was, of course, the obvious response – from someone with something to hide. 'One's not going to be doing any talking for a long time. The side of his face was shot away. I hit the other one so hard the last I heard he's still unconscious. The police know who they are, but they haven't told me. Well, the bloke I knocked out could still sue me for assault, in this topsy-turvy world, on the ground I used unreasonable force.'

Damn, I'd diverted her again. 'And did you?'

'Sue, if someone was charging towards you ready to kill you, someone who'd been torturing another human being with the threat of a killer dog, how long would you take to work out how big a swing to take and when to pull back? A nano-second, I'd think. I just walloped, I make no bones about it.' I winced at the unintended pun but didn't explain. 'Tell me – are you doing what the Law may do: taking the side of the criminal against the intended victim? Because if you are, I'd like you to leave, now. And you can take those ledgers with you to show the police when they turn up.'

'You mean you'd –'

'After what I witnessed today? In thirty seconds flat I'll be spilling every bean I know. I'd rather you did, of course. And I'd rather you were rather more frank than you've been with me. I know the village has a culture of secrecy the Mafia would envy, but you shouldn't endorse it. For God's sake, Sue – you won't even be able to read the funeral service over him, because he's so much blood in a black pudding!'

Her own blood drained from her face. At last I might be getting through to her. Through white lips she said, 'The person who could have told you most can't any more. He's dead.' She gathered up the precious ledgers and stowed them in the deplorable bag. 'Ted Gay. Yes, Lucy's father. The man who blew himself up.' She stood up, ready to depart in umbrage.

I flapped her down again and leaned towards her confidentially. 'I know he blew himself up. But I don't know the whys and wherefores. Even the hows. Except that was fertiliser, wasn't it? But how could even a dimwitted alcoholic blow himself up with his compost heap?'

Her snort might have been laughter. 'Fertiliser's used for other things beside crop improvement, as even townees like you should know. It's used for bombs, Josie. And that's what he was making this afternoon. A bomb. And because you've been so lovey-dovey to young Lucy, no one's quite got round to telling you who it was for, have they? That bomb was meant for you, Josie. It was meant for you!'

'I'd no idea they hated me so much,' I said, still battling with what Sue had said and how I was to digest it. I fended off the glass Nick was pressing into my hand.

'Don't be so daft,' he said. 'Did Tony hate the people he had dealt with? Of course not. It was a business he was running, something he did with rivals and subordinates. They wanted to take you out because you were too damned close to a lucrative business and none of the other hints had worked. Come on, think about all that cash in the Wetherall office. It wasn't Monopoly money. It was real. Like the guns.'

Maybe I nodded, but, like all the other little warnings, it felt personal. 'Shopping Sue won't have helped to re-establish myself, either,' I muttered.

'You didn't shop her. She gave herself away with that phone call,' he insisted. 'And as far as you knew, while you had your heart to heart Short and Evans were still ensconced in the comfort of your flat – or reading stories to the kids as you suggested.'

'Ted Gay, Reg Bulcombe, and those two characters still in hospital – not the nicest selection of neighbours, all the same.'

'True. What'll you do? Hitch up your skirts and run?'

'Not exactly me, that sort of thing. In any case, I don't have any choice as long as those kids need me. I'll just run the White Hart as an orphanage till they're ready to move.'

'I know Social Services'll pay their maintenance and board and lodging. But it's not the same as a lucrative pub, Josie.'

'The pub never made a bean. The bar food, yes. And there's nothing to stop my plans for the restaurant. Provided the locals can refrain from vandalising my customers' cars. And will work for me.'

'No news of Tom and Sharon?'

'I still think they wanted to escape Sharon's incestuous father. Not me. If Lindi comes back – and to give her her due, she's the sort of kid who may well brazen things out – I may keep Robin. Lucy'll finish all her school exams, work for me full time and do a day-release course or two. Then university, if I have my way.'

'All that costs money.'

'Not a problem.'

'Tony's loot?'

It was too late and I was too tired to mess around with tact. 'One more jibe about that and you're out. Out of this room, out of this pub, out of my life forever. Final notice. Not negotiable. Do I make myself clear?' Pity I had to spoil it with a sob I couldn't quite turn into a yawn. Or a yawn into a sob. Whichever.

Chapter Thirty

It was one of those bright March days that God had spring-cleaned especially for me. Now with my own pilot's licence, I had my usual Friday morning session, but without the services of Piers. He'd had his uses, not least as a repository of photos, many of which were logged as evidence when Luke Greville's case at last came up before Exeter Assizes. All the roads had led to Greville, him and his duplicitous mother. Police research – how nice to have someone else doing the dirty work – had shown that Wetherall had been one of a chain of once quite legal rending plants right across the country stretched to capacity and beyond so they could undercut competitors and force them out of business.

After seeing all those overflowing, leaking, stinking vats, I could never look at a vitamin capsule or a new lipstick quite the same way. The illicit Kings Duncombe abattoir had been a bonus for Wetherall, springing up in response to food standards legislation all but small, hard-pressed beef producers could see was entirely sensible. And beef consumers, of course, who were unable to pay the sort of prices I felt were justified for organic meat. And the national minimum wage, as Robin pointed out, which was all most of the villagers earned, if that, didn't run to much in the way of organic anything. He'd stayed, and was rubbing his hands with glee at the sight of the new staff accommodation, though Lindi had never returned. Rumour had it she was working as a picker on a mushroom farm near Weston-super-Mare, which saddened me: she could have done better than that. Lucy was doing just as well at school as she had before her father's death, and Nick was settling into the role of favourite uncle. Both men had of course been strictly vetted officially, and I kept my beady eye on them all the time. Just in case. You never knew with officialdom. Especially as Lucy was rapidly flowering into a quite lovely young woman.

Any day now my gourmet restaurant would open, with lots of nice media coverage, thanks to Nicola and her friends, who were now regulars. The villagers goggled from behind twitching curtains, and women were herding their menfolk to the new snug in the hope of their getting autographs. In any case the snug, clean but with the antique pub furniture I'd acquired, had started to attract back the men who'd once huddled round the fire to the exclusion of everyone else. Reg Bulcombe wasn't doing any huddling, not in the pub, anyway, though maybe wherever he was being held pending his trial. It was his fertiliser that had taken Gay to kingdom come, and although the police believed he'd mixed it with the other bomb ingredients on Greville's orders, doing what you were told was no excuse in law.

Sue had been promoted to another parish, in the time-honoured way in which big institutions deal with troublesome but useful staff. The paperwork she'd produced – and that it turned out she'd planted in my outhouse – made it clear that Fred Tregothnan had been dabbling in a variety of drugs for which he'd forged prescriptions, so he'd have been struck off by the RCVS if his activities had been made known. I don't know what they'd have made of his visits to hardcore porn sites, but the police wouldn't have approved. The grass? Bulcombe, for my money, though he was currently denying all knowledge. Sue had been replaced temporarily by a lad who looked about sixteen, who trotted round the parish in his cassock, Adam's apple a-bobble, demanding to be called Father.

Neither Tregothnan's Land Rover nor Nick's rental four-by-four had ever been found, despite my inevitable photographic evidence. The trouble was, as I'd once told Nick, Somerset was a big county with lots of remote farms on which a car could be disappeared.

It wasn't quite by chance I was circling over Exmoor now. I didn't like loose ends. Never did – any more than Nick does. He'd still love to run to earth Tony's fortune, which I suspect is on reason why we'll never progress far beyond our shared-home-but-not-shared bedroom status. Another is the fact that though he now has occasional flashes of colour, he's still only a pale, washed-out shadow of a man. Like a man who's spent too long in gaol, maybe. No, he can't help it. That stabbing incident made him more of a prisoner than my Tony ever was.

I can almost feel Tony now, telling me to stop musing and get on with something I can't do every day of the week – enjoy my flying.

Yes, it's just like it is on TV. All those fields, with little dark patches where the clouds scud between them and the warm spring sun. The early crops are greening the fields, and Easter lambs are busy preparing themselves for my organic table. But there – yes, down there – is what looks like a graveyard for giants. There they lie, side by side – Gog and Magog, maybe.

Hang on: they were further east. So what on earth would be buried in this corner of an English field, where the tilth merges with the moor? A couple of enormous horses? Or – yes! – a pair of big vehicles, one not missed by its owner, the other still the subject of endless insurance haggles.

I take a couple of snaps, and buzz for home, breathless with delight. Home? To hell with that. I've got another ten minutes before my time is up, and I never was a woman to waste anything. I whirl over Barnstable bay, singing aloud. Yes! God's in His Heaven, all's well with the world. And I know of a very good way to celebrate my find. The moment I land, I call up Mike Evans. Get yourself back to your flat, I say, and get that champagne on ice.